HELPLESS

The stillness of the room only served to enhance her dread. What could he be bringing back? If only it was the key to the manacles that confined her.

Too soon Jonathan returned, carrying a knife, a surgical knife.

"I've proven my love for you. Now it's your turn, sweetheart." He moved slowly across the room, the smile on his face maddening in its warmth, his eyes cold and clever.

"What the hell are you going to do with that?"

"That? Please be more specific, honey. Do you mean my erection or the knife?"

"I wish to hell you'd cut that fucker off."

"Good. You're almost catching on. Except as I said I have already proven my love for you and have allowed you to reverently feed from me. I must worship you in the same way. Shall it be a little bit of breast, or . . ."

She watched his eyes search her naked body.

"You've become much too thin, honey. Ah, but you do have a little excess on the tummy." He patted her abdomen as if she were in a Kansas meat yard. . . .

MARY ANN MITCHELL

Ambrosial Flesh

LEISURE BOOKS NEW YORK CITY

As always, this book is dedicated to John.
A special thank you to Jennifer Toth for her book
The Mole People

A LEISURE BOOK®

August 2001

Published by

Dorchester Publishing Co., Inc.
276 Fifth Avenue
New York, NY 10001

ISBN 0-8439-4902-3

The name "Leisure Books" and the stylized "L" with design are
trademarks of Dorchester Publishing Co., Inc.

Printed in the United States of America.

Visit us on the web at www.dorchesterpub.com.

Ambrosial Flesh

Who made you?
God made me.

Who is God?
God is a Supreme Being.

What is a Supreme Being?

Part One

Chapter One

1956

Jonathan sat intently watching the spinning laundry. He could sit for hours in the laundromat, mesmerized by the circular motion of the driers. There goes a blue strip of cloth, a yellow, a bright red. How merry it all appeared to him, like circus artists flouncing up and down solely for his amusement. Pajamas, socks, and hankies whirled and churned themselves into dancing clowns.

"Jonathan, bring me the detergent."

Jonathan reluctantly lifted himself up from where he was seated and sidestepped his way to where he knew the detergent had been left, without moving an eyeball.

"Yelp!" Mrs. Simpson's toy poodle was under Jonathan's foot.

"Get away from my dog, you little shit."

Jonathan's mother snapped her fingers in the middle of a clown's tummy. He followed the snapping fingers until they stopped in front of a worried face.

"Sorry, Mom."

Jonathan apologized both to the elderly Mrs. Simpson and her poodle. He then walked to the table and picked up his mother's detergent. After handing the detergent to his mother, he tried to return to his circus, but was prevented by snapping fingers.

"Jonathan, you spend too much time staring at the driers. I think you become hypnotized by the motion. Why don't you run down the street and pick up a comic book?"

With a sour, squinty look he shuffled across the linoleum floor. As he opened the laundromat door, he looked back and saw a striped clown bob and weave and tumble in a merry farewell. Jonathan waved. He saw a movement from the corner of his eye. It was his mother waving to him. He nodded in her direction, but then gave a secret wink at the drier before he exited.

The pavement was hot, and as he stepped off the curb he could see high-heel marks and tire treads

in the tar on the street. Ninety-six degrees for the
past three days. The prickly heat on his neck stung.
Jonathan pulled his T-shirt up to his chin. It was
air-conditioned at the laundromat. *Why did Mom
send me out into this heat?* he asked himself. In all
of his ten years he could not remember it as hot as
this.

Jonathan quickly bought a comic book. It didn't
matter what it was. He wasn't going to read it anyway.

When he walked back into the laundromat, Mrs.
Simpson was unloading her drier. The rambunc-
tious clowns, now weary, slipped languidly into the
laundry bag.

"I'll fold these when I get home," Mrs. Simpson
said. "I'm missing my favorite show, and anyway,
they'll still need to be ironed."

Jonathan's mother nodded at Mrs. Simpson, and
then caught sight of her son.

"Did you get what you wanted?" she asked.

Jonathan hadn't wanted anything except to stay
there, he thought. He raised his comic book up so
that his mother could see what he had bought with
his allowance.

His mother frowned. "Batman. I wish you had
picked up something less violent."

Jonathan crossed in front of Mrs. Simpson's poodle, which snapped at his ankle.

"He never forgets," whispered Mrs. Simpson to Jonathan.

He backed away from both the dog and its mistress. Then he saw a perky pink and yellow clown fall to the floor. The poodle seized it in its teeth. The dog shook its head violently, then laid its paws on the edge of the pink and yellow clown. The cloth ripped. Jonathan lunged for the material, and the dog instinctively snapped at his hand.

"Get away from my dog!" Mrs. Simpson's hand swept across the back of Jonathan's head.

"Mrs. Simpson!" screamed his mother.

A cacophony of raised voices backgrounded the demise of the pink and yellow clown. Jonathan could do nothing but watch the poodle shred the fabric as the women argued. By the time Mrs. Simpson left, bits of the clown, formerly Mrs. Simpson's bed jacket, were scattered across the floor.

"Wicked woman," muttered his mother.

Jonathan brushed away his tears with the back of his forearm.

Late that afternoon, Jonathan stretched the top half of his body out of his tenement window to view the other clowns dangling limply in the summer heat. Their appendages and shoulders were attached precariously to clotheslines. They had a free and daredevil style that the clothes in the drier didn't. They hung without nets three, four, sometimes even five stories above the cement yard. Once he had seen one crumpled on the ground, badly soiled. *The Emmet Kelly of the troupe,* he had thought.

Suddenly a group started to dance. The ringmaster was yanking them back into their domicile. There they would disguise themselves as mere possessions and blend into the humdrum around them. The squeak of the clothesline was their only ovation. Jonathan silently cheered as the last clown quivered and flapped from the line's vibrations.

Every string of clowns would disappear before nightfall. Each would be stretched, smoothed, flattened out, and then folded to be tucked away inside a drawer or closet. They would be silent and motionless until freed in a revolving burst of hot air or shaken to life on a simple rope.

By dinnertime, only one queue of entertainers was left. Jonathan assumed they would be gone by the time he finished supper. But they weren't, and night was hovering.

"Jonathan, come away from the window. I swear, people are going to think you're a Peeping Tom."

Jonathan moved into the living room and sat at the feet of his parents. He wondered what a Peeping Tom was. The family spent the next two hours in silence. They watched the picture tube spin out homogenized yarns. Jonathan preferred the clowns.

By nine o'clock Jonathan was tucked into bed. He peered out the open window next to him and saw that the entertainers were still hanging out. They swung high above the ground, spread across the fourth-floor windows. There was a giant sheet that fluttered and foiled, dragging the others with it in each burst of energy. Down near the end of the line, just above Jonathan's fire escape, was a red-and-white clown. Its legs occasionally brushed the rusted steel of the railing. The tips of the feet pointed downward ballet-style.

Jonathan sat up in his bed. His green eyes, brown hair, and freckles were a blur in the darkened room. He watched the clown kick and swing in the air. He stood atop his mattress and stared into the mirror across the room. One more look at the clown, and then he too spread his arms wide and kicked his feet. The mirror reflected only a very real little boy, who looked pudgy and clumsy. There was none of the breeziness that the fellow on the line had.

Jonathan jumped a few times and then landed on his behind. His bare feet touched the spongy carpet, and he walked to the window. While climbing onto the window ledge, he noticed that one of the clown's legs had become wound around the handrail. It pulled and tugged in the wind but couldn't pry itself loose. He was afraid the clown would be hurt, like the pink-and-yellow one earlier that day, so he climbed onto the fire escape.

The steel slats were scratchy and cool against his feet. Loose pieces of paint and rust stuck to his soles. His own pajamas rustled to life in the summer breeze. Jonathan couldn't reach the red-and-white clown from his landing; he had to climb the steps. Jonathan was a sensible child and knew the danger. But he was excited—so he climbed. He climbed three steps before he could reach the desperate clown. As he reached for the cloth he looked down. Suddenly his body was swirling in little circles. He grabbed the handrail, and was elated by the thrill. His pajama sleeves fluttered in glee as his free hand touched the red-and-white clown. He unfolded the fabric and set the clown free. It gaily shimmered in the summer night, performing especially and only for Jonathan.

My jammies never get to hang in midair, he thought. He remembered the sweltering heat of the driers as the breeze of the night sent a tiny chill through his body. Jonathan clutched the handrail with both hands and leaned over the railing.

"Wow!" He sighed.

Jonathan started moving up the steps, pulling on the handrail as if it were a mountain-climbing rope. He paused to dangle one foot in the air, without the feel of solid ground under him, while he continued to stare down at the courtyard. Then he put the foot on the next step.

When he reached the red-and-white clown's shoulders, he stopped. He held one hand out over the railing, and his pajama sleeve trembled in delight. He flicked his arm back and forth in space, and the sleeve started crawling up his arm.

"Don't be afraid," he whispered.

The sleeve stopped at his elbow and loosely swung in time with his motion.

"You're not scared." He giggled. "I bet you'd like to be out there with the red-and-white clown. So would I."

He leaned as far as he could over the railing and removed one of the clothespins attached to the red-and-white clown. The clown dropped quickly, but like a circus performer he remembered seeing, it was caught at the last minute by the other shoulder, which still had a clothespin.

Jonathan's eyes sparkled. The suddenness had halted his breath for a mere moment, and then elation followed. Soaring and swinging high above the solidity of the earth was his dream.

Ten minutes later, after some of his own acrobatic maneuvers, Jonathan's own pajamas were dangling free in the world. And all that could be seen of Jonathan was his bare behind crawling back across his window ledge.

Chapter Two

Jonathan woke to raised voices coming from the kitchen. He couldn't figure out what they were saying, but the tone sounded like an argument was in progress.

He stretched, threw the blankets back, and ran naked to the window. They were gone. All the clowns had been taken indoors, including his own pajamas. He wondered what the new family would do with his old jammies. Did they have a little boy who could use them? Did they get yanked indoors by mistake? Perhaps no one had noticed that there were two foreign clowns in their midst. Aliens. Spies. He smiled and his eyes sparkled with intrigue.

Quickly, he dressed in the clothes he had worn

the previous day. Slowly, he opened his squeaky bedroom door, hoping that his parents wouldn't hear the sound, and ran for the bathroom.

"Jonathan."

He flushed the toilet and swept his hands under the tepid water of the faucet before entering the hall.

"It's about time you're up." His father stood with his hands resting on his hips.

"For heaven's sake, let the boy sleep if he wants," called his mother from the kitchen.

"Hey, he's already up and dressed." His father lowered his voice. "Your mother's always babying you. She doesn't understand us men. We don't need no stinkin' coddling, right, Jon?"

Jonathan enthusiastically nodded his head.

"Run into the kitchen and grab some grub, and maybe I'll take you along to watch me play handball today."

"Pancakes or cereal?" his mother asked as Jonathan entered the kitchen.

"Cereal," shouted Jonathan, thinking it would take less time to prepare and eat.

"But you love pancakes." Mother turned toward him and squinted. "Aren't those the clothes you wore yesterday? Did you even take a shower?

"Young man, I am not going to let you leave this house looking like an orphan. What would the

22

neighbors think? Besides, all of Father's work buddies are going to be at the game."

Jonathan took a secret smell of his shirt. No odor. He had even kept his clothes relatively clean-looking.

"Your choice. Either take a shower while I prepare your breakfast or after you've eaten. Which will it be?"

He might as well go for the pancakes and shower while she made them, he thought.

"Hey, we ready yet?"

"Steve, I'm not sending him out without breakfast and clean clothes."

"Sorry, kid, I can't wait. That's what you get for sleeping so late." His father shrugged and opened the apartment door.

"Stop teasing him."

"I ain't teasing nobody. I'll just about make the game if I leave now. Bye."

Father pulled the door shut behind him, and Mother ran to do up the three locks on the door.

"Doesn't matter. You'd probably be bored sitting around staring at grown men running after a ball.

"Now, I know you like pancakes. How about my cooking up some while you shower and change?" His mother's painted-on eyebrows arched as her forehead wrinkled.

Jonathan nodded and returned to his bedroom,

where he removed his clothes and let them fall to the floor.

He had to check once again for his jammies. Maybe the ringmaster, not wanting to take in freeloaders, had hung Jonathan's clowns back on the line again. Naked, Jonathan ran to the window. Empty. The line just above his window had no performers today. He stretched the top half of his body out the window to check all the other lines. Most were empty, except for one line that had several midgets drooping from it. Midget socks and undershirts looked petrified hanging five stories above the cement ground. No breeze rustled them to life.

"My God, Jonathan, what do you think you're doing?"

Jonathan pulled himself back into the room and turned to his mother.

"You're naked. You can't stand at the window naked. What if one of the neighbors saw you? They'd think fine mother he has, lets her son run around without any clothes on. Come away from that window before someone sees you." His mother made frantic arm movements.

Jonathan looked down at himself and saw that his weewee was extended. Embarrassed, he ran over, picked his pants up, and quickly pulled them on.

"Go take your shower. The pancakes will be

ready before you are. And I don't want to hear any complaints about the pancakes being cold."

Later that afternoon, Mother spread a blanket over the slats of the fire escape and allowed Jonathan to have lunch under the afternoon sun.

A bony gray alley-cat wandered out from between two buildings. Maybe the cat was hungry, Jonathan thought. If the cat came near Jonathan's building, he could throw down his tuna sandwich. Jonathan slipped his legs between the side rails of the fire escape and attempted to angle the sandwich just right so that the cat wouldn't miss the treat. The cat lazily walked closer to Jonathan's building, its bones rising and falling on its back with every step it took.

Gleefully Jonathan anticipated the moment when he would drop the sandwich. When the cat was almost under the fire escape, Jonathan let go of his sandwich. One slice of bread immediately broke free, while the other slice remained glued to the salad. Halfway down the lettuce also broke free. Instantly when the cat saw this manna dropping from the sky, it took off, running in the opposite direction.

Jonathan was disappointed. He crawled back into the apartment to make himself another sandwich.

Chapter Three

"Where the heck are your Pluto pajamas?" His mother was collecting clothes in preparation for the Monday morning laundry.

"I don't know," Jonathan said. He didn't know where they were. Had the ringmaster thrown them out, donated them to a charity, or were they being used by another little boy of similar size?

"When you get back from church, I want you to check under your bed. So many things seem to get kicked under your bed. And you'd better put on a jacket; Indian summer is over," she said, handing him his Sunday-best navy blue blazer.

Jonathan grabbed the pink donation envelope off the table before leaving. Once he had forgotten the envelope, and he had been called into the principal's office on Monday morning and asked why he hadn't gone to church. He explained that he had forgotten the envelope but had it with him now. The black-garbed nun sitting very straight behind her desk seemed appeased when he handed her the pink envelope on which was a depiction of a seated Christ surrounded by many children.

He climbed the steps of the church, preparing himself for the smell of incense that always seemed to penetrate the air inside the church. He dipped his fingers in the holy water font, made the sign of the cross, and hurried down a side aisle to join his class. He slipped quietly into the pew. After a nudge from a classmate, Jonathan realized that he had forgotten to say a prayer. He dropped down onto the padded kneeler. He was glad he wasn't in eighth grade yet. The eighth-graders got to go to the adult Mass in the basement of the church, but those kneelers had no padding. In the lower church, the congregation had to kneel just as much as those in the upper church, but they had to put up with more pain.

When the priest approached the altar, Jonathan and his classmates stood. His stomach growled. He was going to receive Communion today; therefore, he hadn't eaten breakfast. His tummy was empty to receive the body of Christ.

The sixth-graders in the choir loft sang the opening hymn. He twisted his head around looking for Sister Mary Elizabeth. She was missing Mass. What a relief, Jonathan thought. He wouldn't have to keep track of the ritual, answering the priest's words with the correct responses.

At Communion time Jonathan lined up in the aisle to receive Communion. As he drew closer to the Communion rail his mouth started to dry out. *Oh, please don't stick to the roof of my mouth,* he prayed. They were supposed to stay at the Communion rail until they had swallowed the host, and they weren't supposed to mutilate the host and cause Christ any more agony than He had already suffered for mankind.

An altar boy extended a gold-colored plate beneath Jonathan's chin, and the priest placed the host on Jonathan's tongue. He closed his mouth and instantly felt the cardboardlike host stick to the roof of his mouth. His tongue instinctively peeled the host off the roof, bending the host into a rolled-up cylinder. Quickly he swallowed. On his way back to his pew he prayed for forgiveness. He hadn't meant to mangle Christ; only it was so embarrassing to remain at the altar rail longer than everyone else.

He dropped down on the kneeler, rested his head on his hands, and prayed like hell.

"Please forgive me, Lord," he repeated over and over. His stomach replied with an irritable growl.

Chapter Four

The school year had passed quickly and Lent had come upon them along with a late snowstorm. But Jonathan got up early every morning to attend Mass and receive communion. He was determined to have a complete row of gold stars on the chart in his classroom. Some kids had nothing next to their names; others had only silver stars. He wondered what terrible sins they could have committed to be forced to abstain from Communion and not get a gold star.

Entering the church during Lent always brought a slight chill that shook his body as he walked to his assigned pew. Now the statues were all covered by purple cloth in mourning for the last days of Christ's agony. The angles and curves of each statue and cross pushed hard against the material covering them. Sometimes, if he stared long enough at a statue, he could almost swear it moved, rebellious against the laws of the Church, fighting to free itself from the ignoble shame the Church had fitted onto it.

Faceless and bodiless witnesses surrounded him, and he always made sure he was not the last one out of the church. He didn't want to be alone when one of those draped statues wriggled its way free of the purple cloth. He wondered if at night each pulled itself from the sacking. He smiled thinking about the statues running around in early morning covering each other up. Probably St. Francis made the last check; after all, he had the tiny birds and squirrels to help him wrap up again. The Blessed Mother would always be the one to cover the Infant Christ, who seemed to wave out at the congregation—that is, when he wasn't covered in purple.

After services Jonathan ran around to the small bakery just up the block from his school and bought a sugared jelly donut and a glass of milk that he gulped down before heading for his classes.

The principal rang the handheld brass bell, and everyone froze before walking slowly to their assigned line where students were arranged according to height.

Through all five grades Peter had led his class in

and out of the school. He was always the shortest boy, but the girls didn't seem to mind. Even the gawky girls at the end of the line dreamed of pairing up someday with Peter. *They had a long wait,* thought Jonathan. What did the girls see in the munchkin? Peter even wore short pants and knee socks during the warmer months. *Blah! What a jerk!*

Chapter Five

"Summer vacation starts next week," his mother announced at the dinner table. "Dad and I have a surprise for you."

"Hell, I worked overtime all year for this. Shouldn't be a surprise to anyone who noticed I was gone from the house a lot," grumbled Dad.

"We've rented a house upstate. There's a lake nearby and a small town a short drive away."

Voiceless silence pervaded the room while flatware scraped china and Jonathan kicked one leg of the table.

"Please stop, honey."

Jonathan bent his leg underneath his small body.

"So what do you think?" his mother said.

"I think we made a pretty good deal considering

how many weeks it covers, and we get every week-end during July and August. Pass the buns, Jon."

"I was speaking to Jonathan."

"Answer your mother."

"Sounds like fun, I guess."

"What's wrong with the idea, Jonathan?"

"Kinda hard for me to play with my friends."

"We only have two full weeks in June, and in July and August we can only use it on the weekends, so you'll still get to hang out with your pals."

"Some of the times."

"Jonathan, this is such a great opportunity to get out of the Bronx and see trees and water."

"They got trees in St. Mary's Park. No lakes, though."

"See, Jonathan, you'll be able to swim and boat."

"Whoa, who said we'd rent a boat?" questioned his father.

"It can't be that expensive to rent a boat one or two weekends, Steve."

"Don't get the kid's hopes up too much, Elise."

"Is this opportunity meant for you or me?" Jonathan asked.

"For all of us. Sometimes you can even invite a friend up for a weekend."

Jonathan recalled the fights, his father's burps and farts, his mother slathering on cold cream, his mother nitpicking both him and his father. Naw,

33

no way he'd ever invite a friend for a weekend.

"You got any more beer in the fridge?"

"Steve, look at your gut. You don't need more beer. Matter of fact, I should stop buying it. You don't know how to . . ."

The summer house was tucked away in the midst of a farmer's property. The house had belonged to the farmer's mother, but she had died during the last frigid winter.

Saturday night his father did what he usually did in the Bronx: practice handball and watch television.

"I wish you wouldn't use the side of the house as a handball wall. What if you should break a window or leave scuff marks on the siding?"

Jonathan lay in bed listening to his parents' conversation and the squawking of the television. He hoped they wouldn't stay up too late, since one of them would have to drive him to church in the morning.

"Oh, Jonathan, you don't have to go to church every Sunday."

"That's not what they say at school. It's a mortal sin not to go to Mass, and if I die with a mortal sin on my soul I go to hell, where Satan will torture me."

"God wouldn't send a boy like you to hell. Besides, you have many years to go before you have to worry about dying."

"Hey," yelled his father. "Can you two quiet down? I'm trying to get some extra shut-eye."

"Look what you did. You woke your father up. Bad enough you sneak in the bedroom and shake me awake. I thought something awful had happened."

"Something awful will happen if I don't go to church."

"Your father and I never go to Mass. Think we're headed for hell?"

Jonathan didn't answer.

"Go back to bed or at least stay in your room until your father and I get up. You can take some breakfast back to the room if you want."

"I can't eat before Communion."

"Well, you're not receiving Communion today, so either starve yourself or I'll bring you some milk and cookies."

Jonathan didn't answer.

"Back in that room, young man, and I don't want to hear a peep out of you until I knock on your door. Go." She pointed in the direction of his bedroom. When he didn't move, she merely shrugged and went back to bed herself.

He sat down on the orange shag carpet to sulk.

His right knee was itchy. He had fallen off his bike earlier in the week, and now a scab had formed over the cut he had gotten. Folding his right pants leg back to view the wound, Jonathan remembered how he had once seen an animal licking some scabs on its stomach. Would that help to relieve the itch? He bent over while pulling his knee toward his mouth. His tongue flashed out in a quick lick. He looked around to make sure his parents weren't spying on him.

If we're made in the image and likeness of God, could we eat our own flesh and satisfy the Sunday obligation? he wondered. He scratched at the scab and noticed that it was loose. He picked harder at the brownish red crust. The intact scab fell onto the palm of his hand. He raised the hand above his head.

"Body and Blood of Christ." Delicately he placed the scab on his tongue. Because the scab had a bumpy texture it didn't stick to the roof of his mouth. However, he felt a slight irritation in his throat, as if the scab hadn't gone down all the way.

Jonathan went to the kitchen and turned on the faucet, filling a tall glass with water. He took several gulps and felt the irritation slip away. He placed the glass into the sink and opened the refrigerator, pulling out a gallon of milk for cereal.

* * *

He spent a careless summer attempting to inflict wounds on his body in order to be assured of a host for Communion by the weekend. He even carried his missal with him so that he could read the Mass before taking the host.

One weekend he had no scabs. Several bruises decorated his skin, but no scabs. He had already decided on an alternate plan if this should happen. With missal in hand, he went to the kitchen. He read the Mass up until Holy Communion, then he placed the missal on the table and opened the knife drawer. He selected the one he thought sharpest. Mother always used that knife when cutting tomatoes. She had always praised the fine edge, and Father had routinely sharpened the blade.

He rolled up the right leg of his pajama bottom, exposing his calf. He was glad he leaned toward plumpness and was not one of the frail-looking kids that had thin arms and legs. Heaving a great sigh, Jonathan took the knife to his flesh. If he did it fast, it would hurt less. But he couldn't make that initial incision. He wet his lips, grimaced, locked his leg into a rigid position, but he noticed his hand shook. He closed his eyes and recalled the flogging and crown of thorns Christ had suffered. This was merely a small slice off a plump leg. He felt the cold steel touch his calf. His hands were working without the guidance of his eyes. He let out a hiss from between his gritted teeth and felt the blade slice through his skin. He let out a squeak when he looked down at his handiwork and completed the slicing motion he had started. Blood rolled down his leg like drops of water after a shower. He bandaged the wound and noted that he probably would have quite a scab by next Sunday.

He placed the moist flesh on his tongue and it slipped down his throat easily.

Chapter Six

Jonathan came to enjoy the eating of his own flesh. He had a preference for the freshly sliced meat. The dried-out scabs were not quite as tasty as the moist bloodied flesh from his calf. And the cutting jolted his senses into a heightened awareness.

Secretly Jonathan continued his flesh-eating, even when he returned home and was able to attend Mass. Sometimes he got hunger pangs when he saw fresh wounds or scabs on his fellow classmates. He wondered what the others' flesh tasted like. Probably the taste was similar to his own flesh, since they all were made in the image and likeness of God. But he wondered whether there could be a slight difference. He knew the odor of sweat could vary. His father had a heavy, brutish kind of sweat.

His mother seemed to have a lighter, fluttery sweat like her motions. She even called it perspiration; far more sophisticated than sweat.

He never did get his jammies back. Not that he felt that he owned them. They were free to travel the world if they wanted, but he wished that they had left a tag behind to remember them by.

By the age of twelve, Jonathan was living alone with his mother. He only saw his father one weekend a month, when his father played handball in St. Mary's Park. He and his father would take in a movie at the Paradise Theater on the Grand Concourse. Jonathan always thought the Grand Concourse was where one lived when one had money. It certainly had more charm, fancier buildings, and cleaner streets than where he lived. Inside the Paradise Theater he felt as if he were seated in the courtyard of a fancy castle with the stars shining down on him. As he grew older, the castle glaringly presented itself as only a facade and the stars were merely decorations for the ceiling. The glory of the Grand Concourse wilted under his maturing glare.

Dad remarried and Mom approved, since she said that alone Dad would have drunk himself into an early grave. Dad fathered twin daughters with his new wife, and died shortly after their birth.

"He was always way too heavy," his mother said, shaking her head and slipping a pearl necklace around her neck as contrast to her black dress.

He never did meet his half-sisters. At the wake the new wife didn't even acknowledge Jonathan. He wondered whether it would be okay to ask the new wife if he could visit with his half-sisters. But he had never seen his father's new place while Dad was alive; how could he ask this stranger, Dad's new widow, to bring him home with her?

Mother leaned on Jonathan as if he were strong enough to support both their griefs. He wasn't, but he had to pretend.

Shortly after the funeral, Mother got a job and Jonathan was expected to pitch in with the housework. He didn't have time to watch the clothes in the drier, because he had homework to complete and a grocery list to fill.

The union his father had belonged to offered to give him a partial scholarship for college, but where would the rest of the money come from?

Summers were no longer spent in the country. He now was able to attend Mass every Sunday. The Brothers at the high school he attended suggested entering the seminary as a way to attend college and serve God. However, Mass didn't satisfy anymore. He prayed, but life became more complicated. Mother no longer accepted the cuts and bruises found on his calves. He began to shave thin slices of skin from his feet, and he always wore socks.

When he removed too much flesh, the pain when he walked caused him to sweat.

A New York State Regents Scholarship took care of his tuition at one of the four-year city colleges. One of his girlfriends at college picked at herself. She pulled out strands of her hair by the roots. She squeezed budding pimples until they burst. She'd bite her cuticles until they bled. She'd pick at blisters, and Jonathan would watch the warm clear fluid flow.

"Ouch! What are you doing, Jonathan?"

"Nibbling at your fingers."

She had blisters on her fingers from note-taking and from building a doll house for her little sister. The paper-thin bits of dead skin teased Jonathan's taste buds.

"You're really eating my flesh, aren't you? Kinky."

"I can be kinkier than this." Jonathan smiled with a leer in his eyes.

He no longer had to eat only of himself. Seemed his girlfriend was fascinated by his appetites. Their relationship went well through college and only ended after graduation when she moved out of state.

Jonathan found replacements in fetish clubs and at private parties. But he learned quickly that his addiction was financially draining. However, his

Wall Street employment covered his expenses well.

Some attempted to turn him on to blood-letting. The precious drops sprinkled on his tongue spiked his desire for flesh. Tiny bits of flesh sufficed to feed the hunger. He did not require serious mutilation or death to appease his appetite. Matter of fact, he shivered at the concept of true cannibalism. Ripping apart human bodies to feed his meager taste seemed inappropriate.

Eventually he stopped attending Mass. The Church wouldn't understand his particular passion; therefore he felt like a hypocrite sitting in church, planning his next absolute Communion with God. The silly wafer merely served as a poor man's way of faking his connection to the Lord.

He still muttered the words "Body and Blood of Christ" just before receiving a bit of flesh touched by the hint of the life's blood. But he only whispered the words to himself. He didn't share the connection with his partners. His secret of confidence and power existed in the skin shaved or cut from his own body or from the bodies of others.

Chapter Seven

At the age of forty-two Jonathan met a woman who captured his fancy. She worked in his office, and they were able to become close friends. They'd compare methods of doing business, discuss how the political climate could affect the stock market, occasionally took in the cultural advantages New York afforded the wealthy, and soon embraced in his seventeenth-century bed.

"Were you once a star in one of those old porn movies?" she asked.

"What?"

"You never take your socks off when you come to bed." She teased his nipples with her long reddish-gold hair.

"Bad circulation."

"At least you have good circulation in the important parts of your body," she said, rising to spread her legs across his hips.

Jonathan approved of this woman, and debated with himself about whether he could give up his almost lifelong need to connect with the Lord in a very intimate way. The Communion host was a fraud, a deceit foisted on the faithful to keep them filling the church coffers.

If he and Cindy married, he would want to be true to his wife. This would mean giving up the others that offered of their flesh, not only in a sexual but also in a nutritive way. He would have to regress again to limiting his feedings to his own body. Was Cindy worth the sacrifice?

"Know what?" she whispered. "We could make our own porn movies. You with your black socks, and I could get myself some garter belts and silk stockings."

"So they are no longer two, but one flesh."

Chapter Eight

"You remember, of course," she said.

Jonathan dropped his spoon into the cereal bowl.

"Oh, my Lord, it's today, isn't it? We've been married seven years today."

"The magic number," she whispered in his ear. "It's time for our itch." She scratched him on his upper thigh, not far from his genitals.

"I'll always have an itch for you to scratch." He pulled her down onto his lap and kissed her.

The years they had spent together had been good; not the best, Jonathan reminded himself, but good. He still missed the taste of others' flesh. His own feet were now badly scarred. He never showered with Cindy; he'd be way too embarrassed. She would tease him about that. She thought he was

47

sensitive about how his body looked. She reminded him that he was still in good shape, with a flat abdomen and "bulging" pectorals. Cindy was right; he still had the body of his youth, but his flesh was scarred—not only on his feet. Scars from playing sports, he had told her, but the sports he had played were not written about in *The New York Times* sports section.

"Hey, dreamy eyes, you concocting a surprise for me in that marvelous brain of yours?" she asked.

"Maybe."

"Give me a hint."

"You could never guess at the surprises I could spring on you."

"I don't have time to beg now, but why don't we plan on meeting at a restaurant tonight? Anything special you'd like to eat?"

"You."

"That could be arranged for tonight, big boy."

He wished that it could.

"Did I tell you about the Tomb?" she asked as she rummaged through her handbag, ticking off the essentials she would need at the office.

"Tomb? Someone die?"

"You're so 'not with it,' as my kid sister would say. It's a big plush restaurant that opened in one of those old empty packing factories down by the docks. They have all sorts of Egyptian paraphernalia cluttering up the place. However, their food is supposed to be fantastic. Want to call and check to see if they still have a table available for tonight?"

"What's Egyptian food?"

"Don't worry, the mummy stuff is just a gimmick. They actually serve a light French fare. No heavy sauces. The cream and butter is held to a minimum."

"What fun is that?"

"Do you have a suggestion?"

"I'll cook tonight."

Cindy began to giggle and the giggle grew into a hysterical laugh.

"I cooked for you once before we were married," he said.

"You'll never get me to believe that." She sniffed while gaining control over the laughter. "I know you had that dinner catered. You had to. With those thin slices of meat marinated in herbs and wine. I've never tasted anything like that. And if you had cooked the meal, you would have been able to tell me how to prepare the meat. Tell you the truth, Jonathan, I think it's a secret you don't know."

"I'll leave work early today and prepare dinner."

"The same meal you made before we married?"

"No."

Cindy smiled.

"I don't have access to those special cuts anymore," he said.

"Eight o'clock. This is going to cost you big bucks to get a caterer at this late date."

"Do I lie?" he asked.

"Only about your cooking skills."

Chapter Nine

Jonathan waved farewell to his wife as she pulled out of the driveway. A quick shower, a call into the office, and then he would have the day free to prepare the evening meal.

Before going into the bathroom, he stopped into the bedroom to lay out the antiseptics and bandages that he would need for his feet. Gently he pulled off the cashmere socks and took a deep breath as he hurriedly pulled off the tape covering the bandages. He didn't like the look of one particular cut that seemed to be on the verge of festering. He would give that one an extra cleaning. Wiggling his toes, he enjoyed the luxury of naked feet. Sometimes he would put a layer of Vaseline over the wounds to prevent the burning sensation caused by the soap and hot water. This morning he would bear the pain in order to give the scabs and cuts a complete cleaning.

Having a separate bathroom from his wife was a must, not just because of the numerous tapes, bandages, and antiseptics that he kept, but also because Cindy was a slob. When he turned on the light in his bathroom the white tiles shined, the towels were warming on a rack, the floor-to-ceiling mirror was unsmudged, and the open shower stall was mildew-free. And before he left the bathroom he would wipe off the tiles and neatly place his towels into a hamper. The cleaning lady came only twice a week, and Jonathan couldn't abide waking up to soggy towels and mildew. Cindy, on the other hand, called herself a free spirit and claimed to be open to all kinds of experiences, including a little dampness and a slight blackening of her bathroom's pink tiles.

He turned on the water nozzles and regulated the temperature. Water spurted from the mouths of gold dolphins affixed to opposite walls of the shower. As he stepped into the spray, his feet tingled at the sting of the water droplets bouncing against his flesh.

"Ow, ow, ow, ow."

Several minutes passed before he could tolerate the agony of his feet. Finally he mellowed to the sting and rubbed his skin vigorously, only dabbing lightly at the flesh on his feet.

He washed his neatly cut hair last, and added a slight bit of rinse to the last pass.

Jonathan shut off the water and stepped onto the heated marble tiles of the bathroom floor. The warm, plush, Egyptian cotton towel felt good on his wet flesh. Cindy had bought some cotton/polyester towels at a sale. She had even expected him to use them. He had immediately taken them out to the trash.

He looked down at his bulky thighs. Could he slice off some meat from each thigh and give a repeat performance of the meal she held in such awe? Of course, that flesh hadn't come from his own thighs, but his thighs might taste as good as the slices he'd used before. Making love would certainly be difficult tonight with the fresh cuts.

Jonathan walked into the bedroom and sat down on the champagne-colored goose-down comforter. He'd have to shave the inside of his thighs, but that could be done later, closer to mealtime.

With the bandages laid out before him, he began applying antiseptic to his feet.

The bedroom door opened, and his wife rushed into the room.

"Forgot the papers I was working on last night.

They must have gotten shunted under the bed when I—"

Cindy knelt down on the floor directly in front of his feet. He heard her gasp, and watched as she raised her right hand to almost touch his wounded feet.

"What on earth happened to your feet?" She looked up into his eyes.

Jonathan swallowed the lump in his throat and offered to explain, but she interrupted.

"Is it a disease? Do you have diabetes?" And then the big question. "Is it catching?"

"I did it myself," he admitted.

"What the hell are you talking about?"

"I eat tiny pieces of flesh. Not every day. My feet would be in far worse condition if I did. I probably wouldn't even be able to walk if I allowed myself to overindulge. I eat far less flesh than before we were married. I mean, I haven't been unfaithful to you."

"Unfaithful?" Her forehead wrinkled. "Wait. Wait. You used to eat other people's flesh?"

"Sometimes we'd exchange."

"Your right knee for somebody else's elbow?"

"It was a bit more . . . How can I say?"

"Say freak." Cindy's eyes darkened to a deep violet. Her mouth compressed into a thin line.

"I'd let you taste . . ." Jonathan instinctively

stretched his right foot out to Cindy, and she fell backward onto her behind.

"Cindy, you eat strange animals that you don't even know where they've been or how they've been fed. Why not eat from someone with whom you are close?"

"Because it's cannibalistic."

"I've seen what you do when you cut a finger. You put the finger in your mouth and suck on it."

"I do not."

"You don't even think about it. Basic instinct takes over. Rather than let your lifeblood be wasted, you take back in what is dripping out. The next time you do it I'll call it to your attention."

"How long have you been doing this?" She nodded, indicating his feet while her face wrinkled in displeasure.

"Since I was a child."

"Oh!" Cindy slid her body across the carpet, attempting to place a wide distance between herself and her husband.

"Didn't you ever do anything like that as a child or know of someone who did?"

"Eat flesh?"

"I started with scabs and progressed."

Tears shimmered in her eyes.

"Listen, I'll show you how to do it without too much pain. Once you've tasted your own flesh, you'll be hooked. You'll have a mystical experience. You believe you're eating the body and blood of Christ when you take Communion, don't you?"

"There is no way you can compare this to taking Communion."

"Why not?"

"Because . . ." She fell silent, shaking her head.

"Because the Communion wafer is bread and the blood really wine? No, you can't say that, Cindy. If you truly believe your religion, you know that the bread and wine have been changed." Jonathan knelt down on the carpet in front of his wife. "And you do believe." He reached out and took hold of her right wrist as she tried to jerk away. "You nibble on your own nails. That's why you have to wear these fakes on your fingertips." He lifted her fingers to his lips and ripped off a fake nail with his teeth. "Look at the stubs you have underneath." He rounded her finger with his tongue, finally settling into nibbling on the jagged nail.

"Oh hell, you're sick," she screamed, trying to pull her hand from his.

He yanked her closer to him.

"I've wanted to taste you for so long. Please join with me."

The towel that had been wrapped around his waist fell to the floor, revealing a solid erection.

"Pervert! Bastard!" she yelled, whipping her left hand around to slap his face.

He let go of her wrist, and her arms flailed about connecting sometimes with his body, but mostly stirring the particles of dust around her. He watched the spinning particles in the halo of the sun that crept in from the window.

"It's a religious experience, Cindy. Try to understand."

His wife got to her feet and glared down at him.

"I can't live with the kind of twisted person you are." He watched her turn and run from the room. Several seconds later the front door slammed.

Chapter Ten

"I miss you." He gripped the telephone tightly. No response.

"I've become totally nonfunctional. Can't do my work. Hell, you should see my bathroom. Towels on the floor, water staining the tiles. I keep the nightlight on at night now. I hate waking and reaching for you and you're not there. At least with the light I can orient myself faster. It's been, what? Forty-eight hours, and your clothes in the closet and knicknacks on the dresser are driving me crazy. Believe it or not, I can't even eat."

"You never know when to shut up, do you?" Cindy asked.

He sighed and lay back upon two pillows. The

bed had remained unmade. The champagne comforter was stained with antiseptic.

"It can't be comfortable in that motel," he said.

"I'm making do. Where else can I go? I can't imagine telling friends why we split up."

"Hey, we're not officially separated. This is just a misunderstanding between us." He shoved his feet under the comforter.

"No, Jonathan, this is more than a misunderstanding. You need to get help. And I can tell you that I will never return to that house until you do."

"Help?"

"Like from a psychiatrist."

"Come back and help me, Cindy. Talk to me. Hold me. You don't have to understand; just be here for me."

"When you can prove that you've started to get some help. Until then, I don't feel I can trust you."

"I would never harm you."

"What do you mean? You're talking about eating me."

"A small taste of your flesh." He kicked the comforter to the floor. "You're right, I don't know when to shut up."

"Does your mother know?"

"My mother?"

"She's known you all your life; she must have

some clue as to what you've been doing."

"My mother is one of the most clueless people around."

"Talk to her. She'll give you the support you need to get help."

"You won't."

"It's so gross. But yes, if you start to get help, I'll also support you."

"Let's leave my mother out of it completely. She has her own problems with the hypertension and diabetes. She needs me to support her, not the other way around."

"But she's such a good woman, Jonathan. I'm sure if you . . ."

Jonathan took one of the pillows from beneath his head and flung it across the room.

"Stop with my mother, Cindy. What you're really saying is that you can't cope with the situation."

Silence was his answer. Jonathan slammed the receiver back on the cradle.

Jonathan spent the next several days slogging through the work he had taken home and eating the garden burgers Cindy had stocked in the freezer.

He was picking corn kernels out of his teeth when the front doorbell rang. He had asked the office to send a messenger over, and therefore couldn't afford to ignore the bell.

Wearing a T-shirt and khaki shorts, he peeled himself off the leather couch and walked barefoot to the door.

"I got a shitload of papers I'd like you to take back to the office. Naomi should . . ."

He had pulled the door open and started back to the living room assuming the messenger would follow. He sensed no one was behind him.

"I'm sorry, Jon, if this is a bad time. I just thought it would take me at most fifteen minutes to get what I want."

He turned and saw Cindy standing at the threshold, and behind her was a burly six-foot-four male. Hair sprouted out from under the man's shirt. His black shoulder-length hair gleamed under the light of the sun.

"Oh, I'm sorry. This is Mario. He works at the motel where I'm staying, and he offered to help."

"Help fend me off?"

"Please, let's not make a scene. Mario came along to help me lift some of the suitcases. I didn't expect you to help me."

He hadn't remembered Cindy being so scrawny. He knew she constantly dieted, but hadn't noticed the amount of weight she had lost over the past few months. Her breasts were still firm and full, but her calves looked slight, lacking muscle.

"Is it all right?" she asked.

He looked at her quizzically.

"If we come in and get some of my things."

"I don't like strangers in my home," he warned.

"We'll only be a few minutes, and I promise not to come back again." She must have realized how this sounded, because she attempted to clarify. "I'll be back alone, of course, if you get help. I really don't want to move out."

"I don't want Mario moving in."

"Jon, he's only helping. We started chatting and I . . ."

"Told him about our problem."

"Not completely. He just knows that we've been having difficulty in our marriage."

"I eat human flesh, Mario."

"Stop it, Jonathan. Don't try to scare him."

"Like I scared you."

Mario started to shuffle his feet and glance back toward the car in which they had come. Finally he seemed to make a decision, and turned back to speak to Jonathan.

"Hey, she offered to give me a C note if I carried some stuff away. I don't know nothing about what kind of marriage you two got. I can go wait in the car until she's packed."

"Maybe that would be best, Mario," she said. Immediately he turned and lumbered over to her Jaguar.

"How could you bring that idiot along with you?" Jonathan demanded.

"I've already explained. May I come in and pack my things?"

"You live here, Cindy. Why didn't you use your key?"

"Because I don't live here anymore."

"Instead you've taken up residence at Mario's motel."

"It's not his motel. He's a maintenance man."

Jonathan laughed. "What were you having maintained?"

"He was replacing some lights in the hall when I got off the elevator one day, and I was so distracted by our situation that I almost walked into his ladder. I felt bad about almost knocking him over, so I stopped, apologized, and we started talking."

"About our marriage."

"I was explaining why I was so distracted."

"Pack up your stuff, Cindy, and get the hell out of here." He walked back to the living room and plopped himself down on the mauve leather couch.

"This isn't my fault," she called from the hall. "If you'd admit you have a problem and get some help . . . I should call your mother myself. She'd be shocked to hear what you've been doing."

Jonathan threw a legal-sized pad at the living room doorway and jumped to his feet.

"Don't you dare say anything to my mother," he yelled.

Quietly and slowly Cindy came into view.

"I don't mean any of this to hurt you, Jon. I love you. Please, I want you to get help, and I'm frustrated because you won't listen to me. I'm trying to find a way to get through to you."

"My mother's not the answer."

"You've never yelled at me like this before." Her bottom lip pouted out and her eyes shimmered with tears. "Don't you even want to try?"

Jonathan fell back onto the couch.

"What the hell have I been talking about, Cindy?"

"About eating me."

"I've done that lots of times." Jonathan smirked.

Cindy shook her head. "I think you're beyond help." She turned her back on him and headed for the bedroom.

Chapter Eleven

"She's been calling me and hinting that something's wrong with you. I don't understand. And she tells me not to call her. And now you're telling me that she's not there. Jonathan, I'm too old to be worrying about you. Is the marriage on the rocks? I never liked her all that much, you know. I tried to accommodate her the best I could. She always made me so nervous the way she's such a busybody."

"Mom, calm down."

"How can I calm down when that wife of yours spends the weekends on the phone with me complaining? And she does it in such a way that I don't even know what she's talking about."

"I didn't know she was bothering you, Mom."

"She's ruining my health. I take a hypertension pill the minute I get off the phone."

"If you don't settle down, you'll be taking another one soon."

"I have them in front of me."

"I will speak to Cindy and tell her to stop calling you."

"That won't do any good. Besides, she asked me not to tell you that she had called. What if you two get back together? She'll never trust me again. The relationship would be so awkward."

"Mom, do you really care what she thinks of you?"

"She's been telling me that I should come over and look at your feet. What's wrong with your feet? When you lived at home there was never anything wrong with your feet."

"She doesn't like my feet. They gross her out."

"Your feet? You've been married seven years. Hasn't she gotten used to them yet?"

"She hates feet. All sorts of feet."

"Your cousin, Eddy, was like that. Used to scream and yell when his poor parents tried to cut his toenails. I don't know whether he ever got over that."

"Let's not drift, Mom. I'll telephone Cindy and . . ."

"Don't say I called."

"How about you visited?"

"No, don't even mention my name."

Jonathan could hear running water over the phone. His mother had probably started making her own dinner.

"You know I can't travel far; otherwise I would come and visit," she said. "Would it satisfy her if you visited me?"

"Mom, relax. I'll take care of the situation from here."

Jonathan began flipping through the Yellow Pages.

"I just don't want her calling me anymore. She's making you sound like . . ."

Jonathan stabbed his finger on "Psychiatrists."

"Sound like what, Mom?"

"She makes it sound as if you were engaged in some sort of peculiar behavior. Personally, I think she's the one with the problem. Sobbing to me over the phone and threatening to leave you. But now you tell me she already *has* left you."

"Sometimes marriages don't work out. You certainly know about that."

"Do you think this is all happening because your father left us?"

"No, Mom. I married a nut-job all on my own. Not your fault. Not Dad's."

"May he rest in peace."

Jonathan ran his finger down the column of names. He needed a name that would impress Cindy, or maybe a well-known clinic.

"I have to go, Mom."

"You promise you'll do something about your wife?"

"After I hang up with you, I'll make a quick call that should help solve our problems."

"You don't have to stay with her, Jonathan."

"I know that."

"Don't force yourself to stay in a relationship with an unstable person. She can only make your life hell."

"Hey, I know."

"What are you going to do?"

"Call a mental-health specialist."

"For marriage counseling?"

"Yeah, that's what we'll get, some marriage counseling."

"You're still in the house, right?"

"Mom, you called me. If I weren't here you wouldn't have been able to reach me."

"Don't give up the house, Jonathan. You work hard for your money."

"So does Cindy."

"But you've had the house far longer than you've been married. Stand firm. Don't let her drive you out."

"I've already driven her out, so I don't think we have to worry."

"Thank God you never had children with her. I remember how sad you were when your father left, and then he hardly ever bothered to visit with his own son."

"Dad's dead, Mom. He'll never be able to disrupt our lives again. And I won't allow Cindy to make our lives miserable."

"Your dad and I saw a marriage counselor for a while. Didn't do any good, obviously. Seems like she took his side in every confrontation. His drinking and carousing didn't seem to amount to much to her. Every time I started complaining about one of those issues, she'd tell me to get in touch with my inner self and talk about the real problem. I think the real problem was her. Hell, she encouraged him to leave me. Do you believe that? She asked him why he stayed with me, and when he couldn't come up with an answer he packed his bags and left the house. Left the two of us behind as if we had never meant anything to him."

"Maybe we hadn't."

"Oh, Jonathan, I don't want to put bad ideas in your head about your father. He'll always be your father."

"Whether he liked it or not."

"Jonathan, he can hear you."

"Six feet under?"

"Wherever he is. May—"

"May he rest in peace. How about letting me go so I can drum up some peace for us?"

Chapter Twelve

Cindy leaned back in her chair and smiled. Jon had made an appointment at a clinic and was starting this coming Thursday. Relief seemed to spread through her body. She'd see him the night before the appointment. She shook her head. Mario had been starting to look good to her. Not that he hadn't before, but she had started to feel super-horny. Knowing that she'd get laid Wednesday night would help deter her lust for the maintenance man.

Jon had promised to make that special meal he had made for her before they were married. She still teased him about needing to find a caterer, but she knew he personally would make the dinner and spend enormous time doing it just for her.

Mary Ann Mitchell

She hadn't thought he would come around this easy. Maybe his mother had paid him a visit or called or done something. Cindy couldn't ask. He would be furious with her for speaking to his mother about his problem. Cindy couldn't understand why. Elise seemed like the perfect mother. She had raised Jon by herself for years, and then, when his father died, Jon had bonded even closer with his mother. Lord, he hadn't gotten married until he was forty-two. Not that he had lived with his mother, but he had spent every other weekend flying down to Miami to visit Elise. Unfortunately, after they had married, they hadn't had as much free time. But his mother had understood and had always been so gracious over the phone.

Cindy loved, lusted, respected, and worshiped her husband. It was so sad that he had allowed himself to get mixed up with some really twisted people. How else would he have come upon this freakish fetish of his?

She'd have to buy new clothes. Something with which to seduce him. He loved the color red on her. Perhaps a slightly sheer outfit; she could wear a light coat while she was outdoors, and then slowly slip her arms from the sleeves. The slower, the better. Hell, they could do it right there on the hall floor. They had before. They could eat after their proper reunion.

Should she call his mother and tell her the good news? Elise would be so relieved. Besides, Cindy should thank her for whatever she had done to turn him around.

Cindy pulled up Elise's telephone number on her Palm Pilot. She was so nervous that the cellular phone almost slipped from her fingers. What if she gave his mother false hope? Yes, he had agreed to get help, and she knew he meant it, but . . .

After pacing the room for fifteen minutes, she put the cellular phone back in her briefcase. She desperately wanted to share her good news with someone, but was too embarrassed to tell friends. Bad enough she and Jon had separated, but to have to tell people why . . . *My husband's been eating his feet for years. No, I never suspected. Why should I? He always kept his socks on. Guess it wasn't just cold feet, he-he.*

Pathetic. There was Mario, though. He'd be out of her life as soon as Jon got help. She could curl up in his muscular arms and . . . Cindy pointed her right index finger at her right temple and pulled an imaginary trigger. A married woman didn't even consider curling up in another man's arms; or at least she didn't actually do it. However, hot fantasies can get one through a lonely night.

Chapter Thirteen

Jonathan hated these sudden New York downpours, especially when he was wearing a fifteen-hundred-dollar suit. He stomped his feet in the vestibule of Saint Anthony's church. He heard the thunder crack. He was glad he couldn't see the lightning from where he was standing. Lightning had always been scary for him. He opened the church door a crack, and decided that the rain wouldn't go away soon. Gently he closed the door and turned to enter the central aisle of the church. Walking down the aisle, he felt the emptiness of the church surround him. Cindy still practiced her faith, in a way. Sometimes she made it to church, and she never failed to confess her sins at least once a year. Communion martyred her. Without sausages and eggs in the morning she would declare a torture day.

She didn't know pain, did she, Lord?

He decided to kneel at the Communion rail. His knees sunk into the red vinyl pad. He rested his folded hands on the rail. Cold. The marble. The metal rail. The aloof statues. All so cold.

Eager to seek warmth, Jonathan rose to his feet, pushed open the railing gate, and walked toward the center altar. He climbed two steps and laid his hands on the cloth covering the altar. He looked up at the cross.

"Lord, why hast Thou forsaken me?" He whispered the words, sensing the odor of incense and a punishing chill.

"What are you doing there?"

Ancient hands pressed down on Jonathan's. Surprisingly warm, the hands lifted Jonathan's hands from the altar.

"I wanted to get out of the rain."

"That's fine. We don't mind you sitting in one of the pews until the storm lets up, but please stay outside the railing."

Jonathan turned and looked into faded blue eyes. Weary eyes. Eyes that were tired of saving souls or perhaps tired of the futile attempt. Except for his collar, the priest was dressed in black. He had been tall and straight, but the elderly stoop now gave him a sad appearance. He pulled Jonathan along, down the steps and out the railing gate, the priest's movements slow and careful. Jonathan grabbed the priest's hands tightly before he could pull away.

"How long have you served God?" Jonathan asked.

"All my life. If you would please let go, I was on my way to the sacristy."

Jonathan looked down at the priest's hands and saw the knobbiness of the joints, the skin shriveled and purpled by veins.

"Did you worship Him when you were a boy? Did you ever sin against Him? Has He ever punished you?" Jonathan asked.

"If you are having a crisis of faith . . ."

"I've gone way beyond the crisis point." Jonathan could feel the priest attempting to pull away. "Father, do you know that you're the only warmth in this church? Look at me. I'm wet and cold. That plaster statue of Mary and the metal cross on which the Lord rests are cool to the touch. But you are stoking a fire from within. Why?"

"Sir, I would be happy to make an appointment with you to discuss—"

"What about now? It's raining outside, and the Lord doesn't need your ministrations at this moment. Here, sit with me." Jonathan led the priest over to the front pew and sat, dragging the priest down with him. He loosened his grip, and the priest immediately pulled away. "Tell me, Father, how you've managed to maintain your faith after all these years."

"Perhaps you'd like to tell me how you lost yours," the priest said. He settled back against the pew, and turned slightly toward Jonathan.

"I didn't. I changed allegiance. I have faith in myself. I taste of my own body and blood because they are there. They are real. They have taste, odor, texture."

"This is mockery."

"No. I want to know how you can believe in something you can't touch."

"I have kept my faith."

"But how? I would follow anyone that acknowledged me, showed me his flesh, and allowed me a taste."

"The Lord does at every celebration of the Holy Eucharist."

Both men heard the church door open and close. Turning in unison, they saw a man enter. His hair, slick and black from the rain, clung to his scalp. High cheekbones, hollowed-out cheeks, and a straight narrow nose dominated his features. His eyes were small slits and his lips thin. His black trench coat shimmered raindrops, and his suit and tie spoke of wealth. The stranger left three pews' distance between himself and the priest and Jonathan.

The priest seemed uneasy. He looked back at Jonathan.

"This is a sanctuary; I cannot drive anyone out, but please don't blaspheme while you are here."

"Father, do you know the man who has just joined us?"

"No, I don't know either of you." The priest stood.

Nor does he want to, Jonathan thought.

"You are both welcome to stay," the priest said, turning his head from Jonathan to the stranger. "I must go back to certain church matters." He turned away from the interlopers and walked back to the altar, genuflecting briefly and with obvious pain before retreating.

Jonathan looked back at the stranger. The man had closed his eyes. He didn't even seem to breathe, so still was his body. Jonathan wished that his conversation with the priest had not been disturbed. Cranky and resentful, he turned back to stare at the altar. He could hear the man a few pews away shrug out of his trench coat; the belt loudly rapped on the wood. The stranger must have been moving around, because the pew creaked. A steady whine of wood adjusting to the tensions torquing it.

Jonathan had enjoyed the former solitude of the

church. The stranger's invasion had electrified the air with unrest. The same restless feel that Cindy had initiated in him. It was time for her to taste of his flesh and to share hers with him.

Chapter Fourteen

Cindy stopped at a familiar bar restaurant not far from Jon's house. She sipped a dry sherry to gain courage and confidence. The synthetic lining of her black leather coat pressed against the bare spaces of skin that were not covered by the torchon lace of her blatantly sexy dress.

She liked this family-oriented place. No one bothered her at the bar, and she watched the bartender pour as many Cokes as shots of Jack Daniels. The children were often loud here, intruding upon her and Jon's dinner conversations, but the children also reminded them that it was time to start a family. Cindy smiled while watching a female toddler run from her mother. The scene sparked laughter and an ease that made strangers nod at each other.

She didn't need to build up her courage anymore. She needed to be with her husband.

After paying her tab, she drove her Jaguar the short distance to . . . no, not Jon's house, but *their* house. Jonathan had evidently parked his car in the garage, since the driveway was empty, leaving plenty of space for her to park.

As she exited the car, Cindy started to undo the buttons on her leather coat. Her bare legs chilled to the night air, causing goose bumps to form.

Cindy walked past the kitchen window, and saw her husband busily working over the gas range. He wore the navy cashmere sweater, her favorite. The one with the elbows peeking through the material. The sweater had been her first gift to him, along with a magnum of champagne that hadn't lasted quite as long.

She put her hand in her right pocket and fingered the key to the house. Was it too forward to barge in and surprise him in the kitchen? She weighed the key in the palm of her hand and bit down on her lower lip. Better not take too long to decide, she reminded herself. Jonathan had said that he had to get up early in the morning for his psychiatric appointment.

Pulling her hand out of the pocket, she marched to the front door and slipped the key into the lock, turning the bolt slowly in order to surprise him.

As soon as she pushed opened the front door, savory smells caused her mouth to water. She slid the coat off her shoulders and let it fall to the floor. Should she leave the coat there? Not if she were trying to get on his good side. Lifting the coat off the floor, Cindy took a deep breath and started for the kitchen. She held the coat at her side as she filled the doorway with her lusciously laced body.

Several minutes passed before Jonathan sensed her presence. He turned away from the salad he had been preparing, still holding the half-empty balsamic vinegar bottle.

"Wow!"

Awkwardly, he placed the bottle on the counter and rushed to Cindy.

"You look fantastic," he murmured, reaching for the coat in her hand.

Cindy wished he could forget the coat and make love to her here on the tile kitchen floor. But being Jonathan, he neatly hung her coat in the hall closet.

Coyly she rubbed against him as he reentered the kitchen.

"Don't you like?" she asked, holding her arms out wide from her body.

"Of course, but if I stop now the meal would be ruined. The delicate slices of meat can marinate just so long. Since the meat is uncooked, there is nothing to mask the herbal power flowing through this

82

prime cut." He never stopped his movements as he spoke. He hadn't even looked at her. "This is a very special dinner. I don't want the meat to be wasted."

Shrugging her shoulders, Cindy walked over to the refrigerator, found a bottle of white wine, and took it out.

"No, no," he said, taking the bottle from her hand. "Champagne is already chilling in the dining room. Everything shall be perfect."

It would be so perfect, thought Cindy, *that she'd get bored and go home before the meal was even on the table.*

She managed to outwait the preparation, and was glad she had when she tasted the paper-thin sliced meat on her plate.

"I thought you said you wouldn't be able to duplicate that first meal you made for me."

"I decided to go to extra lengths to please you tonight," he said.

The champagne bubbles tickled her palate. She couldn't quite recognize the kind of meat she was eating, but the taste was delicate and light.

"I guess this is all there is," she said, indicating the last bite of meat on her plate.

"Couldn't afford any more than what we have before us."

"Come on, Jon, how expensive can this be? Hell,

we can afford to go out to four-star restaurants at the spur of the moment."

"Restaurants couldn't afford to sell meat of this quality."

Hours later with the lights dimmed, the softness of leather teasing her flesh, and her shoes thankfully forgotten under the dinner table, she relaxed in Jonathan's arms.

"I love you, Jon. I never wanted to leave. It's just that initially your problem seemed so creepy. But now that you're getting psychiatric help, I know you're serious about changing." She gave him a peck on his smooth right cheek.

"I've thought long about this, Cindy. I knew I had to make a decision."

"And you've made the right one." She leaned her breasts against his chest and began licking his lips. When he opened his mouth she moved to the tip of his nose. He closed his eyes and laughed. Lightly she licked each of his eyelids. His hands grabbed at her body, nails catching in the delicate strands of the lace.

"We need to get to know each other all over again," she breathed into his ear.

The fingers of one of his hands lightly pinched the tip of her right breast, while his other hand fumbled to find an opening in the dress. She giggled at his clumsiness and began to undo the buttons on his cardigan.

"Let's have a race," she said.

By the time she was naked neither cared about who had won. Still wearing his jeans, Jonathan carried her into the music room and stretched her out on a Le Corbusier chaise-lounge chair next to the baby grand piano.

"I love a man with imagination," she said, fingering the padded cuffs that hung down from the sides of the chair.

"And I'm turned on by adventurous women." He swept his denim-covered erection back and forth across her mons while manacling her to the chair.

She stretched her legs out, enabling him to manacle her ankles to the foot of the chair.

Cindy lay back and allowed Jonathan to play with her flesh. The heat of his body, the wetness of his mouth, the flutter of his breath, and the coarse hairs of his chest spun her into a whirlwind of sensations, every touch inspiring her body to greater heights of pleasure.

He lifted himself off her body and undid his jeans, sliding the denim down over his slender hips. As the jeans fell to his ankles, Cindy saw the bandages covering both his inner thighs. He ripped the bandages off and whispered so that she could barely hear.

"Bon appétit." And he jammed his erection into her mouth, the wounds on his thighs rubbing against her cheeks, opening to allow blood to slide across soft skin and drip down upon her chin.

Chapter Fifteen

Jonathan watched his wife cry. He didn't think he had ever seen her cry before, at least not with this kind of passion. She was still manacled to the chair, making it impossible for her to wipe away her tears. Her lips shivered, her nose bobbed, as she attempted to breathe through her clogged nostrils. She hadn't looked at him since he had torn the bandages off his thighs. Instead she'd kept her eyelids tightly shut. Well, if she was going to ignore him, he could do the same to her. He walked out of the room, closing the door behind him.

She could scream and yell, but no one would hear her. That had been assured years ago when she'd decided to take piano lessons and had had the room soundproofed. Didn't want neighbors being bothered by all those wrong notes. *Such a good idea, Cindy,* he thought.

His thighs stung painfully, but he liked the sharpness and precision the pain awakened in his brain.

Knowing that Cindy would check, Jonathan had made an appointment at a clinic, and had canceled it immediately before starting dinner. A meal that she had savored.

He showered while thinking about how he liked the high emotional pitch both his wounds and making love had brought to him. He had hated the emptiness of his depression, had hated having to listen to his mother's whining voice. Had hated the disgust in Cindy's voice. And Mario . . . That stallion could nose around somebody else's wife.

Jonathan felt in control again.

Once he had toweled himself down, he brought out the antiseptic and the bandages. When he finished, he slipped on a terry-cloth robe, tying the belt tightly.

Haltingly he pushed open the door to the music room. Silence. Not a whimper. Only if he stood perfectly still could he hear her breaths. Ragged breaths.

"Cindy?" He kept his voice soft and gentle. "I'm back, honey."

He walked over to where she was lying on the chaise lounge. The anger in her eyes astonished Jonathan. He had expected fear. Instead she stared back in defiance.

"I wish I could puke up that meal right in your face." The gravelly sound of her voice informed him that she was truly angry.

"Don't you understand why I did this?"

"Because you're a perverted bastard," she shouted.

"Sometimes I can be a bastard, but I never think of myself as a pervert."

"You're sick!"

"And tired of trying to explain myself to you. Don't you feel the rush from the meal? You ate my flesh. I'm your lord. Let me show you."

Jonathan ran from the room to retrieve a knife. The one he kept for these occasions.

Chapter Sixteen

Cindy's body ached. Her hands were becoming numb. She looked around the familiar room and was amazed how different it now looked to her.

She had loved the Michael Parkes fantasy painting they had bought in Chicago, but now it had become part of her nightmare, staring down at her, inviting her to let loose inside its world. A world where human and beast made contact in very personal and sensuous ways. She wished she could have a tiger basking next to her, his head softly creasing the white linen of her gown. That asshole wouldn't be able to play his terrible games.

The stillness of the room only served to enhance her dread. What could he be bringing back? If only it was the key to the manacles that confined her.

Too soon, Jonathan returned, carrying a knife, a surgical knife.

"I've proven my love for you. Now it's your turn, sweetheart." He moved slowly across the room, the smile on his face maddening in its warmth, his eyes cold and clever.

"What the hell are you going to do with that?"

"That? Please be more specific, honey. Do you mean my erection or the knife?"

"I wish to hell you'd cut that fucker off."

"Good. You're almost catching on. Except, as I said, I have already proven my love for you and have allowed you to reverently feed from me. I must worship you in the same way. Shall it be a little bit of breast, or . . ."

She watched his eyes search her naked body.

"You've become much too thin, honey. Ah, but you do have a little excess on the tummy." He patted her abdomen as if she were in a Kansas meat yard.

"Get away from me!" She lunged forward and felt pain gnaw at her ankles and wrists. Her fingers tingled half-asleep, half-awake.

"I only want a taste. Don't you want to share your body and blood with me? I take of you for my strength and you take of me for yours. Amen." He bowed his head.

"Christ . . ."

"Yes," he said, smiling benevolently down at her.

"Take these manacles off now or I'll tell your mother about this."

"I'm not a little boy. Reporting back to my mother doesn't change anything."

"Then you know I've spoken to her and she realizes there is something seriously wrong with you. Do you want me showing her wounds made by her only child?"

"Certainly not. I simply want you to enjoy this as much as I do." He laid the cold of the steel blade atop her abdomen. "Your nipples are hardening. You're excited."

Cindy shook her head. "I'm scared. Don't frighten me like this, Jon. Please unlock the cuffs, and we'll talk."

"Talking is your only solution, isn't it, Cindy? You talk to my mother. You talk to Mario, the maintenance man. You tell them all about our lives together. You keep nothing private for you and me.

"Only a nibble, that's all I wanted. I didn't want to lop off huge layers of flesh." Jonathan got down on his knees. "Just an itty-bitty taste."

Her breath faltered as the knife slid in and out of her flesh.

He held up the bleeding flesh for her to see. She watched her own blood drip from between his fingers. She lifted her head up and saw the open patch he had made in her flesh. She lay her head back against the chair, wondering why it didn't hurt more. Suddenly she became aware that Jon had moved closer to her face.

"Do you want first taste?" He held the ragged flesh close to her lips. A drop or two of blood wet her lips, but did not whet her appetite. Instead she felt the gorge in the pit of her stomach rise up into her mouth, and she almost choked on her own sickness. Her day's intake of food spurted from between her lips, staining her chin and jowls with the burning liquid.

Jonathan tsked. She looked toward him and watched as his tongue lapped the slimy flesh from the palm of his hand. The remaining blood he wiped off across his chest.

"Are you going to tell Mommy about my bad manners, honey?"

The smell of her vomit faded. The shape of Jonathan's body became a shadow as she realized a deep faint was about to rescue her.

Chapter Seventeen

On his way home from the office Jonathan passed a church. A small church that he had never noticed before. No elaborate ornamentation decorated the front of the church, and there was but a single set of doors to enter. He climbed the few steps, noticing at the top step that the doors were slightly ajar.

Definitely an invitation, he thought, pulling one of the doors open. Odd, the smell that drifted out at him. Neither burning wax nor incense. Something more human. Blood, he thought at first. But it wasn't only blood. Sweat, vomit, waste, flesh all mingled in equal parts. Abhorrent, but also inviting.

He suddenly realized a man stood behind him trying to get by and into the church. Immediately

Jonathan entered the church, not because he wanted to. No, actually he remembered that he had been about to turn away. However, he didn't want to cause confusion by getting in the man's way, so in he walked, followed by the man, who muttered some words. He couldn't tell if the words were "Thank you" or something else since they seemed so slurred. A drunk, Jonathan thought, seeking asylum.

Wrong. The man passed him, dressed in a rich dark cashmere coat. Hair cut precisely but fuller than Jonathan had remembered from . . . He had seen him somewhere else.

There was but a single aisle, and the man traveled slowly across the marble floor, passing pew after pew. Sometimes touching the varnished wood of a pew, the man stopped directly in front of the Communion rail and waited. He didn't kneel. He stood tall and waited.

Curious, Jonathan followed the man's path until he stopped to sit at the first pew. The odor wasn't as oppressive as it had been when he first opened the door. And there was a chill in the church. The altar, a bit shabby with torn and stained cloth covering it, filled the center. The center cross looked rusted. A greenish tint sharpened the creases of the Christ figure that hung from the cross. The altar candles were almost burned down to the bottom of the wicks.

"Kneel."

Jonathan looked back at the man, who still stood with his back to him. The man didn't move. Jonathan waited to hear the man speak again.

"All hail, my Brother," the man's voice boomed out. However, the man showed no homage to anyone.

Jonathan waited now, excited by the mood the man had set.

"The Siberian Yakut have a story they tell about my family. My Father, a powerful man, controlled my Brother and me. We moved nowhere without his following. He was present inside our minds and watched our physical movements with precision. I would twitch, and Father instantly was wary. Of course this made me more anxious, so that I could barely hold myself still.

"My placid Brother watched us and feigned his love for me. But I knew the truth and so did Father, even though he never admitted it. For our Father is all-knowing. He is not a dupe in this conspiracy, but an active participatant.

"Father always claimed that I sought to be more powerful than he. Perhaps I did. Is that wrong?"

Silence. Jonathan didn't know whether to answer or not. Is it wrong to want more power over others?

He certainly couldn't see anything wrong in that. Power drove all the advancements man had made. One man says I can do this better than you. The next man picks up the challenge and improves on the idea the first man had. No, nothing wrong in seeking more power.

"One day my Father demanded that I dive into the deepest water to bring up a bit of sand. But I could not do it, for the sand kept leaking through my fingers before I could rise up out of the water. Wisely I changed shape. For brief minutes I became a swallow and dove deep, carrying up a bit of sand in my beak. I dropped the bit of ooze into my Brother's hand, and he blessed it and formed the earth.

"That did not satisfy my Brother. He feared me and my powers. He hit me on the back of the neck, forcing the small amount of sand that I had kept for myself . . . A paltry amount. Forcing me to spit out the excess sand, splattering the earth with mountains. Mountains for my Brother's earth.

"I anger quickly. My immediate reaction was to throttle my own Brother. Forgetting the presence of our Father, I turned on my Brother."

Here the man turned toward Jonathan. The thin slits for eyes burned a deep lava red. The thin lips trembled with rage, and the nostrils pulsed to the man's heartbeat.

Too frightened to move, Jonathan sat frozen in the moment.

The man took two steps toward Jonathan, and stopped just short of being able to touch the pew in which Jonathan sat.

"I lifted my hand to my Brother, the first and last time. I never touched Him. A windstorm came up and whirled me away into the land in which I now live. Hades."

Jonathan's right foot instinctively flexed to leave.

"You smell a hint of my world here infiltrating a broken-down mausoleum built for my Brother, so that he can lie in state before his worshipers.

"Do you smell the flesh that you so enjoy partaking in? Not the cardboard host that my Brother offers, but real flesh. The kind that is moist and salty. The kind that glides down your gullet."

Jonathan nodded his head, sniffing the air.

The man raked his fingernails on the back of his right hand, drawing blood, scraping off flesh, exposing muscle and bone. He offered the pieces of flesh to Jonathan.

"Eat of me. Worship me."

The flesh gleamed even in the dimly lit church.

"Eat!" yelled the man. "Eat and join yourself to me."

Jonathan stood.

"I can't." He violently shook his head.

The man slipped the flesh into his own mouth.

"Then go home and serve up a portion of your wife for dinner. Will it be a breast? Or perhaps you would like to taste of her thighs."

"How the hell . . ." Jonathan stepped into the aisle.

"The mere morsel you take from her will not satiate you for long. My flesh will. But go back and seek to tame your appetite on an inferior being. When you are ready to join with me, I will know."

Jonathan ran from the church. He slid down the outside steps, falling to his knees, catching himself with his hands, scraping his palms raw.

Chapter Eighteen

Jonathan rushed home, constantly looking over his shoulder for the man he had met at the church. No one followed, although he did get a series of looks from bystanders, some of whom he almost knocked over in his flight.

How could the man know about his wife? The windows of the music room all had been heavily draped. Could there have been a small space where someone could peek into the room? Jonathan doubted he had been that careless. How did the man know, and what did that gibberish oration in the church mean?

Jonathan barely missed being hit by a cab. The cab driver pounced on his horn. Jonathan didn't have time to give him the finger. He needed to see whether his wife was still manacled.

He got within view of his front door, and saw Mario pacing on the cement sidewalk just outside the entrance. What the hell did he want? Did he help her to escape? Nonsense, if he had, he wouldn't be waiting around for . . . For what?

Jonathan stopped just out of Mario's view in order to catch his breath. Mario jerked his head, and his hair flew back from his face; Jonathan watched the dark strings of hair slowly work their way back to cover Mario's left eye. After a brief check behind him, Jonathan walked up to his front door, attempting to pretend he didn't notice Mario.

"Hey!" yelled Mario.

Jonathan turned and looked at Mario with a carefully practiced blank look.

"You don't remember me, but I work at the motel where your wife is staying."

"Oh, Martin."

"Mario."

"I'm sorry. I do remember you. You were kind enough to help my wife move out of our home."

"I told ya I did it for a C note. Nothin' personal."

"She sent you back for more items, did she?"

"Nah, I thought you'd like to know she didn't stay at the motel last night. She's still registered;

101

just, one of the maids was talking about not having to do much to the room. Seems your wife didn't sleep in the bed."

"Maybe her back was bothering her and she used the floor."

"She do that?" Mario asked.

"I guess you haven't been sleeping with her long enough to know her quirks."

"Man, I ain't been fucking her. Don't need to 'cause I got lots of other places to dip my salami."

"Why are you here, Mario?"

"Just thought you'd like to know. Besides, I could watch over her for you for a few dollars."

"How many dollars?"

Mario used his right hand to pull his hair back off his face, and looked perplexed.

"If you're going to try to extort money from people, be prepared with a price," said Jonathan. "Take that stupid look off your face. I am plain not interested." Jonathan reached in his pocket for the house key.

"Don't it worry you that she didn't come back to the motel last night?"

Jonathan paused a few seconds to think. "No."

Mario smirked.

"Ya gotta care. I see one of my women slipping around, I'm going to do something about it."

One of his women, thought Jonathan. He looked

down at the oversized buckle on Mario's belt. He couldn't make out whether the profile was a wolf or a German shepherd, so poorly was it sculpted.

"How many do you have, Mario."

"Varies with the day."

"Sometimes they dump you, huh?"

"But not for long. They always come back to Mario. Women say I look like one of those male models on those paperback romances." Mario stood straighter and offered his profile.

"Don't read the trash myself, so I couldn't tell."

"They like the feel of my hands too." Mario turned his hands palm up.

"They look pretty rough to me."

"A lot of women like rough." Mario grinned.

"Like my wife?"

"See, I got your goat. Nah, your wife seems more the prima-donna type. Needs to be coddled."

"Amazing, Mario, you really have her pegged."

"I have to peg them fast if I want to . . ."

"To what? Fuck them for money? I bet if I asked you to, you'd make sure my wife would be caught in a compromising position. Right?"

"Got any beer in there?" Mario pointed to the door of the house. "Better talking business off the street. Never know who will overhear."

"I got an idea. Why don't you come over for dinner tomorrow night? I'll even pick up some beer for you. What do you drink? Bottled, canned, or on tap? Or maybe you'd prefer hard alcohol?"

"Then you're interested in talking?"

"I'll make something tasty. You look like a big meat-eater."

"All kinds," Mario said with a lopsided grin.

"Yeah, you have to come back tomorrow for dinner. You're just what I need."

Mario slipped his hands in his jeans pockets. "Time?"

After arranging their meeting, Jonathan went into his house. On his way to the music room he noticed several messages flickering the light on his answering machine.

Business call after business call had him yawning until he reached the last message.

"Jon, are you there? She's calling me again. This time she's hanging up when I answer. Have you spoken to her yet? Why is she calling me?" His mother's voice sounded high-pitched.

Jonathan paused a second to remember whether there was a telephone in the music room. There wasn't.

Jonathan threw open the door to the music room. She evidently hadn't been able to control her bladder or bowels. But she was still there. Some of the padding had been rubbed off one of the manacles, and he could see how raw her wrist looked.

"Honey, there's no way you're going to make it out of those cuffs. Isn't it too bad you can't reach your wrists? Animals when trapped often chew off a paw to escape. Would you munch on yourself until free? Now that would be an interesting experiment. With all your indignation about my eating flesh, would you be willing to eat of yourself if you thought you could break free?"

Her eyes stared blankly at him.

"You have permission to speak, honey." He waited several minutes. "Nothing to say. I'm disappointed. I expected some sort of lecture. Are you trying to spite me by not talking? Well, you're not very much fun this way." His nose twitched. "Guess I had best clean you up."

He turned to leave, then stopped.

"By the way, Mario was just outside the front door." He watched her eyes light up. "Yeah, seems he figures I can send more money his way than you can. I won again. What's the score now?"

"Bastard!" she screamed.

"Oh, and the best part is that he's coming by for dinner tomorrow night. Yeah, he'll be just beyond the door to this room. Just out of reach. Wonder if he prefers the breast or the thigh."

He left the room to get towels and soap and water. He enjoyed hearing her softly whimper as he departed.

Chapter Nineteen

"I tell you I know it's her on the line. Once there was kind of a breathy sigh before she hung up."

Jonathan wondered whether his mother had a secret admirer.

"I'm sorry about that, Mom. I've been trying to contact her, but she's been acting so chaotic I can't track her down."

"If this keeps up, I'm going to need a new telephone number."

"That might be the best idea, Mom. I'll pay the fee. Why don't you set up something with the telephone company?"

"I hate changing my number just because you're married to a lunatic. How are my friends going to reach me?"

Jonathan didn't recall his mother having a lot of friends. A few, but certainly she could inform them of the change in a couple of telephone calls.

"If you make a list I'll see to it that everyone is notified."

"What if I forget someone?"

"Then they'll be added on later. Honest, Mom, I have no idea what is going on inside Cindy's head. I'd feel better if you had a new number."

"Think she'll come down here and look me up?"

"Doubtful."

"But if you think she's so dangerous over the phone . . ."

"I don't think she's dangerous. I just don't want her bothering you and ruining your health."

"She still going to work?"

Shit, he had thought he had it all covered.

"Don't know, but I'll check tomorrow."

"Haven't you stopped by her job to speak to her? You say you can't reach her, and you don't know whether or not she's at work?"

"I don't want to get her fired by being a pest."

"I have to change my telephone number, and you're still trying to preserve her job." The indignation in his mother's voice sounded so typical.

"If she has a job, she won't be tempted to take a trip down to Florida to see you."

This seemed to leave his mother speechless for a few moments.

"She always has been career-oriented," his mother finally said. "Do you think she's stable enough to still be?"

"Who knows? One day she may freak out and shoot everyone in her office."

"Don't say things like that, Jon. She might hurt you or me. I mean, why kill an office full of people who have nothing to do with her problems?"

"It happens, Mom."

"I think I will call the telephone company tomorrow and see how soon they can change my number. Actually, it may be a good time to visit with my sister in Connecticut. Want me to stop over in New York for a visit?"

"Not a good time for visiting, Mom."

"I guess I can stop on my way back. That is, if everything's been settled."

"Yeah, sure. Always enjoy seeing you, Mom. Hey, I could even go up to Connecticut to see you."

"I don't want to put my sister in danger, Jon."

"That why you're going up there, Mom?"

"No. What do you expect me to do? You go off talking about Cindy killing people, and I'm going to sit here for target practice."

"Go to Aunt Lora's. Send my love and tell Uncle

Harry he should come down and have lunch with me sometime."

"You're not taking him to that awful club you took him to before."

"It's just a topless place the guys like to cool off in after work."

"Cool off, right. I'm surprised your Uncle Henry didn't get chest pains."

"He probably did after he told Aunt Lora about the place."

"She was so pissed." He heard his mother chuckle. "She went out and bought herself a cat suit a week later. Can you imagine your seventy-five-year-old aunt in a cat suit?"

"Did Uncle Harry appreciate her effort?"

"She claims he did."

He could almost visualize his mother's head shaking as she spoke.

"Sometimes she acts like a teenager," she added.

"As long as she and Uncle Harry enjoy."

"If you do come up, let us know in advance. Aunt Lora loves to make fresh rabbit for you. She knows it's your favorite meat."

Chapter Twenty

Mario showed up for dinner in tired, wrinkled jeans and a torn sweatshirt. Even though it was seven in the evening, Jonathan figured the guy had just gotten out of bed.

"You did say Wild Turkey, didn't you?" Jonathan asked.

"Yeah, that'll be fine," Mario said, walking around the living room. "You got a lot of artwork here. And it sure is different from the stuff at the motel."

"I buy from a different gallery," Jonathan said, handing a glass to Mario.

"They don't go to any gallery. They order their stuff through catalogues."

"That's a surprise."

"You ain't been around to see your wife, have you?"

"She made it clear she doesn't want to see me."

"And you're willing to let it go at that?"

"Let me go check on the meat."

Mario followed Jonathan into the kitchen.

"Man, you have a really nice house," Mario said. "She could rip you off bad."

"My wife has a good job herself."

"Not this good, or she wouldn't be staying in a motel. She'd be down in the city in the Plaza. Hate to see a guy bled by a woman."

"Why don't you take a seat at the dinner table?"

"For the few bucks you pay me, you'd be saving yourself a really brutal battle."

Jonathan pulled the meat out of the oven.

"Smells good." Mario was already smacking his lips together.

"Why don't you carry in the salad while I move the meat to a platter?"

"Who gives a fuck about the greens? Just bring on the meat."

"I like you, Mario. You have good taste. And you know what? If there's any leftovers, I'll give them to you to take home."

"Just stick 'em in a brown bag."

"I have some plastic wrap."

* * *

"You were a success, honey. He loved you. Thought you had the most tender flesh he had ever tasted. Raved about the flavor too. He's not such a bad guy. I gave him five thousand dollars to 'fuck' you. Excuse the language, but I'm repeating his word. I tried to be more delicate in my request, but 'fucking is fucking. Nothing wrong with straight talk.' Again, I quote Mario."

Jonathan looked at his wife and wondered whether Mario would want to sleep with Cindy now. He'd seemed eager at dinner, but he hadn't seen Cindy minus one breast and some muscle. Jonathan had bandaged the wound delicately, trying not to cause more pain than necessary. Perhaps he should offer her something to relieve the pain; however, he had already used up all his own prescription drugs, and all that was left was aspirin. Wouldn't help much. He could offer her what was left in the Wild Turkey bottle, but she really didn't go for that kind of alcohol. Would she care now?

She had passed out during the cutting, and had wavered in and out of consciousness while he administered to the wound. Now she seemed lost in her own mind. Her eyes were open, but she never looked at him. She stared at one section of the ceiling, one that had started to peel.

"I'll call in the painters after . . ."

After what? After he chopped her up. After he

killed her. Cindy had been right. His mother would never approve of his current behavior. How foolish of Cindy to threaten to tell his mother. She had sealed her own fate.

Wait. He saw a flicker of emotion in his wife's eyes. Tears fell down both cheeks now, but she didn't sniffle or sob. Quietly she let her pain out.

He could kill her immediately. Take away all the pain. However, he felt conflicted. He had never killed anyone, and he had loved Cindy. Still loved his wife. He couldn't stop now. He had gone beyond the point of forgiveness. Even if she promised to forgive, he knew she would report him to the police at the first opportunity. There was a big divide between mutilation and killing, and somehow he had to coax his way across.

"Cindy, you could help me make a decision." He saw no response. "Do you want to die?"

His wife turned her head toward him and shook her head.

"I mean, you must be in a considerable amount of pain, and I don't have anything to give you. You realize I can't let you go. I'd end up taking you apart piece by piece."

Her bleating cry stung his ears.

"I could cut your throat and you would die very quickly." He reached out and touched her neck, locating the pulse. "Yes. Right here. That's the spot.

I need your approval, honey. I know it may sound stupid, but I want you to will your death."

"You want me to beg."

The hard edge of her voice soured his stomach, and he walked out of the room.

Chapter Twenty-one

Jonathan couldn't remember the exact location of the little decrepit church. He had never seen the church before, but he desperately wanted to find it again. He swore it had been on one block, and then, no, he decided it was several blocks over. No church.

He did find a neighborhood church with school-children filing in the front door. The girls' skirts flapped in the breeze just above their knees. All wore navy knee-socks and navy oxford shoes. The plaid of the skirts gave some of the girls a sensuous plumpness. The girls wore white, short-sleeved blouses with Peter Pan collars.

The boys fidgeted more than the girls. They took whacks at their buddies while the nun's back was turned, and their attire looked more disheveled than the uniforms the girls wore.

Hell, Jonathan felt that he could get in line and follow the class, fit right in without even being noticed. He realized the gray in his hair might give him away, or even the wrinkles looping his face with experience.

He followed the last boy into the church. The boy did a double take when he felt Jonathan's presence.

Jonathan gave a soft "Hi," and the boy instantly faced forward until he had seated himself safely with his class.

Jonathan sat in the last pew. Funny how the church was filled with children but so still, he thought. Feet shuffled up to the confessionals and then back to do penance.

He wondered whether the man or Satan or whoever he was would show himself here in the midst of all this adulation. Dare he enter this church and rave about his own power? This church was alive with the smell of burning wax and incense. Rows of candles flickered vibrantly under the Lord's scrutiny. All the prayers being offered up stood as a barrier to evil. Youth marked most of the present as innocent. *Where are you?*

A hand touched Jonathan's shoulder. Fear, relief, and a recurrence of the odor of flesh took away his voice.

"Excuse me, sir."

The voice sounded old and feminine.

"If you need to confess, I can put you ahead of the children."

There was a moment's pause.

"Do you need to confess, sir?"

"Yes," Jonathan answered without turning his head toward the woman who had approached him.

"Then if you follow me . . ."

"I'm not quite ready yet."

"When you are, go to the rear confessional, and my children will let you go straight to the front of the line."

Jonathan nodded his head. Lifting his clasped hands to his forehead, Jonathan bowed his head as if in prayer. To whom had he been praying? Certainly not to the same entity these children were adoring. He could walk ten feet from where he sat and unburden himself. The priest couldn't even report him to the police. He chuckled. Or even to his mother.

He set his hands on the back of the pew in front of him and turned his head to view the confessional the nun had indicated. The wooden doors opened and closed frequently. Children entered and spun off their minor sins, and left with a magical number of Hail Marys and Our Fathers that would cleanse their souls.

If he went in, he'd really back up the line. He'd be there for the rest of the day. He could outdo all the combined sins being confessed by the children. He'd frighten the priest. Father So and So would have a sleepless night with his conscience.

Father, I have sinned and am sinning as we speak. I'm torturing my wife and considering how to kill her and when. The cross above the confessional window would probably come down and conk him on the head. *That's not the worst you can expect,* Jonathan reminded himself.

Jonathan stood and took several breaths. He entered the aisle and started toward the confessional.

Bless me, Father, for I have sinned. It has been . . . too long since my last confession.

He crossed in front of the lead child and settled his fingers in the holy water. The water didn't burn his fingers or make them shrivel into dust as he'd almost expected. He lifted his fingers to his forehead and began making the sign of the cross.

A child exited the confessional. The boy quickly dunked his fingers into the holy water font and moved toward the front of the church. How weird, Jonathan thought. The holy water was the same water that had touched his tainted fingertips. Does the priest's blessing protect the water from the plague carried on mankind's fingers? Where have all the other fingers been? Inside a prostitute's pussy? In-

side the diaper of a debilitated sick man? Or inside
the body of a murderer's fresh kill?

Bless me Father, for I have sinned.

"It's free now, sir."

He recognized the aged, feminine voice of the
nun who had spoken to him previously.

The priest opened his own door and poked out
his head to see what the holdup was. A young
priest—probably all he ever hears are children con-
fessing how they'd lied or cursed or been bad to
their parents.

A flash of black passed by, exiting the church. It
was the man he had been searching for. Jonathan
bolted the church, stopping at the top of the steps
outside to look for the black-clad man. He wasn't
to be seen.

So you are as aloof as your Brother.

Chapter Twenty-two

Jonathan needed to report his wife missing. He would be the first one under suspicion, but they would know he was involved in her disappearance if he did nothing. The police would want to search the house. He couldn't allow that until he had disposed of her body, and he couldn't do that until he killed her.

He had telephoned her place of work and asked to speak to her. The receptionist was surprised to hear from him. His wife had taken personal time, and they didn't expect her back for another week. Slowly the reason for the time off occurred to the receptionist as she spoke to Jonathan. He heard the strain in her voice, the unspoken "sorry" that she wanted to say. He gave a clipped "good-bye" and hung up. The injured husband, trying to reach the wife he has loved for so many years. At least that's what he hoped the receptionist had picked up from the conversation.

He had less than a week to report his wife missing. He should be desperately calling friends, asking whether anyone had seen her. Jonathan sat at his desk and made a list of people to call. He even included his mother on the list. He should call Cindy's family also. These would be the worst calls. *I don't know where your daughter/sister is. We had an argument and she left. I haven't seen her since . . .* There was Mario, who could back up the visit to pick up clothes, but did anyone know that she had come for dinner and stayed? Cindy had been adamant about how she couldn't bring herself to tell people what he did. She'd never tell anyone that she was visiting with her husband instead of living with him. Thank God for her ego.

He couldn't eat all of her within a week. Besides, there were parts he had no desire to eat. He'd have to buy something to dissolve the leftovers.

For how long had her car been parked in the driveway? No more than a few hours, he would guess. Would anyone have noticed? *She came to tell me that she was leaving me for another man. She didn't want to try counseling. She had told me to cancel the appointment with the counselor; then she showed up at my door to inform me that she would never be coming back.*

Jonathan wondered about Mario's history. Mario had the look of a jailbird. *I paid him to set my wife up, not to kill her.* Complications. Setting Mario up to take the blame for Cindy's mutilation and death could backfire. However, Mario could be an excellent cover.

Cindy had started to run a high fever. If he were lucky, she would die from natural causes. Almost natural, that is. Her skin had become cold and sweaty. A blue tinge had been spreading under the skin.

Where the hell was Satan? He needed his advice now. He had said he would know when Jonathan was ready to link. Damn, he was ready now.

Jonathan telephoned the motel and asked to speak to Mario. Seems they had several on staff. Did he know the last name of the Mario to whom he wished to speak? He's in maintenance. That's where both our Marios are, he was told.

"The romantic book-cover Mario," Jonathan said.

"Oh, that one," said the young feminine voice, giggling into the receiver.

Within moments he was connected to Mario.

"I'm calling for an update."

"Hey, your woman still hasn't returned. Heavy

gossip among the maids about how your wife and I got it on. I have a reputation, and some want to decorate it with a few more ornaments than I've had the time to collect." Mario sounded proud.

"What are they saying?"

"They think I have her holed up in my apartment while she keeps the motel room to throw you off the trail. Seems her Jaguar is missing. I think they're waiting for me to drive up one of these days in that car instead of my Pinto."

Jonathan had the Jaguar tucked away in the garage, covered by several old painters' tarps. He couldn't just hand the Jaguar over to Mario.

"I kinda spent your money," added Mario, "so don't expect to get any of it back even if I don't live up to my end of the deal. Ain't my fault your wife decided to take off the way she did."

Maybe Mario would make a better witness in Jonathan's defense than a culprit.

"I'm worried about her," Jonathan said. "She took off personal time from her job. I'm about to call all our friends and family."

"The bitch will show up when she feels like it. When she needs some more cash." Mario sounded worldly-wise.

"Would you mind coming over for dinner again? I'd like to get all the details on the conversations you had with my wife. There might be a clue."

"Sure, the food was good last time, and the leftovers got me through several dinners the next few nights."

"I'll cook more food next time."

"I'm a big meat guy. Just double up on that, and I'll be happy."

"I definitely will."

Once the dinner hour was set, Jonathan hung up the receiver.

What could be flushed down the toilet? Not enough of her. He had to worry about the bones.

The telephone calls became easier as he progressed down his list. Cindy's father had always liked Jonathan, and seemed to take his side without any explanation from his own daughter.

"Just like her whore mother," her father shouted.

"Evidently there was some guy called Mario." Jonathan couldn't resist.

"Her mother came and went for years before I finally put my foot down and changed the locks."

"It's hard giving up on the one you love."

"Don't do that. When she shows her face again I'll give her a talking to."

What if she were unrecognizable? Jonathan's biggest worry might be the Jaguar. But even that could be taken apart, and the pieces sold to some corruptible parts dealers in the South Bronx. Hell, he could probably drive the car out to the South

Bronx and park it. The Jaguar would disappear before the night was over.

His work had begun to suffer. He explained to his coworkers how upset he was over his straying wife. Last time he had seen her, she had left with Mario. She had claimed he was a maintenance man at the motel. At least that's what she had said. Mario had helped her to move out.

"Mom, she's disappeared. I can't find her anywhere."

"The slut took off with another man, no doubt. Make sure you keep that house and cancel all the credit cards you share with her."

"Mom, I'm really worried about her safety."

"I've called the telephone company, and they'll be changing my number. Can't visit your Aunt Lora. She and her philandering husband are taking a cruise."

"All I did was take him to see some topless girls, Mom. He never touched anyone."

"The sin is in the thought. He was humping them in the dark folds of his brain."

"What about Cindy?"

"Thankfully, I haven't heard from her, and if I do I'll give her a piece of my mind."

You don't have more than a few pieces left, thought Jonathan.

Chapter Twenty-three

The music room stank of sickness, waste, and blood. Her wounds kept opening up. The coarse stitching he had done on the breast wound hadn't held for long.

He kept the lights low—didn't want to see more than was necessary. In the dim light her body looked like a shadow mirroring a slender monster.

He heard her babble words that he could not understand, so slurred was her speech. Her breaths were spaced unevenly, as if she were constantly on the brink of death.

"Cindy?"

Jonathan walked closer to her body. Bubbles were rising from between her lips, soapy-looking bubbles that burst and reformed almost immediately.

He doubted that he needed to keep her manacled any longer. She didn't look like she'd be able to make it to the door of the music room, certainly not to the main door of the house to escape. He would have to remember to lock the music room door after he left. Could he possibly make her more comfortable? Or was she beyond pain and pleasure?

"Cindy, I've come to clean you up." And for another slab of meat, but he couldn't bring himself to tell her that. He'd need a small slice for his own dinner tonight and a major cut for the meal he was going to prepare for Mario tomorrow.

"You're going to be needing a hacksaw. A surgeon's saw would do. I happened to have brought one."

Jonathan turned and saw the man from the church, Satan, standing at the threshold to the room.

"How the hell did you get in? Did I leave the door unlocked?" He started to leave the room, but the man's hand reached out and grabbed him at the elbow.

"I do not need unlocked doors. Don't you understand that yet?"

"What shall I call you?"

127

"Yakut."

"Like those Siberians you were telling me about."

"Yes." The man walked over to view Cindy's body. "You could package a good bit of her in the freezer."

"And what do I do with the rest?"

"I can take care of it for you."

"You going to tell me what you'll do with her remains?"

"Do you care?"

"I do if they're found."

"Ah, but we may want them found."

"No, I've been all through this already. She has to disappear. Run away with another guy."

"Can your ego stand up to that?"

"As long as I stay out of jail." Jonathan's voice sounded weak.

Yakut touched Cindy's body, and Jonathan had to restrain himself from pulling Yakut's hands away from her.

Yakut ripped away a bandage and poked several fingers inside the wound. A minor halting of breath was Cindy's only response.

"I could dig inside her cavity and rip out all the precious organs that keep her in this half-death. Do you think she would appreciate my grabbing her heart and yanking it free of her body?"

"Don't . . ." Jonathan's voice caught in his throat.

Yakut pulled back his bloodied fingers and turned to Jonathan.

"You wanted my help, and now you hesitate. Hardly a soldier I want in the war that is to be fought." Yakut dropped the surgeon's saw on her stomach and began to walk away.

"I want your help," Jonathan said, his mouth feeling extremely dry.

"But you want to tell me what to do. You don't trust me. Haven't I offered you my own flesh that you refused? You have denied me twice now. Is there a reason for me to stay?"

"Yes. I'll follow you."

Yakut smiled, his teeth white and even, his lips causing lines to form at the corners of his mouth. Deep lines that appeared to crack the skin and cause beads of blood to trickle out the sides of his mouth. He licked Cindy's blood from his fingers and smeared his own on the palm of his hand. He turned the palm outward and offered it to Jonathan.

Jonathan moved quickly forward, but Yakut prevented him from putting his tongue to the fresh blood.

"Kneel." Yakut's voice was softly seductive, charming Jonathan to his knees.

Jonathan stabbed his tongue across Yakut's palm.

"Bite." A hoarseness clouded Yakut's voice with mystery.

"I . . . My teeth . . . I can't bite your hand."

Yakut tore a finger from his own hand and offered it to Jonathan, who reached out and touched Yakut's mutilated hand. The finger passed from Yakut to Jonathan.

"Lord," Jonathan said before biting flesh from bone.

Cindy screamed and Jonathan looked at her. Her eyes were round, her mouth wide, her breath catching as she attempted to rise. Her wounds broke open and bled in trickles down her flesh.

Jonathan went to her and jammed the chewed bone deep into her throat. He watched her gag, noted the changing color of her complexion, and felt relief when her irises floated up behind her opened eyelids.

"No time to savor the moment, child. You must cut and package while the meat is still fresh."

Jonathan looked down at his wife's body and saw the festering wound that no doubt had been causing her fever. He realized that her body had gone rancid days ago, but he would follow the lord's instructions.

Chapter Twenty-four

"Shit, man! I tell ya that meat in the freezer was given to me by her husband. Go over and ask him what the hell happened to her. I don't go around cutting people up and eating them."

"What were you doing, Mario, when the cops showed up at your door?"

"Having dinner, but I don't know what the hell I was eating. I told you that weirdo husband of hers gave the stuff to me."

"Why'd he give the flesh to you, Mario?"

" 'Cause he's nuts. 'Cause he was real pissed off. He thought I was fucking his woman. He paid me to fuck his woman."

"Then why would he be pissed?"

" 'Cause if that was her in my freezer, he knew I couldn't be fuckin' her."

"The wrapping paper has only your fingerprints on it."

"I told ya. He was wearing those latex gloves, the kind medical people use, the night he gave me the packages. Said he had some sort of allergy. Made me hesitate about taking the meat. Thought he might have something catching."

"But you took the meat anyway."

"The meat tasted good, although I gotta admit that my stomach has been on the verge of barfing ever since ya told me that it was her flesh."

"We found parts of her in garbage bags in the trunk of her Jaguar, Mario. And the Jaguar was parked in your neighborhood."

"Hey, lots of cars get parked in my neighborhood, but I don't drive them around. I told ya I don't know why she'd leave the car on my block."

"We doubt she parked it there, Mario."

"*I* sure as hell didn't." Mario kept rubbing the palms of his hands up and down his muscular thighs. The thin faded denim of his jeans started to tear apart.

"Most of your fellow workers at the motel believe you were making it with her. One maid is sure of it. Claims there was evidence in the room. A wrapper from your chewing tobacco in the wastebasket."

"I don't know how the hell it got there. Maybe I dropped it in the hall and she picked it up and threw it in her trash."

"Do guests frequently pick up after you, Mario?"

"I don't know what kind of a clean freak she was."

"According to her husband she wasn't a 'clean freak.' The opposite."

"Maybe she thought she was doing me a favor so's I wouldn't get fired."

"That's right, Mario, you had been given warnings by management against mingling with the guests."

"Hey, I never laid a hand on a woman unless I was invited."

"That's why management couldn't prove you were sleeping with the female guests, but they had strong suspicions."

"Suspicions don't make me guilty."

"Know what makes you guilty, Mario? Having several pounds of a motel guest in your freezer. Did you like it sautéed, fried, or baked?"

Mario's stomach ached. He needed to take a shit, but was afraid the police would take a sample as evidence.

"That bastard is a prick," Mario said. "Serving

his wife up for dinner and trying to blame it on me. This is worse than one of those old folk tales my mamma told me."

"You enjoy hearing those stories, Mario?"

Mario sneered at the detective, and wished he had stayed with the cheap burgers from the neighborhood diner.

Part Two

Mirror Image

The mirror image stalls in my mind. The black surface shaded by the form of a man. The dark skin penetrates the glass. His white eyes glare their brilliance into the dark reflecting image. The eyes search the smooth surface, looking for a real world. Behind him extends the earth that has repudiated him. But in front of his vision is a contained space, acknowledging his individuality. He seeks a refuge from the dirt and hunger that cling to his rags. His belongings are heaped about him, always within his protective reach. He touches his hair and twists it around his fingers. Is he now viewing himself or a reflection of us? There is no way one can know, because his beaming eyes flash in every direction continuously. Will he see me watching him? What will he do if he notices that he has gotten my attention? Will there be rage? Will it be directed at me, at the world in general from which I come, or will he smash his own reflective pool of shiny material just to be free of me and our snubs?

But he remains almost still, except for the slow winding of his long black tresses encircling his fingers. His hair soiled by desperate years flares out into stiffened wisps haloing his face. The tendril wrapped and woven through his first two fingers on the left hand has coiled into knots almost like prayer beads. What does he see? His eyes seem so attentive. His private visions escape me. Maybe I'll never share them. I pray that I do not.

Only his fingers and eyes move. The outline of his body lies hidden, covered in mountains of black cloth. I cannot even tell whether his chest is heaving its breaths. He could be a statue with little batteries moving irises and fingers in circles. When the batteries wear down he will pause forever to confront himself.

I leave but carry him with me into my nightmares at night. Even in my dreams he hardly moves. He emits a stench that I never got close enough to remember. But the odor is here in my sleep. No matter how far I back away from him, the smell is with me and pulls me back closer to him. The pungency causes my head to ache. And still he sits. I think

*that when he does move it will be to spring at me.
He will leap toward me with arms spread wide. He
will wrap me in his arms, close to his body, and
cover me with his rags. The diseases of mind and
body will seep into my pores. It will blacken my
flesh and dull my mind. On my skin will appear
waves of dirt dripping down my forearm until they
reach the elbow and then suddenly end in a splotch
of grime. The skin upon my legs will thicken and
ooze into runny sores surrounded by the peaked
whiteness of scales. My belly will bulge into a
bloated, gaseous mound. My soft breasts will
shrivel and sink. Meanwhile my sex will dry out
and fall into disuse. Physical illness will fade next
to the sickness of the brain that slowly deteriorates.
Lucid moments will mingle with memories. I will
fight to gain them back. But they will break apart
into a delirium of madness. There will be no comfort in this man's embrace. He will steal my unique
being into a vacuous cloud of panicking souls. His
putrid smell will cling to my hairs. And soon I too
shall find a tolerance for the stink.*

*Eventually he will drop me onto the curb where
I shall lie in my own fetid excrement until I shall
find a reflection. A window blank enough to wash
over me. A glass so distorted that my world could
exist within fifteen square feet of me. I shall argue
for hours and win. I shall have the wit to make*

myself laugh. I shall cry and be comforted by a guardian angel. Suddenly this black-and-white world in the shimmer of the glossy pool will evolve life-forms that only the insane appreciate, even if they cannot share the idiosyncrasies with their brothers and sisters.

I am told that I toss and turn now in my sleep. I never awake refreshed anymore. I realize how close this torment is to all of us. It can be looming over a hunched shoulder or stand naked and tall in front of us. But how many of us will know of its potentiality?

We all fought our way out of our mother's womb and staggered our first steps. We learned what we were taught and what they tried to keep secret. Sometimes we stumbled, and most of us picked ourselves up. But what if I fall in a gray, slender alley alone? What if my feet become too heavy to travel? Will my mind mull over my fall forever in this cobblestone passageway?

I look in my bathroom mirror at the redness of my conjunctiva and the half-moons lying on their backs under my eyes. The craggy lines upon my face are betraying me and my jaw sags too much. I go into the shower to wash it all away. And when I open the shower door, my body dripping water, I see two brilliant eyes looking for something in that bathroom mirror.

Chapter Twenty-five

"It's kind of you to help out at the food kitchen, Jonathan."

"No problem, Sylvia. Keeps my mind off my late wife."

"I'm so sorry."

"You've said that too many times. Listen, you're doing me a favor by inviting me down to help out at the kitchen. I need to help other people right now."

Sylvia patted his arm and turned toward the food line. Her hair was a pure white color that shined under the reflection of the ceiling lights. She had quickly twisted her hair into a casual bun as soon as she had entered the kitchen, and strands had

collected around her face making her look younger
than her sixty years.

Sylvia had baby-sat Jonathan when he was a pre-
schooler. On evenings when his parents would disappear, Sylvia would sit next to him on the couch
and read fairy tales. Sometimes she repeated the
same stories, forgetting where she had left off, but
Jonathan hadn't minded because he loved the mu-
sical sound of her voice and the dramatic tempo
she would build.

Yakut had been right when he suggested that
Jonathan look her up. She made Jonathan feel safe,
protected from the world, which might find his life
ungodly. The world couldn't understand Jonathan's
god, and had never given his god any room to grow
and spread. Yakut had definitely been there for him
with his real flesh that bled and the plan to shaft
Mario with the blame. Jonathan hadn't had to do
anything except hand the parcels to Mario and give
Cindy's car keys to Yakut.

"You must be hungry yourself."

Jonathan saw Yakut standing in front of him,
dressed in rags and with a five o'clock shadow.

"What are you doing here?" Jonathan tried to
pull Yakut to the side, but Yakut wouldn't budge.

"I'm watching over you. So many bodies. Surprising how some look chubby, considering they're
homeless. One would expect weedy people stand-

ing in line, happy to be given a crust of bread. Instead, many look well-fed. Don't you wonder what that woman over there tastes like?" Yakut pointed at a plump teenager nursing her baby.

"She's a child," Jonathan answered.

"Better, since then there will not be stringy bits to catch in your teeth."

"I can't eat anyone else."

"Why not? Don't you miss the taste? I made you give me all Cindy's flesh and that left your refrigerator empty."

"Thank God. I mean, thanks because the police dropped by with a search warrant and headed right for the freezer."

"I don't expect you to do a penance, Jonathan. I want you to enjoy life, and I know one of your pleasures is fresh human flesh."

"We shouldn't talk here."

"No one is listening. If someone were, don't you trust that I would protect you?"

"I've got to rein in my appetite right now until Mario is finally convicted of Cindy's death."

"He will be." Yakut looked around the room. "How many of these people go missing every day? How many die in an alley or choke to death on their habits? Most will be wasted in rotting or cremation. Shame. They should have a chance to serve a purpose just like the rest of us."

"What is your purpose, Yakut?"

"I do not serve, Jonathan. That is why I am homeless." Yakut smiled and indicated his attire.

"It's only a facade, Yakut. There must be some reason for your existence."

"To cast doubt on my Father and Brother."

Sylvia called out Jonathan's name from across the room, and Yakut stepped into the food line. When Jonathan reached where Sylvia stood, he found that she was attempting to comfort a crying young man.

"Maybe you can help Seth here. He says his girlfriend died and he doesn't know what to do with the body." Sylvia turned away from the youth and spoke an aside to Jonathan. "So many of these people are afraid of the law. Perhaps you can take the time to win his confidence. At least see if he'll tell where he left the body."

Jonathan nodded and stepped back to let Sylvia pass.

"Where's she going?" asked the young man.

"To help some of the other people. She thought maybe you and I could talk awhile."

"She wants me to tell you where Florry is, don't she?"

"Wouldn't it be better if Florry could have a final resting place?"

"She wouldn't have wanted to stay down there."

"Down where?"

The young man looked smug, and pulled his tray closer so he could eat his meal. Jonathan pulled up a chair at the same table and sat. He glanced around the room, and noticed that Yakut fluttered around Sylvia, always getting in her way, touching her as often as he could. Making her laugh. What the hell was he up to?

"So I ain't telling you."

Jonathan looked back at the young man and thought, *I don't give a damn.*

"She was a little older than me, but we loved each other," Seth said.

Jonathan nodded. He tried to locate Yakut and Sylvia, but couldn't find them.

"Ten years."

"What?" Jonathan's attention turned to the young man.

"Florry was ten years older than me. Maybe more. Didn't matter. Her and me could really get it on. I slept with young girls, but they were never in the same league as Florry. She'd do anything. One night she . . ."

Did Yakut know Sylvia? Was he dogging her because he wanted to . . . To what?

"And she let out the biggest fart." The young crying man became the young laughing man in a split second. "We had so many good times like that."

145

"Sounds great, but I have to find Sylvia," Jonathan said.

"No, you don't, because here I am." She stood directly behind Jonathan's chair and rested her hands on his shoulders. She leaned to whisper in his ear. "Any luck?"

A tinge of guilt frustrated Jonathan, but it was only momentary. Who the hell cared where the dead body was? Let this guy stuff her and keep her in one of his shopping carts.

"No, Sylvia. I noticed you were helping a guy—"

"Yakut."

"You know him?" Jonathan asked.

"For a long time."

"Know what else she used to do?" The young man hesitated, looking up at Sylvia.

"I interrupted your conversation. I think I'll check to see how the cleanup is going in the kitchen." Sylvia, dressed in jeans and a white poet's shirt, headed back across the room. The heels of her boots tapped against the linoleum floor with a firm beat.

"She was into water sports."

Jonathan didn't want to listen to any more of these stories.

"Where the hell's the body, buddy?" Jonathan demanded.

"Down where we was living."

"Downtown, down the street?"

"Under the street."

"In a sewer?"

"Nah, we lived better than that. We got ourselves a little niche near the subway station."

"You're living in the subway tunnels?"

The young man nodded.

"You can't leave her body down there. The rats will get her body."

"Fair play. Once in a while we ate them rats. Seen that man down there sometimes."

"What man?"

"Yakut. Once in a while he passes through. Sometimes he talks people into going down several levels with him. He scares me."

"Has he ever hurt anyone?"

The young man shrugged. "Just never again see the people who go deeper with him. Don't know what happens to them."

"But he's never taken anyone by force?"

"Don't have to. He's got enough people dumb enough to follow him."

"Why do you think the people are dumb—I'm sorry, I don't remember your name."

"Seth. I get this icy thrill running up and down my spine when he's around. I almost break out with goose bumps. Florry always missed her period after he showed. First time it scared the hell out of both of us. We were thinking that she might be pregnant. Shit, what you do with a baby down in the tunnels? Not that there aren't some, but I don't want my kid growing up in the dark."

"I bet some of those parents feel the same way, but they don't have a choice."

"They could get rid of it before it come out."

"Seth." Beads of sweat broke out across Jonathan's forehead. "I shouldn't do this, but why don't I help you bring Florry's body aboveground. We can call an ambulance and tell them where to find the body."

"Mean we don't have to talk to the cops?"

"We should; however, if you show me this underground home, I'll help you and you won't speak to the police."

"You got some perverted interest in the place?"

"I want to help, Seth."

"And you want to find out more about Yakut, right? You afraid he's going to talk your lady friend into going below?"

"Kinda." Jonathan extended his hand to consummate the deal.

Chapter Twenty-six

Jonathan's eyes hadn't become completely accustomed to the dark of the tunnels. He sometimes skidded on wet debris hidden along the tracks.

"Watch yourself!"

Jonathan looked around, wondering what he had done.

"Your getting way too close to the third rail," said Seth.

"Shit." A flattened rat slipped out from under a track and ran across the top of Jonathan's right shoe.

"Over here," Seth called.

Jonathan followed the voice until he came to a niche in the wall. Soft candlelight invited him inside. Seth stood with his hands in the pockets of

his Army fatigues in front of a painted statue of
Christ that stood two feet tall on a slab of plywood.
Smaller statues surrounded the Christ. Some were
of the Virgin Mary, while others were of saints. All
appeared to have small chips in their plastic or plaster. In front of the statues was a movers' mat that
covered a bulging mass.

"Here she is," Seth said.

"She looks a bit bloated."

"She's always looked like that. You know,
healthy." Seth paused to think about what he had
said. "At least, I thought it was healthy."

"We can probably prop her up in the nearest station, then call the ambulance."

"I don't like leaving her alone up there."

"You can wait with her if you want."

Seth quickly shook his head.

"Will that mat wrap around her?"

"Don't know. Probably come close to."

"Maybe you could tuck it under her to make
sure."

"You afraid of her?" Seth asked.

Afraid, no, disgusted, yes, Jonathan thought.

"You want to see her?" Seth pulled the mat away
from the body.

The smell of decay hit Jonathan in a flash. Already the woman's chin had started to blacken. Her
limbs were pencil-thin, but her trunk seemed to be

blown up as far as the skin could stretch. Her left foot quivered, forcing Jonathan to take a step back.

"Get the hell out of here!" Seth swung the mat, and a rat ran from under Florry's left leg. At first it ran straight for Jonathan, but they managed to go separate ways.

"We have to get her out of here now," Jonathan said. "Cover her up. And wrap that damn mat tightly around her." He looked around and spied a rope and picked it up. "Here, tie her inside. I don't want the body slipping apart while we're carrying her."

Seth forlornly gave a last look at his mate. He whispered a prayer under his breath before following Jonathan's instructions.

Several hours later, after Jonathan had helped Seth leave Florry's body in an otherwise empty train station and had called an ambulance, Jonathan sat with his back to Florry's religious statues wondering whether Seth would come back. Seth had been too nervous to stay with the body and too nervous to sit quietly here with Jonathan. He had wandered off without saying a word.

Jonathan looked around. Was there anything Seth would want to return for? A bundle of clothes sat inside a wooden crate. A few utensils were scattered around, and there were two dented pots. One had a layer of burnt crust. Either Seth and Florry ate out of the pots, or they kept their dishes well hidden, because there appeared to be none. Two unmatched water glasses and three matched but chipped cups were piled in a corner. Black ooze crept down the wall behind the cups, causing little puddles of mud to form under the cups and glasses.

A water bug came into his sight, and instinct caused Jonathan to pick up a pot and lunge forward to squash the bug. He missed, and with vengeance the bug leaped at Jonathan, flapping its wings as it seemed to fly through the air. Jonathan pulled himself to his feet and randomly threw the pot in the air.

"Damn!" The water bug had disappeared, but Jonathan spent five minutes dusting off his clothes in case the bug had landed on him. At first something seemed to be crawling along the collar of his shirt. His attention shifted to a prickly feel that was crawling up inside his pant leg. His whole body began to itch. The odor of the dead woman became stronger. He found a bottle of bleach and poured out the bottle on the space where she had been lying. The smell masked but didn't completely hide the odor of decaying flesh.

Where the hell is Seth? he wondered. Jonathan didn't know the way out. He could possibly be lost down here forever. A stupid Tom Lehrer song started pounding inside his head.

Something could be heard slinking nearby. Whatever it was seemed to have a bad head cold, because several times it blew its nose.

Seth appeared at the entrance to the niche. His eyes and cheeks were wet, and his nose wiggled in irritation.

"You bastard!" Seth screamed. "You promised she'd be all right. They'd come pick her up and give her some sort of burial. You promised me. I wouldn't have let them have her if I'd known what would really happen. I woulda kept her here with me. I coulda . . . I coulda . . ."

"Stuffed her?" Jonathan asked.

Seth ran toward Jonathan and tried to get his hands around his neck. Jonathan fended him off, tossing the young man atop the religious statues. One or two broke apart; the others landed safely on a stained mattress.

"What the hell is wrong with you? Didn't they come pick Florry up?"

Seth freely cried. "I couldn't stay away. I went back for another look. Shit, she was black ash. Her face wasn't hers, it had melted into a pool of jelly. The clothes had been ripped off her. And the smell of gasoline was everywhere."

"Weren't the medics there?"

"The police stood around shaking their heads, and the firemen wiped their brows and sprayed down the platform. Yakut told me that some kids had soaked her body with gasoline and set her on fire."

"Yakut was there?"

Seth nodded, wiping his nose against the sleeve of his filthy denim jacket.

"Why didn't he stop them?"

"How? He said it was a gang. A bunch of juveniles."

"A bunch of juveniles walking around with a can of gasoline?"

Seth shrugged.

"Where's Yakut now?"

Seth rolled his body off two small statues of the Virgin Mary, checking them to make sure they weren't badly damaged.

"Florry loved these things. The last of her hope was with these statues. They'd take care of us, she said. They won't abandon the faithful." Seth lifted the small statues and threw them against the wall. One shattered, and the other slipped down the wall and into the black ooze.

Grabbing Seth's denim jacket, Jonathan screamed out, "Where's Yakut?"

The young man covered his ears with his hands and shrugged.

154

"Did he come back with you?"

"No. He was at the station when I got there and when I left. In the shadows like me, but we got a good view of her. She'll never forgive me."

Jonathan lifted Seth to his feet.

"Florry is dead. She couldn't feel those flames. She's not capable of forgiveness anymore. She was no longer present inside that body. Do you hear me?"

Tears ran down Seth's cheeks.

"I'm gonna die like that, and there won't even be someone to miss me."

Jonathan took the young man into his arms and hugged him.

"I'll help you," Jonathan promised. "If you help me. I have to know more about Yakut. When I truly know who he is, I'll take you aboveground with me. I'll give you a life to live instead of wasting. But you must promise to do all you can to locate Yakut. Find people who may have gone down into the deeper levels with him."

"I told ya. Nobody ever comes back. He promises them food and shelter and they follow him. Where Yakut has been accepted, you don't smell no burning rats on spits. He gives them fresh meat to eat. Eventually they disappear. They go deeper into the tunnels and they're happy when they go."

"Why didn't you and Florry follow him?"

155

"He's mean. He's got a bad streak. Florry warned me against him. She said he was enveloped in evil. Her statues quivered when he walked by. Florry always smelled him coming. She said he smelled like the sulphurous fires of hell."

"Did she ever talk to him?"

"She knew him, but I don't know how. She hated talking about him. Her flesh would break out in goose bumps just thinking about Yakut.

"When he goes to the shelter for food, Sylvia always spends a few minutes talking to him."

"If he brings food to the people down here, why does he need to go to the shelter for food?"

"I think he gets some of those people at the shelter to go down below with him. Sylvia sometimes introduces him to people."

"Those people she introduces to him, do they disappear?"

"Don't know. Very few of the homeless are regulars. They tend to move around. Maybe they go with him, maybe not."

"How long have you been going to Sylvia's shelter?"

"Off and on for the past six months. Sometimes Florry and me go through the restaurant garbage bins late at night. Be surprised some of the great stuff you can find if you're early enough. Practically whole pizzas, half-eaten chicken roasts, lotsa grains."

"You and Florry used to cook down here sometimes?" Jonathan said, indicating the two pots.

"Yeah, when we were too scared to go aboveground."

"What were you afraid of?"

"The people up there. They can be mean." Seth's eyes watered. "Like what they did to Florry. There was no reason to do that to her. They didn't even know her. Why hurt someone who has never done anything to you?"

"What keeps you going back up there?"

Seth removed Jonathan's arm from his shoulder. He glanced around.

"Because I'm scared down here too."

Chapter Twenty-seven

The next day Jonathan stopped by Sylvia's shelter. He hadn't planned on working, but the bossy teenager in charge shamed him into slicing meat and ladling potatoes.

By the time the place emptied out of diners, Sylvia arrived.

"I didn't expect you today, Jon."

"I like helping out."

"That mean I can schedule you on a regular basis?"

"I still have a job, Sylvia. I'll be going back to work next week."

"Great. Then I'll pencil you in as a lunch server all this week."

Jonathan winced as she picked up a pencil and

walked over to the schedule hanging on the wall.

"Do you have a lot of regulars, Sylvia?"

"A few."

"I noticed you talking to a guy by the name of Yakut the other day. Does he come in often?"

Sylvia faced him. Her blue eyes were especially clear today, and her unmade-up face sparkled. "Why?"

"He did a favor for me, and I wanted to thank him."

"He's always doing favors for people, Jon. He makes sure he gets a return on them. Don't have to go looking for him."

"Yeah, but is he really homeless?"

"Homeless? Many of the people who come here aren't homeless. Some have families that live out of cars. Some find alleyways to store their belongings. Some live over heating grates. And some, like Seth, go underground. They make homes where the rest of us throw away our waste."

"Does Yakut have an alley or a tunnel that he calls home?"

"What's this interest in Yakut? He's one of the few that come in that I don't worry about. I can introduce you to lots of others who really need your help."

Sylvia grabbed a sponge and started wiping the tables clean.

"Why don't you worry about Yakut?"

"Because he worries about himself, unlike the other folks who come in here."

"You think he's selfish?"

"If we're going to chat, why don't you go over to the sink and grab a sponge and give me a hand?"

At the sink Jonathan found several sponges sitting in a tub of soapy water. He grabbed a yellow sponge and wrung it out. When he got back to the tables he asked his question again.

"Yakut is special, Jon. He can suck you into his life. Make you want to capture his . . . essence. If that's what one could call it."

"Call what, Sylvia?"

Sylvia stood tall and shrugged her shoulders.

"Don't know what to call it. Have you tasted him, Jon?"

Jonathan swallowed hard.

"Yes, I have. And I take it you have also."

"No, but I've heard stories. Stories about whole families worshiping him as if he were a god. I don't turn anyone away, although sometimes I think I should bar Yakut from coming in here.

"He feeds people, Jon. Rumor has it that he gives of his own body and then immediately heals. Other people say he feeds the homeless to the homeless. However, I think you may be able to tell me whether or not that's true."

"When I said I tasted Yakut, I meant figuratively, Sylvia. He certainly never chopped off a . . ."

"Finger?" she asked.

Jonathan wasn't sure who was doing the digging here.

"Yeah. I meant that I've listened to him and he's . . ."

"Helped you out?"

"Yeah. You know, I think I've given enough of my time to the shelter for today. I've got a couple of errands still to run. I'll see you tomorrow, Sylvia."

"Don't worry, Jon. I only penciled in your name on the schedule. If you don't show we'll still be able to cover."

Chapter Twenty-eight

"I can't believe she's dead, Jonathan. It was her own fault. Going out running around with other men."

"We don't know that for sure. Maybe he forced her. Maybe that's why he killed her. Cindy never fooled around."

"Before." Elise's voice took on the air of authority. "All it takes is just one temptation, and some sinners fall at the feet of the devil."

"I have to pack all her things and send them to charity. A few pieces of jewelry I'll give to her family. I only want the wedding ring."

"What for? Know what I did with my wedding ring the night your father told me he was leaving?" She took in a deep breath. "I threw it onto the subway tracks. I didn't want any part of someone who didn't want me. I flung it as far as I could. Even closed my eyes so that I wouldn't know where it landed. I didn't want to be tempted to retrieve it. The bastard took fifteen years of my life. Cindy took seven of yours."

"Mom, Cindy was never Dad."

"Perhaps she was a bit easier to get along with, but ultimately she amounted to the same thing. Know what your father did just before he left? I never told you this."

"I'm sure you did, Mom." His voice held more than a hint of exasperation.

"No, no, I would never have told you this. I tell you now only so you won't feel so bad."

Because his mother had a worse life than his, he thought.

"He left a used condom on the front seat of the car. Like he wanted me to find it. He and I never used condoms. I was using female protection. And when I called the condom to his attention he just said, 'So what.' He laughed at me, told me I couldn't do anything about it. At the time he was right. I had you and no job."

"Mom, we're rehashing old news."

"No, we're seeing how life moves in a circle."

"I have a lot to do on this end. I can't stay on the phone."

"You don't appreciate your mother calling to help you talk out your problems?" Insult tinged his mother's question.

"You're doing most of the talking."

"Fine. I'll sit quietly and let you talk."

A few minutes of silence ensued.

"I don't have anything to say, Mom."

"No good bottling up all the pain, Jonathan."

He wished he could think of something grand to say. He could tell her the truth.

"Mom, suppose I told you something awful about myself."

"That's the depression talking now. You're blaming yourself for things that you have no responsibility for. It wasn't you who caused the breakup, Jonathan. She chose to leave, giving you some stupid excuse. What was it again? Your feet. Imagine leaving someone because you don't like their feet. Think about it. It makes no sense, Jonathan. How often did she even have to look at your feet?"

"Once was enough."

"Please. Your father had ugly feet, but I didn't leave him."

"Did you ever take a look at your own feet, Mom?" He smiled to himself, but didn't allow any humor to seep into his voice.

"My feet! Your father should have been kissing my feet with all that I did for him. I gave him a bright, handsome son who may have unfortunately inherited his father's feet. I cooked and cleaned and shopped. Never said no when he wanted his way."

"Yes, you did, when he wanted to take home that giant mutt he found outside a bar."

"I meant in the bedroom."

He heard his mother heave a heavy sigh.

"I'm trying to help," she said, "and here you are making fun of your mother. Why did I call if you don't want to seriously talk about the breakup?"

"The breakup was nothing, Mom. Cindy is dead. She'll always be dead. If she weren't, she might have come back to me."

"Wishful thinking. I did that for almost six months after your father left. Then he announced that he was getting married. I vomited all night in the bathroom. Then the next morning with barely a half hour's sleep I had to get you ready for school. Make your breakfast, pack your lunch."

"You really soldiered on, Mom."

"And that's what I expect you to do. This stupid talk about having done something awful."

"I used to shave off bits of flesh from my feet and eat them."

"Jonathan, if you can't stay in reality, I'm going to hang up on you. Why would you want to tell me such a disgusting thing anyway?"

"Remember when I was a kid I had lots of scabs? I caused them."

"All little boys get scabs. Doesn't make you any worse than any other child. I would have thought you strange if you never had a bruise or a cut on you. And I don't want to hear about you eating scabs. Your father caught a glimpse of you doing that. He wanted to confront you, but I told him that it was just a silly thing that children occasionally did. All children have strange quirks that they grow out of. I knew if we made a big deal of it we'd only make matters worse."

"Not like I was going to grow up to be a cannibal."

"Exactly."

"But I did."

"So what. You don't eat scabs today, do you?"

"No, not scabs."

"See? Your father would have caused a big brouhaha over nothing. Probably scar you for life with his condemnation."

"They used to get stuck in my throat sometimes."

"Why are we talking about this? It has nothing at all to do with your marriage. By the way, who's paying for the funeral expenses?"

"I am."

"Hmpf."

"What's that mean?"

"All these years you've had to pay for her. Think her family would offer to help, at least."

"Mom, I can well afford it. Besides, the money I'm using was in her account, so she's really paying for her own funeral."

"Closed coffin?"

"Mom, have you heard anything that I've said? How the hell would I be able to arrange an open coffin?"

"Don't raise your voice, Jonathan. It was merely a question. I suppose you save on the layout. Are you going to have a spray of flowers on the coffin? Roses are beautiful. Perhaps you could have red roses. White hardly suits the kind of woman she was."

"I have someone at the door, Mom. I have to go."

"Reporters? Don't say anything to the papers. Try to avoid any photographs. You don't want friends recognizing you."

"Mom, Cindy's name and mine have been on the front page of the newspapers for several days now. Her father sent, Lord knows why, a photo of Cindy at her Confirmation to one of the papers."

"So she'd look like the innocent victim."

"She was." Jonathan dropped the receiver back onto the cradle.

Yeah, you were always there for me, Mom.

Chapter Twenty-nine

"Seth. Seth."

The footsteps halted. Jonathan had been waiting over fifteen minutes for Seth to show. What kind of game was that bastard playing?

"Seth, you better get your ass over here now."

Jonathan couldn't find his way around the tunnels without a guide.

The footfalls continued until the form reached the shaft of light coming through the ceiling vents.

"Seth, what the hell do you think you're doing?"

Jonathan stepped toward the shaft of light just as Yakut stepped into it. He was dressed in black leather, with a black silk turtleneck emphasizing the whiteness of his flesh. The leather jacket looked scuffed and shiny from some sort of liquid. And he smelled not only of dampness and filth but also of freshly killed meat. Sweat, but not his own, touched his clothes. Fear sweat, the smell recognizable under blood and bodily waste.

"What game are you playing, Jonathan?"

"I'm looking for a friend."

"Have many friends that live down here?"

Yakut's eyes narrowed, the pupils shining a yellow-gold. His features were pronounced and classic, his forehead smooth, worry-free. And his mouth seemed deeply colored in the faint light of the shaft.

"One friend," said Jonathan. "But that's all I need to come down here. I met Seth at the shelter, and I've been trying to help him."

"Ahh. I don't require good deeds."

"Sometimes I require them of myself."

"Why?"

Jonathan ignored the question. "Did you set Florry on fire?"

"Would it matter to you?"

"Yes. There was no reason for you to do that."

Yakut sucked in his breath and seemed to shatter in the light. While he was exhaling, Yakut's body trembled and coalesced.

"She was a miserable woman."

"Because she worshiped your Father and Brother?"

"She invaded my territory."

"Did she follow you down into the lower levels?"

"Once."

"But you allowed her to come back up."

Yakut laughed. His hands reached out to touch Jonathan's shoulders, but Jonathan quickly retreated. Yakut folded his arms in front of himself.

"I didn't invite her. I didn't allow her to leave. She invaded with what she considered blessed holy objects. She laid a barrier of blessed soil and holy water to prevent my wanderings. It reeked in the tunnels for weeks after. Many of my people sickened and almost bolted. But eventually they served to bring in the fresh legion that I knew I had needed."

"How did they do that?"

"I fed their flesh to the wretched who had been subsisting on rats and roaches and water that trickled down from rusted pipes."

Jonathan recalled the sludge that oozed down the wall of Seth's niche.

"I gave them fresh, clean, sweet, tasty meat. I mixed my blood in with the stew and they grew strong."

"You killed those people because they wanted to leave you?"

"Because they were weak, because they were

hopeless, because they were of no further use to me."

"Why didn't you kill Florry?"

"I didn't need to. Father had already placed a blackened tumor inside her abdomen that festered around her bowels, causing greater agony than I could bestow."

"Sometimes He does things better than you, huh?"

"Sometimes He knows the exact strings to pluck."

"Then you desecrated her body."

"I merely matched her outside flesh to the erosion and rot that already was eating her insides."

"Why did you bother to make up that story that you told Seth?"

"He's simple and easily tricked."

"I would have thought you'd be bored by such a person."

"If *you* don't bore me, why assume Seth would?"

"I've had enough of your shit!" Jonathan took several steps toward Yakut.

"No, you haven't." Yakut touched Jonathan's face.

He felt his flesh burn. Steam escaped from under Yakut's hand, and rivulets of flesh trickled down upon Jonathan's clothes. Jonathan pulled away, tripping over a rail, and watched as sparks lit up the wool hat that he had been carrying in his hand.

Yakut bent over him and began scraping the flesh off Jonathan's jacket, rolling it into a ball, and forcing it inside Jonathan's mouth.

The texture was slimy, the smell burnt, the taste bitter and sweet and salty. By the time he had swallowed, Yakut was gone and Seth stood over him.

"What the hell happened to you, man?" asked Seth, his hands pushed deep into his jeans pockets.

A shivering Jonathan brought his right hand up to his face and felt his fingers sink into sludge.

"You trip and fall or something?" Seth had moved slightly closer to have a better look at the man at his feet.

Jonathan let out a scream, bringing his other hand up to his face as if he could hold the flesh in place.

"Not a good place to fall," responded Seth. "Some of these pigs will take a dump anywhere."

The smell registered with Jonathan, and he slowly brought his hands in front of him. Shit stuck in clumps to his fingers.

"There's a big puddle of water just down the tracks from here. Gotta be cleaner than what you got on your face and hands." Seth almost reached out a hand to help Jonathan up before he realized it wouldn't be such a good idea.

"Damn Yakut!"

"Crap is crap, can't tell who the original owner was," Seth philosophically stated.

Jonathan pulled himself up to a seated position and forced himself to one knee. He used his forearm as leverage against the other thigh in order to lift himself to his feet.

"Where the hell were you?" Jonathan asked.

"Hey, I guess at the time. I ain't like you, running around falling into crap with my expensive Rolex."

Jonathan searched the dimly lit tunnel. Yakut had gone. *Why did Yakut do this?* he wondered. *Had Yakut been near him since childhood? Had his taste for flesh been driven by Satan all along?*

"You gonna clean up? Because I ain't hanging around nobody that smells like you."

"How do I find the deeper levels?" Jonathan asked.

"I can take you to a level with a cool station that ain't never been used by the system. They started to put in tracks and then stopped ages ago. Got a nice group of people living there. They even got a man who used to be a teacher educating their children. Can't send the kids to school aboveground 'cause they don't have a real address, and if they tried, the authorities would probably take the kids away from their parents. But you gotta clean up first."

"Are these people followers of Yakut?"

173

"Nah. He don't seem to pay much attention to them."

"How far down do I have to go to reach Yakut's territory?"

"You don't wanna do that. They give us all a bad name. Know what the track crews call us? CHUDS. Know what that stands for?" Seth didn't wait for a reply. "Cannibalistic Human Underground Dwellers. They think we're down here eating each other up. I'm sure they get that idea from those who follow Yakut. Sometimes it ain't so bad being a CHUD. Some of those guys on the maintenance crews bring down extra sandwiches with them so we won't chop them up and stew 'em." Seth laughed. "Sometimes it's fun giving those bastards up above a scare. They drove us down here. The kinds of bad things they do to us. Like what they did to Florry."

"Yakut set Florry on fire."

"Why would he do that?"

"You should know, Seth."

"She never went back down there."

"Then you know she was on his shit list."

"He waited, what, eight, nine months to get even with her? Nah. He would have gotten his revenge when she first went down to his level. Besides, he would have wanted her alive so she'd feel the pain of his punishment."

"He knew she was dying, Seth. All he had to do was wait."

"She was getting better for a while. How could he know that she'd take a turn for the worse?"

"Because of who he is."

"Hey, I know he's bad, but don't give me any of this bull about him being Satan. I told Florry she was wrong, and if she couldn't trick me into believing it, you can't."

"Where's this puddle of water you were telling me about?" Jonathan knew Seth was too scared to believe that Satan was here in the flesh. Too scared to even bother Yakut.

Chapter Thirty

"Confiteor Deo omnipotenti, beatae Mariae semper Virgini, beato Michaeli Archagelo, beato Joanni Baptistae, sanctis Apostolis Petro et Paulo, omnibus Sanctis, et tibi, Pater: quia peccavi nimis cogitatione, verbo, et opere, mea culpa, mea culpa, mea maxima culpa."

"They speak a funny language sometimes," Seth said, leading the way to a brightly lit subway station.

"They're speaking Latin. They're reciting the Confiteor."

"What's that?" Seth asked.

"The server recited it at Mass when I was a kid."

"What did he serve?"

"The Lord," Jonathan answered, mesmerized by

the way a handful of people carried out the old liturgy of the Church.

"Hi," Seth yelled out.

Jonathan pulled on Seth's arm.

"We can't interrupt them in the middle of a service."

The group of people on the station platform turned toward the tracks and almost in unison waved to Seth. He waved back.

Small children pressed against their mothers' legs, many sucking on lollipops. The older children, who had been assisting the priest, gathered the utensils they had been using and covered them with a white cloth. Everyone was dressed in obviously homemade clothes. No one's shirt or trouser seemed to fit perfectly. The few women who wore skirts wore them ankle-length.

"Jared's their leader."

"He's the priest?" Jonathan asked.

"Ya mean the only guy wearing a dress?"

Jonathan nodded.

"Yeah. He's a nice guy. Invited me and Florry to live here."

"Why didn't you two live here then?"

Seth shrugged. "Florry never wanted to. And I sure as hell wasn't gonna move down here by myself."

"Why not?"

" 'Cause I was with Florry."

"Seth, come up and join us. We were in the middle of a service, but God would forgive us for stopping for you. You have a friend with you?"

"Don't know if he's a friend," Seth yelled too loudly. His voice seemed to echo around the station.

Jonathan grimaced, wondering whether he would instantly be driven out.

"He helped me with Florry," Seth added. "What little help he was."

"Sorry about your loss, Seth. I just heard about it today when Sister Margaret returned from aboveground; else I would have visited you sooner."

"That's okay, Jared. Nothing you could do."

"We are dedicating this Mass in her memory."

"Oh, thanks."

"You're not Catholic, are you, Seth?" asked Jonathan.

"Florry tried teaching me some of that stuff, but I found it very confusing. Three guys in one. The piece of bread turning into someone's flesh. That really grossed me out. Sounded like something Yakut himself would preach."

"May I ask the name of the person accompanying you?" asked the priest.

"Jonathan." Jonathan had called out his name before Seth had gotten a chance, and Seth appeared annoyed because of that.

"Come up and visit, both of you."

The subway station was the cleanest Jonathan had ever seen. The tiles were still a bright white, and the platform looked scrubbed and cared for.

"They got a real bathroom," Seth whispered, pointing toward an open door. "And it's clean."

Jonathan looked across to the other side and noticed that the opposite platform had been segmented with drapes and sheets.

"The station was never used," Jared said. "We were lucky to find such an ideal place to settle our congregation. The city has forgotten that the station exists. Rather like they've forgotten us. But the water still runs in the men's and ladies' rooms and the electricity still flows through the wires."

"It won't for long," stated a tall man with a gray and black beard. "If those crews come down and find it, they'll start taking the place apart."

"Simon's our pessimist." Jared placed a hand on the tall man's shoulder. "In some ways he keeps us from becoming too optimistic."

"Optimistic down here?" Jonathan asked.

"We live better than most of our brothers and sisters down here."

"I'm surprised the others haven't raided this

place looking for better accommodations for themselves."

"Ah, Jonathan, I see you and Simon have something in common."

Jonathan took a closer look at Simon. The tall man's build was muscular, too muscular for someone who didn't work out regularly. The skin on his hands and face seemed blotched with tan splotches that crept across the otherwise pale skin. The man looked as if he hadn't smiled in years. His eyes, dark and penetrating, observed Jonathan.

"I don't think Simon likes me," said Jonathan, still not taking his eyes off the tall man.

"He doesn't like or dislike anyone. He doesn't trust."

"I'm sorry we interrupted the Mass. Actually, I haven't heard Latin spoken in years. Not since I was in school."

"You were raised Roman Catholic then, Jonathan?"

"Yeah. Drifted off over the years."

"We can continue the service, if you'd like."

"I think Seth would get bored."

"Would you mind, Seth? We are saying the Mass in memory of Florry, so it is right that you should be present."

Seth nodded.

The service went just as Jonathan had remembered the old Latin Rite. When it came time for Holy Communion, almost everyone received the host except for the youngest of the children and Seth and himself. At the end, everyone held hands and sang an old hymn.

Seth had chosen to stand a distance from the congregation, while Jonathan had wandered into the middle of the crowd and found himself close to the priest.

"I always thought Mass could only be said in a consecrated church, Father."

"Please, don't call me Father. I would have been excommunicated years ago if the Church knew what I was doing."

"Servicing the poor."

"Not sticking strictly to the beliefs of the Church."

A wiry old woman cradled an infant in her arms. The baby looked feverish, its face was flushed, and it seemed to have difficulty breathing. Once in a while the old woman would fan the baby with flat cardboard from the back of some writing tablet.

"The infant needs medical attention," said Jonathan, turning toward Jared.

"We do the best we can." Jared continued putting away the vestments he had worn at the service.

"He should be taken to a hospital," Jonathan insisted.

"She. Marissa is her name. And what would happen if we took her to a hospital? The grandmother would lose the child to authorities who would pronounce her unfit to care for the child."

"The mother? The father?"

"We don't talk about them." Jared leaned over the old woman and made a sign of the cross on the baby's forehead. When he stood straight, he barely shook his head.

"Jonathan, why are you down here?" Jared asked, still glancing down at the feverish infant.

"I met Seth at a food kitchen, and as he said, I helped him dispose of Florry's body."

"And you became fast friends?"

"I guess Seth still doesn't completely trust me, but he needs someone to look after him. I have the impression he was dependent on Florry for many things. Most importantly, company."

Jared moved away from the old woman and faced Jonathan.

"That's very nice of you. Do you plan on gradually bringing Seth aboveground?"

"If he wants to come up, I'll help him."

"Seth likes the dark best. He likes to blend with the shadows."

"I know that. I thought he was approaching me earlier, but . . ."

"Yes?"

"It wasn't him, it was someone else, and then all of sudden there was Seth."

"What is it about Seth that has you coming back to visit him?"

"Hey, I don't mean any harm to him."

"He's quite vulnerable."

"I know, but I'm just trying to do a good deed. Make up for all the shit I've done in my life."

"Your soul will never be cleansed until you confess, Jonathan."

"Confess! That's behind me. I don't go around telling people what I do in private anymore. That's for schoolkids and old people when they feel the Angel of Death cozying up on them."

"Death walks beside you now, although it may not be you he wants. But he travels with you."

"And I thought Simon was the only one who didn't like me."

"I told you, Simon neither likes nor dislikes. But all of us are suspicious of outsiders. We have to be."

A sudden wailing noise pulled the two men apart. They searched for its source. The old woman had stopped fanning the infant, and now rained teardrops down on the child. No one attempted to take the child from her. Everyone stayed a distance from the anguished woman.

"You see what I mean?" Jared whispered to Jonathan.

"Hell, you can't blame me for the death of that kid. She was ill when I came down here. Whatever she died of had nothing at all to do with me."

"You opened our door to death."

"Right. And no one has ever died in your little congregation. If you want me to leave, say so. I guess you do."

"Will you take the child from the old woman?" Jared asked.

"What? Why the hell would I steal her grandchild?"

"You helped dispose of poor Florry. Could you find it in your heart to do the same for Marissa?"

"Since I travel with death you think I run a pickup service. He robs their souls and I get to keep the flesh."

"None of us will be strong enough to take the child from the old woman. We all know her and care. But you are a stranger to her, and she will not fight you."

"You mean she'll be scared to do anything but hand over the baby?"

"Please, as a parting gift to us. Take the child and dispose of the body in a way that she will not be thrown to the vermin that will take her down here."

"She may not give me the baby."

Seth came up beside Jonathan.

"At least that kid's not suffering anymore," Seth said. "She had looked awfully sick, Jared."

"I have asked your companion to take the child, Seth. He hesitates. Can you perhaps talk him into it?"

"You hear what happened to Florry when I gave him the body? Some kids set it on fire. He told me the medical people would come and take her away if we left her on a platform. Instead some hoodlums spread gasoline all over and lit a match."

"You didn't want to stay with the body, Seth. It wasn't my fault."

"But this is a tiny infant that could easily be brought aboveground without anyone knowing," said Jared.

"And what do I do with the body?"

"Care for it the way you would a family member."

"I just buried a wife. You expect me to bury someone else's kid?"

"You are not a poor man, Jonathan. You wear an expensive leather jacket and a Rolex on your wrist. A simple burial can help you atone for those sins you mentioned earlier."

"I'll feel like a shit taking that baby away from her."

"She will bless you after you are gone. She will

185

understand why you took her grandchild."

Jonathan's stomach tightened into a knot. There was a part of him that wanted to carry the baby away to . . . To what? His hands shook and his arms ached. Slowly he made his way across the platform to the old woman. He squatted beside her.

"I'm sorry about your grandchild. About Marissa. I'll see that she . . ."

Jonathan was amazed when the old woman held the child out to him. He looked up at Jared, but he had already turned away. Seth mutely stared at Jonathan. Looking back at the old woman, Jonathan reached out, and she laid the child in his arms. The blanket was warm. He touched the baby's tiny hand, and felt the heat of life still lingering in a body that no longer carried life.

When he got to his feet, he noticed that most of the congregation was wandering off. Only Seth remained. Jonathan used a tip of the blanket to cover the baby's face, and walked toward the stairs leading back to the tunnels.

Seth followed, and the old woman's sobs echoed behind them.

Chapter Thirty-one

When the light from the station faded, Seth took the lead. Jonathan kept close watch on Seth. He was amazed by Seth's ability to be so silent. Jonathan's own feet slipped on the wet ground. He sloshed into unseen puddles and kicked at invisible barriers. His shoes were always scuffed with a creamy black ooze that he carefully removed before taking them into his home. Sometimes he staggered, thrown off balance by an unexpected pothole or tie. In some areas there were loose tracks that had been abandoned.

His eyesight had started to acclimatize to the darkness, enabling him to see shades and shadows that looked like what they were and not just a hovering black hulk.

He doubted, though, that his sense of smell would ever become accustomed to the smells that prickled his nose hairs.

Seth led him to the exit and turned to face him.

"I hope you're gonna do good by that baby." Seth's eyes held a hint of wetness. He dug his hands deep into his jeans and hunched his shoulders.

"If you took the baby from me, what would you do with it, Seth? That's what you're thinking. That you should grab the baby and defend it from the savages aboveground. But how would you protect her from the vermin down here?"

"I'm just saying you shouldn't let what happened to Florry happen to this innocent little thing." Seth's eyes looked down at the blanket Jonathan carried. The baby was completely swaddled in the clean cotton blanket.

They stood silent for several minutes before Seth moved away from the exit and let Jonathan pass by.

At home, Jonathan laid the infant on the leather couch and opened the blanket to see the body of the naked child. Color had faded from the baby's cheeks, and rigor mortis had started to settle in, the arms and legs freezing into the shape of the tight bundle Jonathan had made of the baby. The baby was pudgy, definitely not undernourished. He wondered what the baby had died from and how long the infant had suffered. He touched the folds of flesh that sagged around the bent elbow, cold now. So cold and lifeless. No longer human, only a butterball of flesh.

He should have taken the infant directly to the funeral home. He knew the director, and could have explained to him how he had come by the child and what kind of preparation he would like for the burial. Why did he bother to carry the child here, to his home, cluttering the rooms once again with death?

"Peckish, Jonathan?"

He knew the voice, and refused to turn to face Yakut.

"Jonathan, this is a tender babe. What a special treat. And no one will miss this meal. No one will ask questions. They'll believe that you properly disposed of their bastard."

Jonathan swung around and saw that Yakut was dressed in a dark wool suit. His white shirt had gray stripes and the black necktie had a subdued gray paisley print. A gray silk handkerchief that matched the color in the shirt flowered from the upper left-hand pocket of the jacket. Yakut's hair had been stylishly cut very recently.

"Now you're in your well-to-do persona," Jonathan said. "How easily you change. Even the hair seems to gain and lose length with your whims."

"Oh, it definitely does, Jonathan. I am whatever

makes people around me comfortable."

"And vulnerable," Jonathan barely whispered.

"Dressed liked this, do I intimidate you? I certainly didn't when we met earlier today."

"You smelled bad and looked vicious."

"I was in our other world, Jonathan. Like you, I change garments to please those around me."

"Not to please, but to throw them off guard."

"As I said, to make them feel comfortable around me. I could never appear to anyone on this earth as I really am. Oh, don't conjure up ideas of those awful demons out of horror books. No, I am as handsome as my Brother and my Father."

"Not more so?"

Yakut smiled.

"I have a touch of my Brother's humility."

Yakut walked around Jonathan and stared down at the infant.

"Do you have a big pot? We could make a marvelous stew from this flesh."

"I wouldn't eat with you."

"No, only of me." Yakut touched the identical finger Jonathan had accepted. "You would hoard this prize solely for yourself?"

"I'm going to see to it that the baby is properly buried."

"The questions. What kinds of answers will you give? From whom did you take the body? Where is this group located? They would go on and on. But then, you figure your money could buy the funeral director's silence. How naïve. He's licensed, you know, and I doubt he would be willing to risk his livelihood for the money you could scrape together. Nothing to do but cook the waif. And how tender she'll be. Much better than Cindy. There was a certain toughness to her that turned me away from her flesh. But this babe shows no signs of the brutality of the world, except perhaps for the rag that was used as a blanket."

Yakut quickly pulled the blanket from beneath the infant. "Now even that has disappeared," he said, throwing the blanket into the air to burn up before it could touch the stained and polished hardwood floor.

Jonathan looked down at the infant and felt the saliva building inside his mouth. He knelt down next to the child and reached out his hand to touch the fatty flesh. He bent his head and lowered his lips—to kiss the babe good-bye, he lied to himself. Upon contact, his tongue touched the flesh and rounded the curves and hollows of Marissa. Marissa, he thought. A little person named Marissa who never got to bring joy into more than a few people's lives. And now she would be taken apart to feed the hunger of a stranger. His teeth nibbled on her toes. His fingertips touched the coldness of death, and his hands went to pull the arms from the sockets. But he stopped, for the babe still had the hint of milk and baby powder, of helplessness. The meat hadn't turned stale as yet. The skin was wrinkled with youth, not age. Marissa had never done wrong, had never sinned against the Lord.

Jonathan pressed his hands against the leather of the couch and brought himself to his feet. He turned to his bedroom to retrieve a better blanket in which to wrap Marissa. As he did, he heard a pot being filled with water in the kitchen. Yakut, he thought, and continued to the bedroom, where he opened a chest and took out a pastel peach cashmere throw. When he returned to the living room, the baby was gone. He dropped the throw on the couch and rushed to the kitchen.

Yakut had laid the infant atop the small butcher block table that Cindy had used to prepare major holiday meals. The knives were lined up beside the baby. Beside Marissa, Jonathan kept saying to himself. Yakut had already turned on the professional-quality burner to heat the water.

Jonathan stretched out his right arm, knocking the pot off the burner and singing the leather of his jacket. The water splashed onto the expensive polished shoes that Yakut wore.

"Not someone this innocent." Jonathan's voice held determination.

"In a few more years, she wouldn't be so innocent," said a somber Yakut. "Anyway, who are you to claim this thing innocent and your wife sinful prey? This thing is a stranger to you, but perhaps that is the problem. You need the flesh of someone dear, someone you desire to consume with all their flaws known to you. Then who will be next, Jonathan? Your mother perhaps?"

The telephone rang. Jonathan refused to move. He stood motionless, waiting for the timbre of the bell to stop. The answering machine clicked on.

"Jonathan, are you there? Pick up if you are, this is your mother. Jonathan? Give me a ring as soon as you get home."

Yakut's laughter echoed throughout the kitchen. The walls vibrated from the lush sound. A knife slipped from the butcher block table and nearly landed on one of Jonathan's socked feet.

Jonathan lifted Marissa from the butcher block table and headed for the living room. He saw the blinking light of the answering machine, and was disappointed that the call had been real and not an illusion created by Yakut. Quickly he wrapped Marissa in the cashmere blanket and slipped into his Sperry shoes. He took a last look toward the kitchen, opened the front door of his house, and left.

He settled his bundle on the backseat of the car before driving away.

Chapter Thirty-two

The dinner hour had ended, but Jonathan saw a dim light shine from the back of the food kitchen. The door was still open, and he had no problem wandering toward the kitchen. Sylvia stood by the double sink, shaking out a wet rag that was used to sop up excess water from the floor.

"You're here, thank goodness." Jonathan heaved a heavy sigh.

"Can I help you with something, Jonathan?" Sylvia seemed startled.

"I have a favor to ask of you. Everyone knows how closely you work with the homeless. You can probably manage to pull this off better than I could." He hugged Marissa close to his heart.

"I don't rob banks." Sylvia chuckled.

"No. It's this." Jonathan settled the bundle on the tile counter. "She was given to me today while I was underground with Seth." He unwrapped Marissa and thought for a second that the baby odor had turned rancid, but the smell quickly dissipated. "She died in her grandmother's arms. Her name is Marissa. I didn't think to ask the last name. I don't even know whether anyone would have told me. Her parents seem to be some unspoken secret."

"Not more than eight or nine months, wouldn't you say, Jonathan?"

"I don't know. In any case, her life was far too short. Will you help her?"

"I think she is beyond any kind of help."

"I mean to have her buried the right way. Not just thrown inside a trash bin or left for a stranger's mercy. I'd pay the cost, of course. It's just that I may be asked questions, and I really don't want to be connected to . . ."

"The homeless."

"The authorities might not understand."

"Or believe you."

"What I'm telling you is true, Sylvia. I went down into the tunnels to meet a group that had set up home in a deserted subway station."

"So you probably went deeper into the tunnels."

"Seth may have taken me down a level. You should have seen the grandmother. She rocked

Marissa the whole time I was there. The baby looked as if she would ignite from the high fever. She died while I spoke to Jared."

"Jared?"

"A priest, I think. Or he had been a priest; he still served that function for these people."

Sylvia carefully hung the rag on a towel rack to dry.

"The authorities will want to know how I came by the child."

"You can tell them that Seth brought her to you. They'll never find him."

"They'll come around here asking questions. If they send a police officer, it will frighten the homeless away. I won't be able to continue this kitchen. There'll be no one to feed."

"I'll give you the name of a funeral director, the one who took care of Cindy's services. I'm sure the police will agree to question you at the station if the director sees fit to report the situation at all."

"You plan on giving me enough money to silence him?"

"I'll do anything. Please, I want to see this child properly buried. Obviously she's never had anything. I want to give her this one final gift."

"Why is she so important to you, Jonathan?"

"It's complicated. I had to rescue her from . . ."

"From what?"

"Her remains had been endangered of being despoiled."

"By whom?"

"Yakut."

"You met him in the tunnels?"

"No, aboveground."

"And he tried to take the infant from you?"

"Sylvia, please stop asking questions and help do something for Marissa. I can write a check." Jonathan pulled his checkbook from his inside coat pocket. "I'll make it out for the same amount that Cindy's funeral cost. I'm sure it will in no way come close to that price, but if we want to buy some silence . . ."

Jonathan scrawled his signature at the bottom of the check.

"Better yet, I trust you," he said. "Why don't I give you a blank check and let you or the director fill out the amount." He ripped the check from the book and offered it to Sylvia.

"You must have something heavy-duty on your conscience to be this generous to an infant you never knew." She took the check from his hand. "Leave the thing, and I'll see what I can do."

"Marissa. The child's name is Marissa. She's not a thing."

"It's getting late, Jonathan; I'd like to close up. Would you mind if I tossed you out?"

"No, I'm sorry. But you will see to Marissa's burial?"

"Just one more good deed for the day."

"Thank you, Sylvia. Thank you so much." He walked to the kitchen door.

"Wait. Don't forget this blanket. It must be yours. I don't think many people in the tunnels have cashmere."

"Keep it for Marissa. You'll need something to wrap her in."

Sylvia nodded, and Jonathan left the kitchen.

He was on his way home in the car when he felt his inside pocket. The checkbook was not there. He must have left it on the tile counter. He turned the car around and returned to the food kitchen.

He felt especially lucky when he saw that the back room light was still on. He tried the front door, and was worried when it wouldn't open. Had Sylvia locked up immediately after he had left? He tried knocking at the door, but got no response. He walked around to the back of the store. The alley was quiet, but he noticed that a garbage can held open the back door to the kitchen. She was probably setting out the day's garbage, he thought. He walked to the door and peeked in. He could make out Sylvia's shadow on the far wall. She seemed to be carrying a meat cleaver. Suddenly she raised the cleaver and brought it down. Blood sprayed onto that same wall. He moved farther in to see what she was doing. Again she raised the cleaver and brought it down. She lifted a tiny arm with her free hand and tossed it into the clean sink. Words could not come out of his mouth; he simply moved closer to Sylvia and watched as she kept hacking Marissa up. The thing, Sylvia had called the baby.

Sylvia wiped off her hands and walked over to turn on the radio. It was already tuned to a classical music station, and Sylvia didn't bother to change it.

"Sylvia," he whispered almost into her ear.

She started, but was relieved to see that it was Jonathan.

"Scared the hell out of me. People are always telling me to keep that back door locked, but it gets so stuffy in here." She continued preparing the baby for cooking.

Jonathan thought he had to be caught up in a nightmare. Maybe everything had been a nightmare. He'd wake and find Cindy asleep next to him. His body would be whole, no scars, no scabs, no open wounds.

Sylvia rinsed out a large soup pot.

"Why did you come back anyway?" she asked.

The sound of rushing water almost drowned out her voice. She looked over her shoulder at Jonathan, expecting an answer to her question.

"You promised me, Sylvia."

"Don't worry, I wouldn't have cashed the check. Then again, I'm never against small donations to the kitchen." She set the pot on the stove and turned on a burner.

Déjà vu, he thought. He looked back at Sylvia, expecting to see her transform into Yakut. Perhaps that was who this really was. He had been tricked. Yakut said he could take on a look that would make the people around him feel comfortable. If he could change the length of his hair and grow and remove a beard from one second to the next, then why couldn't he assume the shape of Sylvia?

"Why so quiet, Jonathan? I would have expected some sort of shock to come from you. This is the best way, though. She—what did you call her?"

"You're Yakut. You tricked me."

Sylvia turned to face him.

"I'm not Yakut, but I do accept his donations at times. Are you horrified? I can barely feed all these people. The government is too busy worrying about businesses to be able to spare some change for the poor. Many of these people can't work, Jonathan, and never will be able to. They're not trained, they become diseased on the streets, they forget or never learned how to act in a work environment. I feed them with whatever I can get." Sylvia picked up his

201

checkbook from the counter and held it out to him. "Want the blank check too?"

Jonathan felt a sharp pain in his gut, and bent over slightly.

"Oh, please don't throw up. I have enough to clean with the mess I just made chopping up that child." She put the checkbook back on the counter.

"You've done this before."

"Not often," she said, splashing the body parts into the soup pot.

"Why did you want me to ask Seth where Florry's body was?" He rubbed his abdomen, feeling a slow settling of his stomach.

"Just as well you didn't tell me. It would have been careless of me to use her flesh. I don't know what diseases she might have had. Couldn't have the kitchen closed by the Board of Health."

"Yakut brings you babies."

"Usually. Most have died from lack of nourishment. No real danger of spreading disease." She used a long wooden spoon to stir the pot's contents before pulling down various spices from the kitchen cabinet.

"Don't you feel dirty?" he asked.

"Dirty? Maybe I look a mess now, but I'll wash up when I get home."

"No, dammit, you know what I mean."

"I feel like I'm helping people. Would it have

202

been better for this child to decay away in some earthen hole, a feast for worms and beetles? I know it wouldn't have been better. Instead, tomorrow she will feed my little family." Sylvia shook several different spices into the pot. "Don't need much tenderizer for one so young."

"You've tasted of Yakut, haven't you?"

She turned to Jonathan. "That filthy man! I wouldn't even kiss his corpse good-bye."

"He's making you do this, Sylvia. He's warped your mind. He can do that. I know he can. I came here to escape his temptation."

"What was the temptation?" she asked, suddenly giving him her full attention.

"He gave me his finger once to eat and I ate the flesh off the bone. I lost track of who I was and what I was doing and . . ." He realized he could entrust the knowledge of his having killed his wife to no one.

"Would you like a taste of the stew tomorrow? All you have to do is come around and help out at lunchtime."

"Why waste it on me? I don't need your food."

She shrugged. "Thought you might be curious as to the taste." She began chopping up vegetables.

"Have you eaten your own stews?"

"Never! The food is for those in need. I thought

203

that since you were a big donor, I'd make an exception for you."

Jonathan leaned his back against a greasy wall and watched Sylvia meticulously prepare the food.

"By the way, I've never noticed that Yakut is missing a finger," she said. "I think you're hallucinating this drama you described. Are you trying to tell me you ate a raw and bloody finger?" Her face took on the look of skepticism. "Maybe you should see a psychiatrist. Sometimes a trauma like losing a mate can send a person over the top. It all fits, though. That horrid man dicing up Cindy and having her for dinner. No wonder you're having these outrageous fantasies."

"What's so horrid about Mario?"

"Oh, come on. He killed your wife and ate her."

"You're cooking Marissa."

"I didn't kill her. I merely used what was gifted to me." She stopped suddenly and looked at Jonathan. "You didn't kill her, did you?"

Jonathan broke out in a cold sweat. Could Yakut have told Sylvia about his killing Cindy?

"You look ill, Jonathan. Maybe you shouldn't spend so much time in the tunnels."

"Why did you ask me if I had killed her?"

"Well, I don't really believe that you would. So many homeless children die from lack of medical attention. I'm sure that's what happened to . . .

Marissa. That's what you called her, right?"

"Marissa. Yes, that was her name." He pulled away from the wall and headed for the back door. In the alley a rat was rummaging through a Dumpster that belonged to a Greek diner next door. He was sure there were other rats nearby. He heard some loud squeaks, and looked to his right to see a pair of rats clashing over the remains of someone's half a chicken. The customer had left most of the meat behind, giving the rats a hardy meal that neither wanted to share.

He staggered back to the car and threw himself into the driver's seat. At first he couldn't find his car keys, and in the process of the search remembered that earlier he had left his checkbook on the counter. He leaned his forehead against the steering wheel and prayed that this was only a nightmare. When he raised his head, he saw that he had left the key in the ignition. Lucky the car was still here, he thought. But the street was empty of pedestrians, and even though one or two streetlights were out, there still seemed to be plenty of light.

He expected to see Yakut walking down the block or . . . Quickly he turned to his right to check the passenger door. No, Yakut wasn't gripping the handle, attempting to come in. By now Yakut had

Mary Ann Mitchell

probably even cleared out of his kitchen.

Jonathan turned the key in the ignition. The car started smoothly, and Jonathan decided to drive downtown to stay at one of the tourist hotels.

Chapter Thirty-three

"Jonathan, I called you several times and left a message each and every time. Why did it take so long for you to get back to me?"

"Mom, I haven't been home much. Matter of fact, I spent the last two nights in a hotel downtown."

"What for? Are you brooding over Cindy? The house reminds you too much of her, doesn't it? Come visit me. We'll take some fun side trips and play pinochle until the wee small hours of the morning."

"I promise I'll visit when I'm feeling better."

"But that's the idea. If you stay with me for a while, I'll distract you from thinking so much about Cindy."

"I'm sure you'd try, Mom; I just know it won't work. There are several things I have to settle here. Why was it so urgent to speak to me?"

"A man came to the door the other day selling frozen meats out of a truck. Never saw him before, but he was very persistent. I should know better than to open doors to salesmen or strangers. The salesmen are a waste of time, and Lord knows what some of the perverts are up to.

"Anyway, he had the nerve to come back two days in a row."

"And you opened the door to him both times?"

"No, I'm not that stupid. Took a peek out a side window and tried to be quiet as possible until he went away."

"Good, Mom."

"Who knows how old that meat is that he's selling. He showed me a shoulder. Frozen solid. It would take weeks just to defrost the meat, and I could never eat it all before it went bad. Tried to explain that to him. He kept insisting that he could bring smaller cuts. I was way too nice and let him go on for at least twenty minutes before I slammed the door in his face."

"Just don't answer the door if you don't know the person ringing the bell."

"As I said, he came back the next day and left his business card in my mailbox with a list of prices.

Does he really think I'm calling him up and ordering blind? When I go to the butcher's, I always demand to see the meat. I never allow whoever is waiting on me to wrap up the cut without my approval. I even do this with Sal, the owner. How do I know what they're trying to unload? Might not even be the kind of meat I ordered. One hears those horror stories of restaurants serving street pigeons or cats or whatever. That's why I hardly ever eat out. Never Chinese. I can't recognize anything once they mix it all together in one of those brown sauces."

"I always wondered why we never ate Chinese when we went out. Instead, we'd wind up at that awful Greek diner with the Spanish-sounding name."

"Miguel's maternal grandmother was from Spain. Rest of the family were Greek. And their food wasn't so bad. Although your father always became annoyed when they were too slow in bringing the coffee."

"I always ordered the spaghetti. I swear it came out of a can."

"That's your own fault. No one stopped you from ordering something else. Can we get back to my frozen meat story?"

"I thought you were finished." Jonathan pulled

the hassock closer, placing his feet atop the maroon leather.

"It turns out that Ruth next door actually tried the meat."

"A reckless lady."

"Said it tasted different. She invited me over to dinner to try it. I'm going over tomorrow night. I'll bring a pie or something. Anyway, if I like I may order some. I still have his card. Let's see, the name of the company is T-U-K-A-Y."

"Spell that again, Mom."

"T-U-K-A-Y. Tukay. Is that how it's pronounced? Don't know what ethnic group he's from, but he was dark with slitty eyes that looked reddish. Probably had been on a drinking binge. His hair was nicely cut, though. You see some of these guys walking around with ponytails or buzz cuts nowadays. Why can't the young people just have normal haircuts? I remember you in college—"

"Mom, don't go to dinner at Ruth's." Jonathan kicked the hassock away and sat upright on the sofa.

"Why not?"

"Because you don't know where the hell that meat comes from."

"You mean pigeons or cats or something?"

"Or something. Rats even."

"How disgusting! You'll make me lose my appetite for the rest of the day. I swear you can be so disgusting. Talking about eating scabs and rats. You got that from your father. He always thought it was funny when he'd come out with those filthy jokes at dinner."

"Mom, don't answer the door if that man calls again."

"Should I call the police?"

"They won't be able to do anything about him."

"They could confiscate his meat and take it to some lab. They'd find out what he was selling."

"They'd have no cause to confiscate the meat, Mom. Just stay away from him and what he is selling. Understand?"

"I'm glad I spoke to you. I had some misgivings about this dinner invitation. The prices looked too good, and he looked too shifty."

"The card, Mom, rip it up and throw it away."

"Maybe I should keep it just in case Ruth and her family become ill."

"Mind your own business, Mom."

"That's not generous, Jonathan. I should look out for my neighbors. I appreciate they're doing the same for me. Remember when I had that pipe that burst while I was up north visiting with you?"

"I know they did a lot for you, but believe me, in this situation, you can't help them."

"How embarrassing. What do I tell them? I mean, they ask me over for dinner a couple of times a month."

"Tell them you've become a vegetarian."

"But what if they see me in the butcher shop?"

"Don't make this difficult, Mom. I've heard awful stories about these people who sell meat out of trucks. I don't think you want me to go into details."

"No. Do you think a vegetarian diet is healthy?"

"I'm beginning to think so."

"Have you stopped eating meat?"

"Certain kinds."

"The red meats. Right?"

"I've been thinking about giving up all meats. Doesn't it seem strange to you that the Apostles were fishermen and pushed eating fish on Friday, while Christ wanted us to eat his body and drink his blood?"

"Silly, it's only a metaphor. Christ certainly wouldn't have encouraged the eating of human flesh. But you always took those nuns seriously, didn't you?"

"They *were* serious."

"When you become an adult, you have to temper the Church's teachings about some things. Of course, I never went to parochial school myself. Neither did your father. We sent you to parochial

212

school only because the public schools were so bad in that neighborhood. You even had some local Jewish kids going to your school, just so the parents could keep them safe. Remember?"

Jonathan nodded, but didn't answer.

"Promise me, Mom, that you'll throw away that card. Promise. I never want you to be tempted to call that man."

"Oh, he wasn't as frightening as I've described him. I was basically annoyed with his wasting my time."

"Promise me, Mom. I don't want anything to happen to you."

"I guess if Ruth's family becomes ill, the police will find Tukay's name and number somewhere in her house. She seems to be ordering a steady stream of his products."

"Promise."

"Yes, and I'll never open the door to him again. Thank you for worrying about me, Jonathan. I love you."

"I love you too, Mom."

Chapter Thirty-four

The next day, Jonathan showed up at Sylvia's soup kitchen. He was looking around the front room when suddenly a bowl of stew was put under his nose.

"I promised I'd give you a taste if you came in today," Sylvia said.

The smell was enticing. A good balance of herbs, vegetables, and . . . Jonathan knocked the bowl out of her hand. The bowl split in two, and the stew splattered all over the front of his shirt and trousers.

"There's a mop in the kitchen, Jonathan, and after you finish with that, you can help Steven at the counter."

"Fuck you, Sylvia."

"Leave." Her voice was low but seething.

He shook his head.

"Where can I find Yakut?"

"He comes and goes, Jonathan. Excuse me, but if you're not going to clean up the mess you made, then I'm going to have to get the mop and do it myself before someone slips and hurts himself."

He grabbed her arm as she turned to move away from him.

"No, Sylvia, I'm not going to let you walk away. I want to know everything about Yakut. Why is he haunting me? Why is he going after my mother?"

"Your mother?"

"He knocked on her door and offered to sell her frozen meat."

"Are you sure it was Yakut?"

"His business card had T-U-K-A-Y on it, and my mother's description was dead on."

He and Sylvia were jostled by a pair of drunks that had come in for a meal.

"We can't talk here, Jonathan."

"He wanted me to join some army. He wants to defeat his Brother and his Father. What happens if he does, Sylvia?"

"The world turns topsy-turvy," she answered.

"And you want that to happen?"

"Look at the people around you, Jonathan. Look at how they're forced to live. Is God the Father or

God the Son helping them? No, instead, these people are made to beg and hide. They're blamed for what they are. Society forgets that most of these people are abandoned early on. Did you know that they've started to lock up churches when services aren't being held? You know why? Because these children of God might want to seek shelter within those hallowed walls. If the Church rejects these people, who will save them?"

"Not Yakut."

"No, but maybe he'll make the ground even so that no one has any more than anyone else. He'd push some of those religious, wealthy hypocrites out onto the streets with these people."

"So we'll all be scavenging for food. We'll be eating our neighbors to keep ourselves alive? That's what he's making us do now, Sylvia. Don't you see it? That baby I gave you and all the others he has given you."

"They died because of the way our society treats the poor."

"But did they deserve to be eaten, perhaps by their own family who came in for a meal?"

"You admitted you ate of Yakut. Who else did you eat, Jonathan? Maybe Mario didn't lie to the police. You can't cast the first stone, can you, Jonathan?"

He let go of her arm and backed away. He knew

that she didn't know for sure that what she suspected was true and certainly couldn't prove it. He backed up into a man and turned to apologize, and there was Yakut.

"A shame someone wasted good food by dropping it to the floor, isn't it?"

Yakut had a scraggly beard, and his hair was pulled back into the kind of ponytail Jonathan's mother detested. His clothes looked familiar. They were shabby. They smelled of dampness and soil. Seth, he thought. Seth had worn that same jacket and pants the last time he had seen him.

Jonathan grabbed for Yakut's collar, but slipped on the very food he had spilled. He fell at the feet of Yakut, who reached out a hand to raise him up.

"I have assisted you many times, Jonathan, and you continue to disappoint me. You shouldn't do that."

He looked at Yakut's hand and saw that the flesh was stained with blood. Seth's blood? He ignored the hand offered to him, and pushed himself up to his feet.

"Why did you kill him? Are you taking everyone away from me?" Jonathan asked.

Yakut sighed. "Here, Sylvia, let me help before someone injures himself." He knelt down and picked the split bowl up from the floor.

"You sacrosanct bastard!" Jonathan yelled.

The room fell quiet. Some people pushed their way nearer to see what was happening. Others took their food and made for the door.

"He's had a little too much to drink," said Sylvia to the crowd, resting her hand on Jonathan's shoulder.

He pulled away from her and noticed the staring faces. Most were curious; some were ready to wager bets on the winner, others were ready to pitch in.

"Ask Yakut where Seth is, Sylvia." Jonathan looked at the crowd. "Some of you must know Seth. Young. Just lost his woman. Lives in the tunnels. Has anyone seen him today?" He spun around looking for one hand to rise, listening for one voice to call out, and hoping to spy Seth himself in the crowd. A hacking cough came from the far end of the room. He pushed the crowd out of the way to reach the man who was coughing. An old man, a man who didn't look anything like Seth.

"Do you know him?" yelled Jonathan. "Seth. Do you know him?"

The old man blew his nose into his hand and wiped the snot onto his peacoat.

"He was sitting right where you are only a week ago. He was eating—" Jonathan looked down and saw a bowl of stew. He reached out, grabbed the bowl, and tossed it toward Yakut, who easily sidestepped out of the way. The bowl fell to the floor, this time shattering into many pieces.

The old man lunged at Jonathan's back, and reached around to slide his forearm under Jonathan's chin. Several homeless joined in with severe punches, and finally dragged Jonathan out of the shelter. They threw him up against a beat-up Chevy Impala that had been rusting away for several days on the street. His head hit the handle of the passenger door, causing a ringing inside his ears. He slumped to the ground, and saw the group of homeless scatter.

Moments later, a policeman squatted down to ask how he was and ask for identification.

"It was a terrible mistake, Officer," said Sylvia. "They misunderstood his intentions. Please, I've never had a problem here before."

Jonathan put a hand up to the back of his head. His hair felt wet. When he brought his hand around he saw blood.

"You okay? Can you hear me?" The officer seemed to be ignoring Sylvia's panicky speech.

"I'm okay. She's right. There was a misunderstanding. I didn't know the bowl of stew belonged to someone, and they thought I was stealing it from the old man."

"What's your name?"

"What do you need my name for? I told you it was a mistake."

"And he won't come back here, will you?" Sylvia asked.

"No. I have no reason to come back." He looked into Sylvia's eyes and saw the fear and displeasure she felt toward him.

"Still, I have to make a report," the officer said.

"Please don't," said Sylvia. "I promise I won't allow him to come into the shelter. He's not homeless. He used to help out at the counter," Sylvia explained. "You know I run a quiet kitchen, Officer. You must know that; that is, if this is your regular beat."

"It isn't, but I'm willing to give you a chance. Just don't come around here anymore, buddy."

Jonathan nodded. He looked around, but Yakut was nowhere to be seen. The officer helped him to his feet and steadied him.

"Be good," the officer said, walking away.

"Idiot! You can't afford getting arrested. Can't afford having questions asked," Sylvia said in a muffled tone.

"What do you know?" he asked, rubbing the back of his neck.

"More than you'd like me to know."

"But you can't prove anything."

"Yakut could. He could twist the situation

around so much you'd be sitting in the electric chair before the year was up. Why make him angry?"

"Because he's destroying everyone I care about."

"Back off, and maybe he'll disappear from your life," Sylvia said, placing her hands on her denim-covered hips.

"He won't. He has a use for me, and he won't settle for a substitute."

She walked away from him and back into her nearly empty food kitchen. With nothing for them to do, the counter people stared out at the street, waiting for someone to explain what had happened. She closed the door behind her and turned over the sign to read "Closed."

Chapter Thirty-five

For the first time, Jonathan wandered the tunnels alone. He tried hard to remember where Seth had been staying, but there was no sign of any of Seth's belongings. He could have sworn that the niche in which he presently stood had been Seth's and Florry's home, but there were no statues, no pots, no cups, none of the clothes that had been piled into cardboard boxes.

A broken-down cradle rested in a far corner, the mattress spotted and threadbare. When he approached the cradle, an overpowering smell of sour milk made him stop. Several roaches scuttled across the mattress. He backed away, knowing that the cradle had never belonged to Seth and Florry.

He took out a small flashlight and searched the

floor, looking for evidence of broken plastic or plaster from Florry's religious statues. Nothing was recognizable. Trash was scattered around, and several milk containers had been placed on a ledge. But he didn't believe a baby had been here. He was sure that this was where Florry had died, and probably where Seth had been taken by Yakut.

He now had to find his own way through the maze of tunnels, avoiding those who would attack him out of fear and predators that lingered in darkened corners awaiting their victims. He switched off the flashlight in order to draw less attention to himself. His arm brushed against a wall that crumbled under his light touch. He looked and found a collapsed box that had been eaten through by insects.

He accidently ran into some trackmen who were making repairs. They glared at him, stopping their work until he had passed by.

The only people he knew down here were Jared's group, and he had to find the entrance to the next level down. A shape glistened up ahead, and Jonathan moved faster to investigate it. He took out his flashlight and shined it down onto a half-eaten face. One eyeball was missing, and the nose had been wiped off the face completely. The lips had been eaten away and the mouth was writhing with maggots. The body was naked, scratch marks tattooing the flesh. He wondered if this could be Seth. Carefully he reached his left hand under the part of the face that touched the ground and turned the head. The features resembled no one he knew, and the one eye was a dark milky brown, unlike Seth's blue irises. He pulled his hand back and wiped the sticky liquid from his fingers onto his jeans.

Had the poor man been killed for his clothes? Had his body simply given up all reason to live? Jonathan knew that in a few days there wouldn't be much left of this stranger, only bones picked at by rodents and vermin or desperate humans.

He backed away from the body and turned off the flashlight, allowing the man some dignity.

Months ago he never would have believed that the thought of eating human flesh would turn his stomach. Flesh scraped off or whittled off in tiny amounts had appeased a part of him that needed a connection to the others around him. He'd turned his fetish into a religion. He'd demeaned the worth of the body by glorifying its destruction. Pain had propelled his hormones into instant highs. He had looked forward to awakening his senses. He'd colluded with hopeless souls who were sparking their own emotions with superficial wounds, superficial relationships, superficial rites that marked them forever as victims.

He would seek out Jared and his group. He

would ask them for help. Jonathan hesitated, thinking of what Jared had said. Did he really walk with death, and was it seeking other lives not his? Did Yakut walk with him even when he stole time alone in his house? In his bed under the covers? In his own head and heart? And did he still retain his soul? Or had Yakut taken over his body, invaded Jonathan's flesh with the flesh Yakut had given to him?

"Where are you?" Jonathan spoke the words knowing there would be no reply. "Where are you taking me? And why me? Do you mean to destroy the world through me, or am I only a disposable helper that takes you a step closer?"

Jared would have to accept him, would have to exorcise the devil that clung to the spirit of his soul.

There was something else he had to do before he could lose himself in the maze of tunnels.

Chapter Thirty-six

"Mom, I want you to go stay with your sister."

"I can't. Don't you remember they're off cruising the Atlantic? What's wrong? Was Cindy's body misidentified? Is she walking around planning some sort of revenge?"

"No, Mom. I'm uncomfortable with that man you told me about. The one selling the frozen meat."

"Oh, don't worry about that. I went over to Ruth's and didn't know how to turn down her offer of roast. I mean, she had obviously spent hours seasoning and cooking the meat."

"You didn't eat it."

"It tasted fine and I'm fine. Nothing's wrong with Tukay's meat. Actually, even though it's been frozen, it tastes fresher than the stuff I buy at the

226

butcher's, and he charges much less. I called him the other day to order—"

"I told you to stay away from him," Jonathan yelled.

"Let me remind you, dear, that I'm the parent. I don't expect you to tell me what to do. Advice is fine, but I'm old enough to make my own decisions."

"But you don't even know what is going on." Jonathan paced the living room with his cell phone. "This man is dangerous. He means to harm everyone around me."

"What are you talking about? Do you know Tukay?"

Jonathan steadied his breaths before answering.

"I know of him. He has a bad reputation. His meat isn't always of good quality."

"Why didn't you tell me that before?"

"I didn't know. Just recently I found out. I have been asking around."

"I don't know, Jonathan. He seems pleasant, a bit aggressive, but then aren't all salesmen? He is trying to make a living. Ruth's never had any problem, and I am expecting my first delivery tomorrow."

"Don't accept it."

"What do I say when he comes to the door?"

"Will he be delivering the meat himself?" He

paused, remembering that Yakut could be anywhere at any time. Perhaps the less she knew, the safer she would be.

"That's what he said. I didn't bother to ask Ruth who delivered her orders. He seems to be doing this on a limited budget. I don't think he can afford to hire drivers as yet."

"Then pay him and accept delivery, but don't eat the meat."

"Jonathan, that's a terrible waste of money. If you know for sure that he's been selling rancid meat, then I'll tell him off when he gets here. I'll cite whatever source you give me. Why should I let him get away with stealing what little money I have?"

"I'll pay you back, Mom. Don't worry about the money. I don't want you to have any trouble with him."

"Is he dangerous? He doesn't look dangerous. I mean, he does have slits for eyes, but he talks nice. Always asks how I am, tells me to have a nice day."

"Mom, I don't want you getting into an argument with him. Your blood pressure is barely under control. Think of your health and don't worry about being a crusader."

"You have a point." She took a few moments to think. "Okay, I'll do what you say; only I feel awkward taking your money since you did warn me against ordering."

"I have the money, Mom. You have a limited budget, and you know anytime you need anything, I'll buy it for you."

"I like to feel independent, Jonathan. I don't want to be one of those parents who's a burden to her child."

"You're no burden, Mom. Was I a burden when you raised me?"

"That was different, you didn't ask to be here."

No, Mom, this is all your fault, he thought.

"Besides, it wasn't such a big order that I can't take the hit," she said.

"Destroy the meat, Mom."

"What if it's good meat? So many people go hungry, and I'm going to toss a couple of pounds of meat into the garbage?"

"Better to do that than to have someone become ill."

"Okay, but Ruth's roast was quite good. Tender. Don't think I've ever tasted such a tender roast before."

"Mom, promise me you won't change your mind. No matter how guilty you feel, throw the meat into the garbage. Even better, take it out with you and dump it in one of those public trash cans."

"I think that's a bit excessive, Jonathan. You'd

think you expect maggots to come crawling out of the packaging. You don't, do you?"

"You never know. Don't open the package. Take it down to the park and dispose of it there."

"What if some poor bum goes rummaging through the can?"

"That's not your problem."

"How cold of you, Jonathan. I hate to think I raised you to have that kind of attitude."

"It won't be cooked. Anyone who finds the package won't want to eat it raw."

"I don't know. Some of these people look desperate, and down by the lake the homeless often have a bonfire going."

"Mom, do what I say. Be there to accept the meat. Show no sign that you're suspicious. Pay him. Take the meat down to the park and dispose of it or take it to the beach and drop it into the water."

"I like that idea best. Hope it doesn't harm the fish."

"Fish eat all sorts of things. They eat rotting dead bodies that they come across in the water."

"Why must you spoil these conversations with some sort of disgusting image?"

"Promise me that you'll do as I say."

"After the description you just gave, I don't think I'd ever be able to eat that meat. I'll toss it into the water."

"Immediately."

"What?"

"Immediately. After he leaves, wait a few minutes for him to drive away, then get into the car and head down to the beach."

"I'll miss my television program."

"Mom, do you want the package sitting in the kitchen, rotting away on the counter, maggots pushing their way through wrapping?"

"You can be so awfully descriptive sometimes. I'll set the video recorder and watch the show when I get back."

Later in the day, he would recall the details of the conversation, hoping he had truly talked her into following his advice.

He walked the streets, attempting to find an open church. As Sylvia had said, all the doors were locked since services were not being held. He thought this odd, because just a short time ago he had been able to enter and leave churches whenever he wanted. He had escaped a bad storm by sheltering himself in a church. One church had been open for confessions, but the old dilapidated building had been empty, had looked as if services had not been held there for a long time. But he had never been able to find that church again, and there were no new vacant lots where the church might have been. Yakut had forced him into that church, forced him into killing Cindy. Jonathan shivered with the memory of how he had mistreated his wife. Yakut had to be the one behind the lifelong obsession that had led to his wife's death.

Rain began falling. The wet streets gleamed under the light that the lampposts threw. People quickened their steps and automobile traffic slowed down. The sky lit up just before the sound of thunder frightened a small dog that had been nosing along the curb. The dog squatted down and crawled under a double-parked Toyota Corolla.

Without giving any thought to the direction he took, Jonathan ended up in front of Sylvia's soup kitchen. The lights were off in the store, and a drunkard was taking shelter in the doorway. The drunk awkwardly sat, falling nearly halfway down. It didn't take long for the man to get comfortable and pull out a small whiskey bottle from inside his jacket. He shook the bottle as if he needed to mix the contents, or perhaps he was measuring his ration, thought Jonathan.

Jonathan checked the street. No one was paying any attention to him. All were hurrying to their destinations, ignoring the stranded. A few cabs passed, their passenger lights on, but there was no sign of police.

He slowly moved closer to the drunk, not wanting to alarm the seated man. He noticed the man had raised the bottle to his lips and had thrown his head back to take a long drink. When he had finished, he brought the bottle down, heaved a sigh, and suddenly noticed Jonathan.

"Ain't enough room here for two of us. Go find your own place," the drunk said, screwing up his face into a hideous contortion of wrinkles.

"The rain doesn't bother me," Jonathan said. "I just want to ask you some questions."

"Shit, are you going to make me move on? Are you a cop?"

"No. I'm looking for a friend."

"Ain't any left these days. Only people walking around are them that'll stab you while you're sleeping."

Jonathan felt inside his trouser pocket. How much money had he brought? He could feel several rough, crinkly papers, but didn't know the denominations.

"How about I buy you . . ." Jonathan hesitated. He could do good and offer to buy a meal or gain the man's confidence by offering another bottle. "You seem to be getting low there," he said, gesturing toward the whiskey bottle.

The man chuckled, reached inside his coat, and drew out an unopened bottle of whiskey.

"Still, that stuff isn't going to keep you for long.

233

I could give you enough money for another bottle or two."

"You could, but will ya?" The drunk smiled up at Jonathan.

"I might. Do you know a young man by the name of Seth?"

"Kid. Skinny. Real pain in the ass. In love with the Queen of the Harlots," the drunk said.

"When did you last see him?"

"Five minutes ago. Five hours ago. Five days ago. Who the hell knows? If it didn't turn light and dark, it'd be the same day for me all the time. Only sometimes I kinda black out during some of those altering hours and can't tell the difference between day and night."

"What was he doing when you saw him?"

"You think ya gonna get all this info for free?" The drunk indignantly sat upright.

Jonathan pulled out the paper in his pocket. This guy had hit it big. He threw a fifty and a hundred onto the ground. The drunk didn't know what to do with the bottles he was holding. Finally he cradled the unopened bottle in the crook of his arm and reached out to grab the soaked bills.

"These real, or am I gonna get into some kind of trouble? You rob somebody?"

Jonathan shook his head.

The drunk pulled the bills closer to his eyes to

make sure of what he thought he had seen. Once satisfied, he opened one of his worn sneakers and slipped the money inside the shoe. One pant leg rose, showing the remains of several scabs on his shin.

"Might even try harder to remember when I saw him. Wasn't today. Probably not more than a couple of days ago. He was running like his pants were on fire. Headed on down the subway stairs on the next block. Wouldn't be surprised if he had pinched something from some street vendor. They're mighty pissy when crossed."

"Anyone chasing him?"

"No, must have given the guy the slip. Wish I could still run like that. Not that I'd go lifting things that weren't mine, but . . ." He paused, trying to think of a phrase to justify his wish. "Good exercise," he finally said.

"Better take care of that leg."

"What? Oh, you mean these." The drunk touched his shin and scraped off the scabs, throwing them out onto the street and into the rain.

Jonathan felt weak. His temples vibrated. He felt the old hunger in his belly. His mouth sagged open, allowing a drop of saliva to roll out the corner of his mouth. Immediately he wiped away the saliva and clenched his teeth.

The drunk fumbled to make it to his feet. Jonathan turned and saw a police car slowly riding by. The car stopped a few doors away, but the cop didn't get out immediately.

"Pigs, think they can hassle ya just because ya don't have a proper living room." The drunk grumbled some more under his breath. Jonathan couldn't make out the words.

A car door slammed, and both loiterers looked around to see the cop slowly moving toward the curb. Both the drunk and Jonathan split up, going in different directions. When Jonathan was far enough away, he looked over his shoulder and saw the cop getting back in the car. Farther down, pressed up against the buildings, the drunk stumbled along.

Chapter Thirty-seven

Jonathan let the telephone ring at least forty times before hanging up. His mother should be home by now. The meat should have been delivered sometime in the afternoon, and it took no more than ten minutes to drive down to the park or ocean. His mother didn't drive in the dark, and the sun had been down for a while now. He picked up the receiver and punched out his mother's telephone number again. The familiar ring went on incessantly. He pushed the switch hook down and dialed the operator.

"Can you tell me if there is anything wrong with the line for . . ." He gave his mother's area code and number.

"No," answered the operator; all calls were going through.

He didn't bother to thank the operator; instead, he made another attempt at dialing his mother's telephone number.

What the hell was her neighbor's name? All he could remember was Ruth. Ruth what? She should have given him a number to call in case of an emergency. She took her need to appear independent too far. His call-waiting signal intruded upon the ringing number.

"Hello," he said.

"I'm sorry to bother you, but is this Jonathan?"

"Yes," he said, not recognizing the voice.

"My name is Ruth Shield. I live next door to your mother."

"Yes. My mother's mentioned you."

"Dear woman."

Get on with it, lady.

"I noticed that the television has been on all day. She has the set facing her large picture window in the living room. Seems it's been on all day, but for most of the day there's been nothing but snow on the screen."

"Have you knocked on her door?"

"Several times, but there's no answer."

"Did you try the door or call the police?"

"Oh, I tried the door, but it's locked." Ruth hesitated. "And I wasn't sure whether I should telephone the police. I saw her around seven this morning, taking in the newspaper. So she hasn't been missing for very long. It's just I can't understand why she would leave the television on when there was no picture."

Jonathan rested his hand on the telephone table for support.

"Get the police, Ruth. Tell them that I told you to call. My mother's been ill, and I'm worried about her."

"I didn't know that. She looked all right the other day when she came over for dinner."

"Do you have another telephone line in the house?"

"No."

"Then give me your number, and I'll call you back in five minutes. That should allow you enough time to call the police."

"Of course. I really didn't know about her illness, or I would have called you sooner. She gave me your number the last time she went up East to visit you."

"It's all right. I'm hanging up now. Get the police immediately."

He paced the living room while the minutes slogged along. Just short of the five minutes he called Ruth's number.

"Hello."

"Are the police coming?"

"Seems they had another call about her house. The back door has been slamming open and closed. I didn't even pay any attention to the noise, since there's an extended family living on the next lot. Kids are always running in and out of their house, and the grandmother has no control over them. Wait. I see a police car pulling up in front of your mother's house now. Why don't you call me back in a half hour? I should be able to tell you something then."

"Take my cellular number and call collect." Jonathan rattled off his number and made Ruth repeat it. "Call me the instant you know anything about my mother."

Jonathan found his cellular phone buried underneath the sofa cushions. He'd go straight to the airport and get a ticket for Florida. When Ruth called back, he'd have the cellular phone with him.

Flight numbers of arriving and departing planes were jumbled together in a whiny voice that seemed to attempt to speak as softly as possible. Jonathan had called ahead and made arrangements to be on the 11:05 PM flight bound for Florida. He dumped out his change into a round plate at the inspection area and hurried through, retrieving the change and lifting his satchel at the other end of the conveyer belt. He walked immediately to his gate, noticing that barely fifteen people filled the area and the flight was due to board.

He presented himself to the airline representative, tossing the e-mailed ticket on the desk.

"I'm sorry, sir, but the flight is overbooked."

"What? What the hell do you mean? I just was booked on this flight, not more than forty-five minutes ago."

"Yes, sir, but the flight is overbooked. And we have a waiting line in case any seats free up." She pointed in the direction of the lingering crowd.

"Listen, this is the only flight leaving tonight. I have to be on it. My mother's ill and needs me."

"We can ask if someone is willing to take a flight tomorrow morning. Otherwise, we will give you the four hundred dollars in vouchers. If you need a place to stay, we can get you a hotel room for the night."

He hadn't noticed what the representative looked like until now. The woman was in her mid-forties; gray hairs were sprinkled among her auburn hair. The coarseness of the gray hairs made them stand out all over her head. *Something like the Bride of Frankenstein,* he thought. Her makeup, though minimal, was meant to hide the many wrinkles framing her blue eyes. Braces held her teeth in position, and were marred by a slight tint from her red lipstick.

"Damn!" he shouted. "I have to get to my mother tonight. I don't want to hear about tomorrow morning, lady. I don't care whose ass you have to pull off the plane I have to get on."

"Hey, buddy, think you're the only one with something important to get to?" a rotund man standing to Jonathan's right bellowed directly into his ear.

"I think you're a drunken sot and smell like a brewery and ought to keep out of this before you end up on your ass," yelled Jonathan.

The man shoved his belly into Jonathan, almost touching the leather jacket he wore.

"Gentlemen, this will not help. If you persist in this argument, I'll call security." The airline representative lifted the telephone headset off the cradle.

The man backed away, aided by a thin small woman who shook her head at him.

Jonathan turned back to the representative.

"So how about it? You going to get me on this flight?"

Just as he spoke, he saw a tall, dark-haired man grin at him from the entrance to the walkway. Yakut was about to board the very plane on which Jonathan had a reservation.

"You bastard!" Jonathan roared, lunging at Yakut. But it was too late. Yakut entered the walkway, and security guards were dragging Jonathan back, his heels skimming the gray carpet.

"Leave my mother alone," Jonathan yelled over and over again as security whisked him away to a small office.

They attempted to question him for a while, then left him sitting at a metal table with a can of Coke in his hands. His cell phone went off.

"Hello"

"Hi. Is this Jonathan?"

"Ruth, what do you have to tell me?"

"Perhaps you should fly out as soon as possible."

"That's what I've been trying to do for the past several hours. What's going on with my mother?"

"Seems she had a stroke. Doctors aren't sure how bad it is. They're talking about doing some tests. I haven't been able to see her. They keep asking for a family member. I told them we were as close as family, but it didn't go over well."

"It doesn't look like I'll be able to get there until tomorrow morning. You have to do me a favor, Ruth."

"Anyway I can help I will."

"The meat delivery man."

"Tukay?"

"Yes. See to it that he doesn't reach my mother."

"Tukay? How would he even know that your mother's hospitalized?"

"He knows, and he's on his way there now." He stopped and thought out the situation. Yakut was already somewhere near his mother. Yakut only got on the flight to enrage Jonathan, not because he needed the transportation.

"Please see if you can stay with her tonight."

"I'm sorry, Jonathan, I'm already home. They told me that only family members were to be given access to her room."

Jonathan smashed the cellular phone against the far wall.

"Hey, let's keep it down in here," said a guard who had evidently heard the noise and opened the door to check. He carried Jonathan's satchel. "Here's your bag," he said, placing the satchel on the floor near the door. "When you calm down, you can leave. Else we're going to have to call the police." The man left the room, closing the door behind him.

Jonathan stood and walked over to his satchel. The zipper was partially open. He lifted the bag and placed it on the table, pulling the zipper the rest of the way. His clothes were shuffled about; obviously they had searched his bag. He looked down at the cellular phone on the floor and realized he wouldn't be receiving any updates from Ruth. If he wanted to speak to her, he'd have to use a public phone.

Chapter Thirty-eight

Elise swam in a wave-free body of water, the vortex of which kept pulling her to the pitch-black center. She paddled harder, but still felt as though she were sinking. From time to time, she'd try to reach an arm up into the air to grab onto whatever germ of life might exist around her. But her hand merely waved in a vacuum, and she'd slip closer to the center of the vortex.

She couldn't remember how she had gotten here, couldn't remember the details of her prior life. There was only water that didn't seem to seep into her clothes, into her flesh, water drier than a desert of white salt. She couldn't splash her face with the sting of cold, brutal, life-reinforcing water. The water skimmed her body, dragging her down. She fought, fought so hard that she began hearing voices. Sounds. Oftentimes words that she couldn't distinguish. Life surrounded her but didn't touch her soul.

A home. A small, well-cared-for home. Dainty Limoges sealed inside a glass cabinet. Each a memory, a memory that she tried hard to recall. And the vortex spun her in circles, clouding her mind, confusing her. Vases filled with flowers, not from her own garden, instead bought on a weekly basis to cheer the home. Dishes and silverware. Crocheted throws made late in the evening in front of the television. Candy bowls, now empty, had been meant for children racing through a home. They weren't her children, not all of them. Only one connected. The chubby little boy. Framed photographs high on the mantel. The same little boy at ten, at fifteen, at twenty-seven, and much older with silver in his hair. Jonathan. The name rebelled against the vortex, helped to push her to the surface. The beeping of machinery steady, monotonous, surrounding her with some comfort.

Jonathan, did I do wrong? she asked. He didn't answer. Was he angry? Was he even here among the shades that moved about her?

She had grudgingly accepted the wrapped meat. The package lay heavier in her hands than she had remembered ordering. Heavy and wet, the smell slightly rancid. No, she didn't want this meat. Take it back. She had been warned and wouldn't be taken advantage of.

A man's hands spread around her own, pushing her into her home. Pushing gently, letting his fingers intertwine with hers.

Jonathan, she cried silently.

The water, a blue-green tinted black in spots, washed over her face and she felt her body succumbing.

Jonathan, she cried louder. The boy, the little boy needed her. Jonathan. The name acted as a lifeline, keeping her from falling all the way into the vortex. Jonathan. Her arms flailed about her, and her lungs ached. Jonathan. Her legs moved frenetically under the water, kicking her away from the whirlpool's center.

Don't let me go, Jonathan. Hold tight to my soul. Keep me with you in your heart. Call me back to be with you. Forgive me. I didn't realize how dangerous he was, nor how cunning. Jonathan, he caused my head to ache. Blindingly ache. His grin blurred. His hands reached inside me. Jonathan, please take me back. Don't let him send me away.

She listened and caught words. Medical terms that she did not understand. And the machinery echoed in the background. The smell of antiseptic and the feel of clean sheets rocked her back into a world that she sensed she knew.

The water puddled at her feet. The vortex weak, moving in slow motion into its own dark hole.

Jonathan, she whispered inside her mind, her body now still, sleep descending on her like a soft cloud. She was tired. She had never fought so hard before. The danger was gone now. Only a hint of danger loomed in the forest of shades that moved about her. She could rest for a while, knowing that she would see her Jonathan, wrap her arms about him, and breathe in his life, strengthening her own with his power.

He seemed so kind, even though he had slits for eyes. Bloodshot eyes, she recalled, amazingly red, like blood on fire. The letters of his name were a jumble with letters spilling over into each other. An anagram with two correct answers. Yakut, she kept thinking, but that wasn't right. The letters folded in and out of each other, never standing still, never staying on the same line. But she did not know a Yakut. She knew only Jonathan. That was the only name that mattered. Jonathan. She wrapped herself around the name and sighed. Here she could find peace. Here she could rest until the stranger came for her again.

Chapter Thirty-nine

Jonathan carried his satchel into the hospital, dropping it onto the floor at the nurse's station.

"I need some help here," he bellowed. "Someone please tell me which room I can find my mother in."

One nurse asked him to wait a second. Another breezed past him, chilling the sweat that had soaked his shirt. A bodiless voice called out a doctor's name. An old woman pulled her IV down the hall with her, her nostrils flaring, her eyelids heavy, her mouth drooping open.

"Dammit! Someone help me now. I have to see my mother."

He had startled the old woman. She looked confused, entering a world that she had forgotten. He caught her eye, but he could tell that she didn't see him. She saw only her memories now, and she didn't want to form any new ones.

He grabbed the arm of a female nurse. It was so thin that his fingers closed all the way around her flesh.

"My mother. She was admitted last night." He pronounced his mother's name and saw the nurse's eyes light with knowledge.

"The stroke victim," she said.

"Yes," he whispered, awed by the diagnosis.

"She's in intensive care."

He tried to keep track of her directions. He'd follow the yellow line until . . . Until what? He turned left? No, right. He had to ask another nurse before he finally found the room.

Stillness, waiting for something to happen, waiting for someone to die, or at least fall into a crisis. Machines uselessly guarding against death. They'd scream out frantically, but it didn't mean they'd save a life.

Jonathan found his mother's bed near the window; the blinds were opened, but not raised. Horizontal lines of sun fell across the neutral-colored blanket. He looked up at his mother's face. One side drooped. The other seemed to have taken on a tic that caused an eyelid to flicker.

"Mom." He kept his voice low and moved closer

to the head of the bed. "Mom, it's me. It's Jonathan. I'm sorry I didn't get here sooner, but you know those damn planes. I had to use the airline you've always warned me against, but they were the only ones with a last-minute flight. A flight that was overbooked."

Strangely, he missed her complaining voice, missed the whiny scolding that she would have given him had she been able. He wondered whether she was doing just that inside her head, frustrated with her inability to teach him another lesson.

A nurse reached out and touched his shoulder.

"You left this by the nurse's station. Please keep it with you at all times. We don't want anyone tripping over it." She handed him the satchel and left.

All he could think of was the confused old woman. Had she fallen over his satchel? She had looked so confused that he was sure she wouldn't have noticed it resting on the floor. He flattened the satchel and slipped it under his mother's hospital bed.

"Mom, did you hear that? I'm already getting into trouble, and I just got here." He smiled and waited for her to say something. This was a rare occasion when she didn't care. She lay quietly atop the white sheet. The pillow lifted her head slightly, not at an extreme angle. He had to lean closer to make sure she was breathing. She was.

Should he remind her that he had told her to stay away from Yakut? Why do that? He could only upset her.

"Mom, I'm going to the house later. I'll take care of any bills that come in the mail and make sure the water deliveries are canceled until you can return home. Hey, I'll even do some yard work."

It was unnerving standing in front of his mother without being able to reach her with his words.

"Ruth did good by you. She watched out for you and made sure you got help. She wanted to be here, but was told only family could visit."

The tick in her left eyelid fascinated him. He kept waiting for the eyelid to open wide, revealing his mother's blue eye. He touched her cheek and was relieved to find her skin warm. He kissed her forehead, taking in the smell of shampoo and antiseptic. They had cleansed her carefully before placing her in bed. Had they washed Yakut completely from her body? The man's closeness would have left a scent on her skin, a scent that would be unmistakable. Jonathan brushed a strand of hair off one of her cheeks, letting his fingers catch in the body of her hair.

"Mom, I'm so sorry. I never wanted any of this to touch you. I didn't even want Cindy's life to end the way it did. He seemed to be completely in control for a while. I didn't have a thought that was mine. I did his bidding without knowing what I was doing. A bit of flesh, a treat to be taken only on occasion."

He hadn't tasted his own or anyone's flesh since feasting on his wife. He found himself drawn and repulsed by the thought.

A patient at the far end of the room moaned, and kept on moaning until Jonathan pushed the call button near his mother's bed.

A heavyset nurse with dark hair and circles under her eyes entered the room.

"That patient over there," Jonathan indicated the now-silent body by the door. "The patient was moaning a few minutes ago."

"I'll have a look. Does your mother need anything?"

"No, I didn't call for help with her."

The nurse whipped the curtain around the distant bed and disappeared behind the hospital green of the curtain.

"Mom, I'm going to see how long it will take to get you moved to a private room. I'll hire a private duty nurse and see what I can do about having you transferred to New York. I'd like to have you near me if they say you can travel."

"She won't be traveling for a while," said the nurse from across the room. "Stroke victim like her is better off staying at one hospital. Our medical staff is quite good, sir."

He turned and saw the nurse swish back the curtain. He could barely make out the profile of the patient lying in the bed behind her. Yakut. He lay with his eyes closed, his lips slightly parted. Suddenly the smell was present. Flesh and vomit and blood.

"What the hell is he doing in this room?" Jonathan started walking toward the bed in which Yakut lay. "Dammit, he's not sick. He can't be. What the hell is he supposed to have anyway?"

The nurse blocked his path, keeping him in the center of the room. The pockmarked flesh on her face sagged, but her lips remained rigid. The hands she held out in front of her were red, raw from some abrasive.

"Can't you smell it, you ignorant bitch? The sickening odor that trails him."

"Sir, this is a hospital. Please quiet down, or I'll call security." Her hands touched Jonathan's shoulders, and his body shivered. "Now if you'd go back and stay by your mother's bedside . . ."

"Shit! What kind of hospital is this?" He pulled back out of the nurse's reach.

"A small hospital that needs to mix the sexes of their patients in intensive care. Isn't like they'll suddenly jump up and start to party. I'm sure your mother will be perfectly safe here. He's terminal, actually. He's not expected to last more than a day or two."

Jonathan kept shaking his head.

"I want to see my mother's doctor."

"He's not in the hospital at the moment, but . . ."

"No, call him into the hospital. Do whatever, just get him here now."

"Please step outside, sir. You're disturbing very ill patients." She pointed toward the doorway.

"I'm not leaving my mother alone with him. I'm going to have her moved now. I want a private room."

"She gets better assistance here, sir."

"I'll hire a nurse. I don't care. He's not taking my mother away from me too."

"Your mother's illness, I'm sure, came as a shock; still, you need to pull yourself together and think rationally."

"A telephone."

"There are no telephones in this room. You need to go down the hall."

"I ain't going anywhere." He looked at the badge on her chest. "Nurse Cantor. I'm staying put." He raised his voice. "You here that, Yakut? I'm staying and taking care of my mother."

"I must ask you to leave, sir." Nurse Cantor huffed up into an indignant yellow ball of flesh.

"Go to hell," Jonathan whispered, and returned to his mother's bedside.

The room fell silent around him. He reached out to pull the curtains around the bed in order to be alone with his mother. A warm hand touched his.

"How is she?" Ruth asked.

"Same, I suppose."

"They finally allowed me in. I've been praying for your mother. Stopped at our local church and lit some candles. I asked the priest to say some special prayers for Elise. I know she's not religious, but at this time she could use some powerful assistance." She looked at him, waiting to see how he would respond. When he didn't answer, she asked whether it was all right.

"Yeah. Listen, I have to make some calls. Think you could stay with my mother until I get back?"

"Depends on how long you'll be away."

"Half hour."

Ruth nodded and took his place by Elise's side.

It took him forty-five minutes to arrange for his mother's move to a private room and for a private duty nurse. He walked swiftly back to intensive care. His mother's bed was no longer in the sunlight; instead, an empty bed with fresh linen waited for the next patient. His stomach heaved. The pressure in his gut forced him to bend over. A flood of heat swamped his body, causing his forehead to break out in salty sweat. The room spun as he whirled around to locate Yakut's bed.

Yakut sat on the bed, his naked legs dangling over the side of the mattress. The palms of his hands lay flat against the hospital gown covering his thighs, his skin like white marble and his eyes glinting amber out of a wrinkle-free expressionless face.

With a drunken stride, Jonathan staggered toward Yakut, reaching one hand out to snatch the devil before he could disappear.

An alarm went off inside the room, signaling a patient's distress, but Jonathan ignored it, fixated on the figure before him.

A rush of white moved past Jonathan. Nurse Cantor stopped to grab his arm.

"You must wait outside. The doctors will do everything they can for your mother."

He turned to the nurse, catching a yellow-red glow in her pupils.

"If you want your mother to survive, you must step into the hall now," she said.

"My mother." The words mumbled from his lips seemed weak, hopeless.

"Come quickly," she said, pulling on his arm.

"Get him out of the way," shouted one of the white figures administering to the patient in the bed next to Yakut's.

Jonathan glanced over his shoulder and saw a doctor directing a small staff near a distressed patient. His mother. Helplessly he allowed himself to be driven from the room. He stood in the hall, lost in bright lights and sweeping movements that came and went from intensive care.

"Here's your bag, sir. You keep leaving it behind. You should take better care of things that belong to you." Nurse Cantor dropped the satchel at his feet.

"My mother. I tried . . ." What had he tried to do? What could he have shared with her that might have prevented her hospitalization?

He lifted his satchel and began to walk back into intensive care, but was turned away by a bulky male nurse.

"Mamma," he whispered and walked down the hallway to the elevator. "Mamma," he said again, the word catching in his throat, his eyes hurting from the onset of tears. "Mamma." The elevator doors opened, and he mindlessly walked on.

"They told me they were moving Elise, so I figured you had managed to get a private room, and I didn't want to be in the way," said Ruth over the oak dinner table stained with years of meals.

"They only moved her to the other end of the room," Jonathan said. "Next to Yakut."

"Yakut? What a strange name. Which patient was he? Not the elderly man with the awful wheezing, I hope."

"Next to Tukay. Didn't you see him?"

"Tukay was there? As a patient? What's wrong with him?"

"Nothing. Nothing. He was there to give me a warning."

"Then he wasn't a patient. Well, he must have come and gone before I got there, because I never saw him. Odd he should be at the hospital. Didn't know your mother well enough to be visiting, did he?"

Jonathan stood, every muscle aching, every movement forced.

"They did say that she was stabilized, didn't they?" Ruth asked.

He walked to the back door of the house. As he put his hand on the knob, he heard the telephone ring.

"Must be for my husband. No reason the hospital should call here this evening."

He heard the wariness in her voice as they both stood silently waiting for the message to come through. Ruth's husband burst out laughing and Ruth and Jonathan took a deep breath.

"One of his bowling team members probably trying to get him to go down to the alley for practice."

Jonathan wordlessly nodded, twisting the knob in the palm of his hand, and opening the door with a sudden pull.

"Come back tomorrow morning, and I'll make you breakfast," Ruth called as he stepped down the cement steps leading to the backyard.

His mother was alone with Yakut, sleeping in the next bed. Yakut could reach out and steal her soul, her life, pass his hand over her skull leaving her mind empty, leaving her son an adult orphan.

He heard the door gently close behind him, and realized he had left it open.

There was a knock on the glass window of the door. He turned to see Ruth waving at him. He couldn't wave back; he was too tired. He remembered the clowns from when he was a child, dancing and waving, just like the bundle now at the door's window. Ruth's mop of curly red hair sprayed out in a splashlike effect, the loose sleeve of her dress animated by Ruth's energy instead of a blast of hot air. He almost lifted his hand in farewell, almost slipped back into those moments at the laundromat.

Chapter Forty

Sometimes the room was too hot. Sometimes the lights were too dim. Sometimes sounds interrupted her thoughts; she lost the train so quickly now.

She didn't have choices to make anymore. People around her made the choices. The nurse with the endlessly boring grin who talked baby talk made the choices most of the time. Her son ceded to the nurse's decisions. He moped most of the time and depressed her frequently with his meanderings about childhood. She wanted to move out of the past, wanted to defeat the hemorrhage that had so limited her life.

The nurse was a bleached blonde, her roots starved for peroxide. He had interviewed several before settling on this one. He had dutifully brought each candidate in to meet his mother as if she could tell him which to choose. When this one appeared on a rainy day, Elise had been groggy, awoken from a nap. She had barely paid any attention to the candidate, since he was having such a hard time making a selection. It was nice having Jonathan around all the time, catering as he had never done before. She hadn't even wanted a nurse; Jonathan would do fine.

The nurse offered Elise a straw. The waxy paper touched her lips, forcing its way inside her mouth. It was time to drink. Which would it be? Milk, juice, never did they offer her soda—or a highball, for that matter. Elise sucked up to the nurse by sucking on the straw. The splash of orange juice slipped down her throat. She never seemed to be hungry or thirsty anymore; the nurse and Jonathan in their prescient way wouldn't allow it.

"Just a wee bit more," the nurse said, puckering her lips as if she were about to suck from a straw.

Elise did as she was told, for that was easier than the fuss that both Jonathan and the nurse would make. They counted her intake of liquids, the calories she ingested, and the number of pills she swallowed. Her stools were tested and her urine measured. Not even infants had to go through this kind of degradation, Elise thought.

The nurse took away the liquid and capped the

tumbler, for later she would again be enticed to take more juice. Elise wondered whether they hid some of her medication in the liquids. Yes, she took a few pills, but surprisingly not many. However, sometimes the juice tasted tainted, a trace of something she could not recognize.

She didn't like being back in New York and cooped up inside Jonathan's house. His decorative style leaned toward the dreary. She had been surprised that Cindy hadn't been able to liven the place up. But as far as she could tell, Cindy had never tried. Perhaps they shared the same taste.

Elise wanted to sit out in the sun, sit by the beach, watch the children play, snoop on the bickering couples who had been sniping at each other for the past fifty years. Elise even missed Ruth. Ruth had said she would visit, but never would. Ruth had placed a rosary around Elise's neck and kissed her cheeks. It was a relief when Jonathan removed the beads before tucking her into bed. The beads had been heavy, and the color had been atrocious, burnt sienna. The silly thought that the crucifix would burn its image in her flesh kept bothering her. Finally, Jonathan forgot about placing the rosary around her neck, or maybe he knew that the rosary wasn't going to do any good except choke her if it caught on something.

Elise surprised herself. Although she had never

been a strict Catholic, she had always shown respect for the artifacts that represented the Church. Before the stroke, she couldn't have imagined being so flippant about a rosary.

Upon bringing her back to New York, Jonathan had taken her to church one Sunday. She had fussed so much during the service that he had never taken her back. She wasn't dead yet, and she didn't intend to go back into a church until she was carried inside a coffin.

Chapter Forty-one

A relaxed-looking Sylvia stood on the doorstep. Jonathan had opened the door to find her standing there.

"Hi, I was just about to ring the bell." The smile she gave him was friendly. Her hands held an aluminum pot. "I wanted to stop by and say hello to your mother. I remember her so well when we were children. I always liked her. One of the best moms to baby-sit for. Always generous with the food and never forgot me on my birthday and Christmas."

"What the hell are you doing here?"

"I brought over some chicken soup. I know it's a cliché, but I wanted to show that I was thinking of her." Sylvia's teeth were a bright white, and every single tooth seemed to be strong and straight.

"What baby did you cook to make the soup?"

"Jonathan, that was an unusual situation. And if you remember, you're the one who brought the baby to me."

"I don't want your damn soup." He backed into the house, ready to close the door.

"But does your mother want the soup? Perhaps she could gain strength from it. I promise it is only chicken soup, Jonathan."

"I can make her some soup and know that it is really made from chicken."

"Jonathan, you shouldn't fight Yakut." The smile disappeared, and worry lines creased her forehead.

"You his messenger?"

"Yakut told me what had happened. Maybe you're right. Maybe he is using me as his messenger, but I feel close to you, and your mother, and wouldn't want the situation to worsen."

Jonathan laughed. "How much worse can it get? My mother needs twenty-four-hour-a-day nursing care. She cannot communicate, although often I get a hint of acknowledgment when I look into her eyes."

"Such a waste." Sylvia shook her head. "Do you think it would help if I visited with her?"

"I don't want you going near my mother." He walked back out the doorway, closer to Sylvia. "I never want to see you coming to this door ever again."

"If not me, then Yakut himself will." Her voice and expression were brazen.

"I can't control Yakut, but you're human; at least you used to be. And I can prevent you from coming into my house. Take that shit in the pot and feed some of your poor with it."

"I will, since there's nothing at all wrong with the soup." She rested the pot on the handrail and lifted the lid off the pot.

The smell of flesh caused his mouth to water. Flesh, human flesh, he conjectured. Bits of meat were visible through a layer of liquid fat.

"You see, Jonathan? Simply chicken soup. I left the gizzards and liver in to add some flavor." She bowed her head to take a whiff of the flavorful air steaming just above the pot.

He raised his leg high and kicked the pot from her hands and off the railing. The contents dripped from the bush unto which it had fallen.

"Take the damn pot and get out of here before I kick your ass next," he bellowed.

Sylvia took a step back, shaken by his behavior. "I'll leave the mess for you to clean up. But I promise that you'll never be able to do it alone." Sylvia left the porch, stepped down the stairs, and headed for her car, leaving the pot and lid behind.

Jonathan reached out to the bush and grabbed hold of the pot; turning, he flung the pot at her car, hitting the driver's door. As the pot fell, he could see that a slight dent now marred the paint job.

"Stupid bitch," he muttered to himself, and turned to see the private duty nurse standing in the doorway.

"Did you want me?" he asked. His voice sounded harsh inside his head.

"Your mother is agitated. She could hear the visitor's voice." The nurse spoke low so that he barely heard her speak.

"Tell her it was a salesperson. No one she would know."

"But I thought I overheard her say that she knew your mother."

"I'll go speak to my mother," he said, charging back into the house.

The nurse stumbled a bit while trying to get out of his way. Jonathan didn't bother to apologize. He headed straight for his mother's room. *His mother's prison,* he thought, remembering how she remained cooped up inside the same room in which Cindy had died. The room had been altered to accommodate a disabled person. All the bedrooms were upstairs, and he had planned on being able to easily wheel his mother into the dining room and living room without having to carry her up and down the stairs.

As soon as he opened the door, the smell of waste hit him. She had lost control over her bowels and kidneys.

"Sara," he screamed, calling for the nurse.

"Yes," she said, running up to him.

"Why the hell can't you keep my mother clean? I pay you well to see that she is constantly cared for."

"I left the room only briefly to find you. She must have needed to relieve herself while I was gone. I certainly wouldn't leave her to sit in her own mess, sir."

His mother stared at him. He almost thought she winced under his glare.

"Not your fault, Mother. I'm sorry. I didn't mean to upset you. Only I want everything to be right for you. I don't want . . ." He didn't want a repeat of what had happened to Cindy.

He looked around the room. A hospital-style bed had replaced the chair where Cindy had died. He hadn't noticed before that he had chosen that spot. His mother's wheelchair sat in a far corner outside her view, and the piano had been covered with a canvas tarp.

The foul odor in the room released the memories that he had managed to block for so long. His mother's helplessness reminded him that Yakut could enter the room and take her life, her flesh, without any protestation from his mother. She was completely vulnerable, and yet he knew that she had to be completely aware by the look in her eyes.

Chapter Forty-two

Jonathan hadn't been down in the tunnels in weeks, and he felt that he had lost the sense of orientation he had attained. Should he take a left? A right? Where was the damn entrance to the lower level? He wanted to find Jared again and ask him what he knew of Yakut.

Evidently he had accidentally stumbled into the entrance, because up ahead he could see a brightly lit station, the platform crowded with kneeling people. He would wait for the prayers to be over before approaching.

"Sanctus, Sanctus, Sanctus, Dominus Deus Saboath. Pleni sunt coeli et terra gloria tua. Hosanna in excelsis. Benedictus qui venit in nomine Domini."

271

Jonathan joined them in saying the last *"Hosanna in excelsis."*

He waited silently through the rest of the Mass, and noticed that everyone seemed to receive the Eucharist, including the elderly woman who had entrusted him with her grandchild.

"We are finished, Jonathan," called out Jared. "Come and join us."

As Jonathan climbed to the platform, he saw the elderly woman scurry away. He was glad that he wouldn't have to face her or talk to her. A child with sores covering his bald scalp went running down the stairs that Jonathan was climbing. The child disappeared into the darkness of the tunnels. To play, he wondered, or to seek out food? A rat? Another human?

"We hoped you would be coming back," said Jared.

"Yes, I have some questions to ask you."

"Join me in a bite to eat. We have plenty this morning, since Bernadette was aboveground yesterday." Jared patted a hassock next to his own and began buttering a scone.

"I've already eaten," said Jonathan. Not true, but he couldn't take food from these poor people. He sat and watched small hands, large hands, fat hands, slender hands, hands wasted by age, and hands barely touched by the years grab at the pile of scones and muffins before him.

"Bernadette is friendly with a baker above-ground. I believe at one time she dated the man. He often will make a special batch of bakery goods for her. Odd how he manages to get word to her. She claims to feel him call to her. I think it more likely that she occasionally sleeps with him. She still. . . . I hate to say loves, but she feels pity or guilt toward him. See, she sold their child. Poor girl didn't know what to do at the time."

"To whom did she sell the child?"

Jared turned away from Jonathan and scolded some small children who were taunting a little boy.

"Jared, I asked you a question. I don't want to be ignored."

Jared turned back toward Jonathan, his face pensive, his hands fidgeting with the coffee cup he held in his hands. "Yakut."

"She sold her child to Yakut. For how much?"

"For freedom. For the freedom of her soul."

The two men sat quietly for several minutes until Jonathan spoke. "And is she now free of him?"

"None of us will ever be free of him. His influence pulses in the air." He pointed to the children who had been doing the taunting. "Causes children to misbehave and sometimes makes their parents overreact to the childish pranks. Forced me out of the priesthood and into this hole where I relive my past, since I'm already dead aboveground.

"And what has he made you do, Jonathan? Why are you down here with us sinners?"

"I'm down here to atone, but I still have a life to live in the world above us."

"Or you think you do."

"I do. I have a mother that needs me. She has suffered a stroke, and I mean to make her as comfortable as possible."

"And what did Yakut make her do?"

"Yakut can't force people. He can only feed on our weaknesses." Jonathan thought of his hunger for human flesh and how he had blamed Yakut, thinking Satan had influenced his cannibalistic urges since childhood. He was wrong to blame something outside himself, wrong in letting the guilt go so easily.

"True, but we are weak, and the Lord sometimes tries us. Why?" Jared shrugged. "Out of boredom, out of spite, out of love for his own Sons."

"We are his children."

"And not his toys?" Jared smiled. "Playthings he can toss about, playthings for his Sons' amusement."

"Why did you leave the Church?"

"I wasn't needed in the small Queens parish. The congregation was decreasing in numbers. The pastor was near death's door; probably dead by now. All sorts of changes in the Mass had begun. I have an affinity for Latin, Jonathan. I enjoy speaking the language. I enjoyed the awe the congregation had held in my words. No more."

"That was reason to drift underground?"

"There was a woman. More than one woman. Several." Jared looked directly at Jonathan. "Seems one woman is happy to corrupt a servant of God and keep it secret, but she will raise hell if she finds she has competition. I was dismissed many years ago from that parish. I drifted about, well schooled but not well skilled."

"How did you end up here?"

"I helped some homeless people. Actually, they helped me. They needed religious guidance. I was the one really homeless. The homeless took me in, Jonathan. They invited me down here. I did help them to find a better place to live. I couldn't believe. this station with running water and toilet facilities had never been . . . homesteaded."

"They build up your ego, and you let them think there is some hope for their souls."

"How crudely put! But true."

"Then you don't believe in those prayers you recite?"

"I do and don't. I believe they make the pain easier, but they don't do away with the pain."

275

"What dealings have you had with Yakut?"

"Very few. I take in those he casts away, and for some reason he considers this place to be off limits. He has never paid us a visit. He has tempted many of my people to join with him, but he never invades my territory. So, maybe there is something to prayer. Thank you for calling that to my attention."

"This is consecrated land as far as Yakut is concerned?"

"Not consecrated. Perhaps not worthy of his immediate attention. I live in fear that one day he will come here and there will be nothing I can do. I will fail all these people that trust me."

"I believe he has killed Seth."

"A shame, but inevitable. He and Florry annoyed the hell, pardon the language, out of Yakut. Florry with the statues and the blessings and the holy water. She even managed to smuggle in Eucharist. I don't have the slightest idea how she got the wafers, certainly didn't come from me. I'm not even sure anymore whether my wafers turn into anything but stale bread."

The elderly woman whose grandchild Jonathan had taken approached the two men. Jonathan watched her progress from the corner of his eye. He thought about leaving before she had time to speak to him. He thought about ignoring her, acting as if he couldn't understand her, saying that he didn't remember her grandchild, but he knew Jared would suspect. She carried baby clothes in her arms, and laid the entire bundle on the floor at Jonathan's feet.

"Ah, she wants to donate her grandchild's clothing. Will you accept them?"

"I'm sure there are many babies down here, within your own group, that need the clothes."

"You cared for her dead grandchild, Jonathan. She wants you to disperse the clothes in any way you want. Perhaps you may have a child of your own?"

"No. Tell her to share them with the mothers who already live here." Jonathan had not acknowledged the woman.

"You tell her. Her name is Louisa."

"Get her the hell away from me." He moved closer to Jared in order to speak in a lowered voice. Hate, fear, and helplessness tinged the words.

Surprised, Jared looked closely at Jonathan. The two men at first glared at each other, until Jared's eyes softened. Jared moved to his knees and picked up all the baby's clothes, folding each so that he ended with a neat pile of pastels.

"Thank you, Louisa." And the words dismissed the elderly woman, who turned and walked away.

"You gave Marissa to Yakut, the same as Bernadette did with her child?" Jared looked at Jonathan.

"No. Not directly. He wanted the baby, but I wouldn't allow him to have her."

"So?"

"Do you know Sylvia?"

"Only from what I have heard about her. Many of the people down here think she's a saint." Jared looked over at Jonathan with a humorous gleam.

"She's Yakut's helper." Jonathan rose to his feet. "I didn't know it when I gave the baby to her. She cooked the infant and then fed her to the homeless, perhaps even some of your own people."

"So, you have heard the stories that have been told about Yakut sharing flesh with the poor."

Jonathan looked down at Jared. The priest's eyes were a sludge brown, his features coarse within the sagging flesh. *How old could he be?* Jonathan wondered. Not as old, certainly, as he looked. The priest's hair was thinning, but still held the rich color of black. Only a few gray hairs marred the deep color.

"I've tasted of Yakut himself," said Jonathan.

Jared's eyes narrowed. "You are one of his followers. Are you here to bring him information about us? About the way we live and how many of us there are?"

"Right now Yakut and I hate each other."

"Why aren't you dead then? Yakut doesn't tolerate what he can destroy."

Jonathan thought of Florry. She had lived only because Yakut knew she would die painfully. Did that mark Jonathan himself as doomed?

"Maybe he has a purpose in keeping me alive. He may need me to fulfill some plan that he has."*Or I may be dying,* he thought.

"Are you a procurer for the bodies he uses?"

"Marissa was an accident. I thought I could trust Sylvia."

"Why are you down here, Jonathan? Certainly not to help the homeless, and you're not without a way to make a living. Why are you here?"

"He . . ." Jonathan paused for several seconds, determining how much this priest could digest without banishing him. "He broke up my marriage. I wanted to know why. Now, my mother is ill and I'm sure he caused it. Again, why?"

"Do you think he'll tell you?"

Jonathan shook his head. "You're probably right, Jared. There's no sense to my following him."

"But you must?"

A four-year-old girl came to the priest crying. She had fallen, and the open wound on her knee seemed to flap open as she limped.

Jonathan's mouth filled up with saliva. He stared at the wound and reached out, not to help the child,

Mary Ann Mitchell

but to touch the delicate young flesh. The golden-haired girl looked up at Jonathan. Her bottom lip pouted out, tears streaming down porcelain cheeks, nose dripping, eyes glassy. Too glassy for a real little girl.

"Where did you come from, sweetheart?" Jared was asking. "Are your parents nearby? Here, sit next to me."

Her eyes shined an icy blue. She allowed Jared to touch her right hand, but pulled away when he tried to sit her on his lap. With her free hand, she reached down to her wound and began picking at the flesh on her knee.

"No, sweetheart. You'll only infect the cut." Jared still tried to calm the girl, but she paid no attention.

When she had a loose piece of flesh between her fingertips, she offered it to Jonathan.

"Bastard!" he shrieked, bringing his hand down to slap the child out of his sight.

Jared jumped to his feet and grabbed Jonathan's arm before the hand could make contact with the girl.

"What the hell do you think you're doing?" asked Jared.

"She's not a child. It's Yakut in the form of a child. He can be anything he wants."

"You certainly won't prove that to me by slapping this child around."

"Look at her eyes. They're glass, not real. If she is not Yakut himself, then she is a demon aiding him."

Jared turned to the child. Her face was swollen from crying. Her body was laden with baby fat. The plumpness quivered with each sob. Her clothes were stained but clean, and her feet were bare. She played with the flesh she held in her fingertips before popping it into her own mouth.

"Now what do you think?" yelled Jonathan.

"She's a child. She has no idea what she's doing. Maybe . . ." Jared paused. "She may come from a family that practices cannibalism. It's known that some of the people down here do."

"Yakut's people do." Jonathan pulled away from Jared. "Get that kid out of this camp before she pollutes everyone and everything here."

"Sweetheart." Jared's voice was soft. "Where is your family? Let me help you." He reached out his right hand to the child. But she turned away from him, walking toward the group of taunting children.

"Stop her," shrieked Jonathan as he backed away toward the exit. "You told me that he hadn't invaded. Now he has, and he won't leave. He'll suck you into his plan. The entire group will break up, and he'll be the winner. He'll take them deeper into the tunnels and won't let them return."

Jared stood frozen to the spot on which he stood. His head turned from Jonathan and back to the child.

"What's the matter with you?" Jonathan cried. "Didn't you hear anything I just said?" He was only a few feet from the exit. The elderly woman, Louisa, approached the little girl and placed a withered hand on the girl's hair, stopping the girl in her tracks. The girl twisted around and viciously attacked Louisa. The child fought like an animal. Her teeth ripped gouges on the old woman's flesh. Blood drops sprayed the air surrounding them. Splotches of blood dotted the faces of the nearby children, who stood awed by the scene in front of them.

The elderly woman tripped while trying to escape, and fell to the ground. Not only did the girl pile on top of her, but the other nearby children joined her lead.

The priest waded into the melee, calling out names of other residents to come help him.

Jonathan ran from the station, acidic fluid bubbling up through his esophagus from his stomach.

Chapter Forty-three

The smoky air caused her throat to tighten. So many charred bodies surrounded her, charred bodies that still moved, hands grabbing at her legs, fingertips dissolving into ashes. She was walking. She didn't remember when she had learned to walk all over again. The stroke had left her paralyzed, so paralyzed that at mealtime the nurse would tie a bib around her neck because half of her food rolled out the right side of her mouth.

With each step she took, she heard a crunch. Synthetic waste? Flesh and bones?

Where was Jonathan? She needed to find her son. He could lead her out of this dark crispy world.

Skin drooped down from a child's chest. Freshly burned, the child was crying.

Elise moved toward the child, and as she did her legs began to give out. The right knee weakened. Then the left. She tried hard to remember how to walk. The harder she concentrated on walking, the more clumsy she became.

The child's features were unrecognizable because of the burns, but there was something familiar in the child's movements, in the child's cry.

Food. She smelled the odor of freshly cooked meat. Roasted. Blanketed by the odors, she became disoriented. Where had the child gone? She turned her head to look around and found that she didn't need to move her body. Her head spun completely around upon her shoulders. Her head kept moving, didn't stop when she had made full circle. Instead her head continued round and round. Her head was spinning so fast that her eyes couldn't see the shapes around her.

Her head ached. A throbbing pulse filled her head with noiseless pain.

"I'm not going to die," she said. "I am *not* going to die. The bastard will not have my life. He'll not cook me with his other sinners." She gripped her fists tightly. She squeezed her eyes closed and her body wavered; her head suddenly ceased its motion. She waited for several minutes before opening her eyes to the sight of Tukay.

"Obstinate bitch." He spoke the words to himself, knowing that she could hear. "What marvels do you have to live for, old lady? What joys are left to you? You are ready for the ovens, ready to mingle with my souls." His arms spread out, engulfing all the charred bodies about him.

She could see burned bodies cowering from the sight of him. Tukay lowered an arm toward a naked female and set her legs afire with a simple wave. The female hit her legs with her already blackened hands, attempting to put out the fire that seemed capable of burning even already blighted and burned flesh.

Elise reached out to help the woman, removed her own nightgown to help smother the flames. The cotton immediately flashed to ash as it touched the flames.

"You're a bastard," she whispered.

Tukay heard. He heard her thoughts. He knew her pain and frustration.

"Come sit beside me," he gently said. Elise looked back toward Tukay, forgetting the female on fire. "I want you to sit down. Come." He reached out his right hand for hers, and she backed away. "How can we come to any compromise if we don't talk?"

"I am *not* going to die," she repeated.

"Not easily. I think even my Father will have trouble reclaiming what is His."

"I don't belong to anyone."

Tukay's eyes saddened.

"Won't you be mine?" He lowered his hand.

"Who the hell are you?" she screamed.

"Your lover, Elise. I am the only lover you will have for the rest of eternity."

"Never. You're too . . ." She thought for a second. "Slimy."

"Oh, Elise, you fail to see my beauty."

"Maybe because it's just not there." She gave an indignant nod in his direction.

"I have patience, Elise. I can wait for a flirt."

"Don't waste your time on me. I'm not yours."

"And what about Jonathan?" he asked, reaching down and lifting the burnt child she had seen earlier. "Jonathan, your mother is here with us."

"He is too young to be Jonathan. Jonathan is a man now, no longer a simpering child. I remember him clearly, Tukay. You cannot fool me."

The child wiggled in Yakut's arms, metamorphosing into flab that melted between Yakut's fingers. The hissing sound as the flab hit the floor transformed into smoke that climbed the air in front of Elise.

"Let me hold you, Elise." Tukay put his arms out to her.

She spat at him. The saliva sizzled when it hit the floor.

"You hurt my feelings, Elise. You stab my heart with your rejection." Yakut took a step toward her, placing his hand over his chest. Yakut ripped the shirt from his chest and pointed. His wet heart became visible, beating out a steady rate in front of her.

"You are mocking the Lord." Shock tinged the softness of her voice.

"I am God, Elise. I am everything to you."

His heart began to drip blood. She watched the rivulets glide down his chest.

"It is you who makes my heart bleed, Elise. You who causes the pain that stalks me wherever I go."

She noted how beautiful his hand was: the fingers long, the nails cut perfectly. The whiteness of the flesh radiated its own light within the darkness that surrounded Elise and Tukay. A beautiful hand that beckoned to her. A hand that she wished to touch to test its softness. The palm of the hand reached out for her. And in that palm she saw a world she remembered, a life she had lived, departed ones awaiting her arrival. . . . But she smelled the burnt meat and felt the warmth of the fire. A fire so hot that her eyes teared.

"No!" she screamed. "I will *not* die."

Chapter Forty-four

"Thank God you're back," called the nurse after Jonathan had opened the front door. "Your mother had a crisis. I called the doctor, but by the time he got here she seemed to have recovered on her own. He's given her something to sleep. He hopes the rest will help. I didn't have a telephone number for you, or I would have called immediately."

"What kind of crisis?" he asked, making his way to the music room, where his mother was bedded.

"It started with a fever that I couldn't manage to bring down. She started mumbling. I even think I heard her say your name. Isn't that amazing? She can't speak, but I'm almost certain she called out your name."

He opened the door to the music room and saw

his mother soundly asleep. Her breathing was regular and her face not flushed.

"Was she upset over something?"

"No. She was sitting up in bed, and I was reading to her, when all of a sudden I noticed a glassy look come over her eyes. Her complexion turned an awful shade. A bluish tint almost made me think that her veins were near bursting."

"Another stroke?"

"The doctor didn't say. He wanted to wait for her to wake up after the sedative to give a final diagnosis."

Jonathan walked closer to his mother's bed. He took her left hand, which lay atop the blanket, and began to kiss each finger, then moved on to the palm and the back of her hand. Tears blurred the vision of her face soundly sleeping, but her hand was warm. *She is still alive,* he consoled himself.

"Next time, you should give me your number. I would hate to have her di . . . Have another crisis and not be able to bring you back to the house."

Without freeing his mother's hand, Jonathan got down on his knees and prayed. He heard the door to the room catch, and he knew he was alone finally with his mother. Through his tears he studied her face and remembered the young woman that she had been, the skin that didn't sag, the lips that were always painted red, not the pale blank color of those chapped lips before him. The nose straight and slender. The eyes unmarred by wrinkles and bags. The forehead smooth. And her hair clean with its deep natural color. All so beautiful and so transient. God the Father had inflicted his own kind of pain on his mother. A slow, progressive loss that worried her mind into depression.

"She can still be beautiful again."

Jonathan looked across the room to see Yakut seated in the wingback chair that the nurse used.

He felt his mother's pulse pick up.

"Get the hell out of here." He contained his anger so that he would not feed into his mother's panic.

"She can always be beautiful in your eyes."

"She is beautiful," Jonathan responded.

Yakut shook his head. "Not to you and not to the world."

"To your Father," Jonathan whispered the name.

"Only he is beautiful, don't you know that? You humans are a minuscule reflection of his beauty." Yakut paused and then added, "And mine."

"Your soul is ugly."

"I have no soul, Jonathan. I am truly one with God."

"What are you saying? That you are God?"

"God the Father, God the *Sons*, God the Holy Ghost. We are all the same person."

"No. You're the snake that tempted Eve. Yours

was the voice that cried out for your Brother's death. You claimed your Father's Church, but could not steal it.

"You want me to believe that you have so much power, but up to now you have failed. You ensnare the desperate and ignorant and the fearful. You stole my youth. You stole my wife. And I let you because I wanted to be more than human."

"You are less than a roach crawling on its belly after ingesting the poisons of man. You mean less to my Father than you could imagine."

"Then why do I mean so much to you?" Jonathan asked.

He felt his mother's pulse slow to normal, and when he looked Yakut no longer sat in the wingback chair. Yakut's influence was gone from the room.

291

Chapter Forty-five

Jonathan stayed close to home over the next few days. His mother passed in and out of sleep. The doctor said she was neither worse nor better than she had been before the crisis.

"I saw your wife once."

Jonathan jerked himself from his reverie to pay attention to the nurse.

"Only once," the nurse said. "She seemed very nice. I'm sorry about what happened to her. I hope that man from the motel doesn't get off. So often that happens. More than we can even imagine as lay people; that is, people not involved professionally with the law."

The nurse crossed her legs, and the white uniform rode up her thighs. Her legs were on the plump side, yet the rest of her was slender and almost perfect in proportion.

"Do you want to know where I saw her?" she asked.

"No," Jonathan replied.

The nurse fidgeted with a paperback she had lying on her lap. Her blond hair and dark eyes contrasted.

"I hope I haven't distressed you, sir. I just thought you might want to talk about her. It's been a while."

"Merely months."

"Terrible way to go," she continued. "Imagine being chopped up and served as dinner. But then you can imagine that."

"What the hell are you talking about?" Jonathan turned his full attention on the nurse, wondering what game she was playing.

"Simply that you can imagine it because unfortunately it happened within your own family."

"Where are you going with this conversation? Spit it out."

"I hadn't realized I had seen her until I read the papers the other day. I live near the motel, and frequently stop by to visit a former patient who lives there.

"She certainly was attractive. Your wife, I mean. A bit fidgety. She didn't seem to know what to do

293

with herself. She paced back and forth in the lobby one day. Until a tall man arrived."

"Mario."

"Oh, no, not her killer. No, no, I've never seen him. No, this man was dark and well dressed. She called him by name. An unusual name that I'd never heard before."

"Yakut." He suddenly felt exhausted.

"Yes, I believe so. I assumed he was foreign. His mannerisms weren't your typical American male."

"What did they do when they met?"

"He hugged her and kissed her cheek. They left the lobby together. Don't know where they went from there."

"Are you telling me that you think she was having an affair?"

"An affair? Funny, it never entered my mind. They weren't lovey-dovey enough."

"They were in the lobby hugging," he reminded her.

"Yes, but it was as if he were an old friend. You know, kinda cursory hug and kiss."

He sensed movement from the bed, and turned to look at his mother. Her body trembled, and even though her eyes were closed he could see the lids twitch.

"You're not to talk about him in front of my mother. Do you understand?" He turned back to the wingback chair and saw that it was empty.

A gentle knock at the door introduced the presence of the nurse.

"Where are you going?" he gruffly asked.

"I'm sorry I'm late. I was delayed by traffic. How is your mother doing?"

"We were just talking about Yakut and the motel."

"Your mother?"

"No, you and I."

"Sorry, sir. I don't know what you're talking about."

"My wife. Her death. Her murderer."

The nurse's face was blank.

"I know nothing of your wife, sir, except what little I read in the newspapers."

"You've seen my wife."

"Never met her."

"At the motel. She met Yakut."

"I'm lost. Perhaps it was someone else you had been talking to."

"You sat in that chair." He pointed accusingly to the wingback chair. "Just a few moments ago."

"I just arrived. I haven't even had a chance to check your mother, which I should do right now."

The nurse walked over to the bed and began her physical examination of the patient.

"You arrived on time, examined my mother, then sat in the chair."

"Perhaps you've been sitting up with your mother too long. I can take over now, if you want to get some rest," the nurse offered.

If not the nurse, who had sat in the chair? he wondered. The answer came to him, but he kept wanting to reject it.

"You were reading that ratty paperback. The one with the bluish cover. I can't remember what the hell was on the cover."

"I never read paperbacks. I love the feel of a hardcover. That's why I belong to so many book clubs." She continued making his mother comfortable.

"What are you reading now?" he asked.

"This has been a really bad day for me," she said, looking up at him. "I forgot my book, and I was wondering whether you'd mind if I looked amongst your library for something to read."

"You're lying."

"Excuse me, sir?" She dropped the cotton blanket she had been holding and confronted him. Her dark eyes stared at him.

"I have to do some work. Just don't leave her alone." Jonathan hurried from the room, closing the door softly behind him.

What the hell do you want, Tukay? Why won't you leave me alone?

Chapter Forty-six

"What are you doing here, Jonathan? I thought I made it clear you shouldn't come back. Is your mother . . . ?"

"My mother is the same, Sylvia."

"Turn around and march back out before you start a riot."

"I'm not here to cause trouble."

"You will if some of these guys recognize you."

"Sylvia, I need to know what Yakut wants." He laid his palms flat on the table before him and leaned toward Sylvia.

"Ask him."

"Is he here now?"

"No, but you know his haunts."

"And this is one of them."

Mary Ann Mitchell

"Not today. Haven't seen him for several days."

"You must be running low on your food supply." The sarcasm in his voice pricked Sylvia's attention. She waved for him to follow her.

She led him out to the back alley in which he remembered carrying Marissa. The lids of the trash bins were thrown open, and the bins themselves were empty. The yard had been freshly swept.

"I wanted to help you, Jonathan. Remember, I came over with the soup and offered to help with you mother. You rejected my offer and managed to dent the side of my car in the process. Now you're here threatening to tell my secrets."

"I'm not." He rammed his hands into the front pockets of his jeans. "The sarcasm was inappropriate. I'm frustrated. I've stayed away from the tunnels, and he's come after my mother and me. He shaped into the nurse and talked to me about my wife. I didn't even know he was there. My mother sensed it, though. She began trembling."

"He doesn't want you to stay away. He wants your obedience," she said.

"What does he want me to do?"

"What he tells you to do. I don't know his exact plans. Just don't fight him, and maybe you'll get to keep your mother alive for a while longer."

"He wanted me to feast on that baby's flesh. I

298

refused. I can't eat human flesh anymore, not since . . ."

"You tasted of him."

Jonathan staggered back against the building's wall.

Sylvia brushed her white hair back from her face. The sun caught the glint of the white strands.

A volunteer came to the door of the kitchen and called to Sylvia.

"I'd better go in and help out. Things fall apart so quickly when I'm not present." She stopped in the doorway and turned to Jonathan. "Go home to your mother. I know she isn't coherent, but tell her I'm thinking about her."

"No, I'm going down into the tunnels. I'm not going to sit and wait."

"You'll wait as long as he wants you to. Haven't you learned yet what the price of disobedience is?"

"I can't be disobedient if he doesn't tell me what he wants."

She walked over to him and placed her left hand on his cheek.

"He wants you to follow. To be a soldier for him. Increase his fold, Jonathan. Bring others in to worship him."

"That's what you've been doing, isn't it? You've been recruiting for him among the homeless, the discouraged, the fearful. People come to you for help, and you lead them into hell.

"How does that make you feel, Sylvia? And what do you stand to gain? You don't do it to feed the poor. No, you do it because you want a seat right next to him when he rules his Father's world."

"I'm willing to take the seat right behind yours, Jonathan, for you are the one who will be seated next to him." She slowly rubbed his face with the palm of her hand. "I'll whisper in your ear, guiding you and protecting you."

"From Yakut?"

"No, from your own stupidity. You need no protection from Yakut. That is merely a childhood perversion foisted on you by those who wanted to rule your behavior."

"Ah, the devil is truly looking out for my welfare."

"Of course not. For his own, but that includes you and me. I'm a bit jealous of you, Jonathan. He has never offered me his own flesh. He's brought me the bodies of others. All dead, nothing fresh." Her hands moved to the back of his neck. "How did he taste, Jonathan? Spicy? Hot? Did his flesh burn your tongue? And when you swallowed, could you feel him filling you up? Blackening your soul with his lust?" She smiled and her eyes sparkled.

"None of that, Sylvia. I felt ashamed. I used his bone to . . ."

"To what? Please, I want to know everything." Her hands gripped the back of his neck tighter.

"He made me kill my wife." Jonathan felt shock at his own statement.

"No. He assisted you in what you wanted. Why keep her alive when you could have him?"

Jonathan shook his head.

"There can't be two strong forces in your life. You've chosen, Jonathan. And you made the right choice."

"I was driven to killing her. I didn't want her dead."

"You were driven by your own desires. No one forced you. You called to him and he answered."

"Are you telling me I must choose him over my mother?"

Her hands dropped away from his neck, and she jammed her fingertips into the waist of her jeans.

"Only if you allow her to come before him."

She turned and walked through the doorway to the kitchen, leaving Jonathan feeling cold, so cold that he shivered in the afternoon sun.

Chapter Forty-seven

The nurse fluffed the pillow and chattered. The words weren't important, but the heat of her breath gave Elise hope. Life was still near. Life was within reach. Elise tried to move her hand to touch the nurse's arm, but couldn't. Her fingers scratched at the bottom sheet, slowly, with great effort.

Why had Jonathan been talking with Yakut? He had allowed the man to sit in the wingback chair and converse. The sneers on Yakut's face had tormented her. Why couldn't Jonathan see the way Yakut had baited him?

The nurse settled Elise's back against two down pillows.

"I'm going into the library to get myself a book.

I'll try to select something we'll both enjoy, and I'll read to you until you're sleepy."

She hated the nurse's smile and hated the color of the lipstick the nurse always wore. Sometimes the smashed raspberry color of the lipstick rubbed off on the nurse's teeth, and Elise would want to reach out and rub the damn color off. *Such a slob*, she thought. The nurse's shoes were the worst. *Old-lady shoes*, Elise thought. Hell, she had to be at least forty years older than the nurse, but she'd never leave the house in a pair of shoes like those.

Ah, she has another run in her stocking, or else she's wearing the same pair of stockings from yesterday, but put them on opposite legs this morning.

The nurse turned back to Elise with a final smile before closing the music room door behind her.

Bugger you, Elise tried to say, but she heard the words come out garbled, unintelligible, just like everything else she said.

Where the hell had her son gone? If only he'd pay closer attention to what she was trying to communicate to him. Instead, he attempted to soothe her with words and the obsequious way he would run his fingers through her hair.

Elise tried to move her legs. At times, she'd think she had made headway, but never could be sure, since she couldn't be sure what distance her leg or foot had moved. Her hands were doing better. The fingers now moved on both hands, except she worried about the tremor that seemed to be developing in her right hand.

She heard the soft sound of something quickly rubbing against a sheet. Intently she listened and waited. If that bastard showed up again . . . The noise became louder and more frenetic.

Her eyes searched the room. Same room. Same empty feel. She breathed in the scent of herself, the sweetish soaps they used to sponge-bath her body, the powdered flesh that smelled babylike. She wanted the smell of good solid sweat.

The nurse reentered the room, carrying a pop psychology book in her hand. *Had to have belonged to Cindy,* Elise thought. Her son would never be caught reading that trash.

The nurse left the door open and rushed to the bed. She threw the book onto the seat of the wingback chair. When she touched Elise's right foot, her own hand started to shake.

"I'll get something to relax you," the nurse said, releasing Elise's foot and walking over to the cart that had been brought in from the kitchen.

Hell, it's my foot that's been making all that noise, Elise triumphantly thought. Any movement right now was better than none. Elise forced her chin downward so that she could see the foot of the bed. Sure enough, her right foot was shaking like crazy.

The nurse came to the head of the bed carrying a small Dixie cup and a glass of water.

"Here, now you take these pills and relax. I'll call the doctor and see what he has to say about this." She placed the Dixie cup to Elise's mouth and coaxed the pills between Elise's tight lips, then brought the water up to the same lips.

Elise shrugged away the glass with her mouth, spilling some water on her chest. When she spat out the pills, the nurse tsked as if Elise were a five-year-old.

"You stupid bitch," Elise screamed inside her head. "I have to move. I have to save myself."

A trembling sensation spread throughout Elise's body, uncontrollable waves of motion quickening her own breath into a pant.

The nurse had picked up the cell phone and was now talking, but Elise didn't pay any attention to the words. She felt saliva bubble across her lips. Her tongue lapped against her teeth, and her throat gurgled. Her eyes rolled back under her lids, and she saw the fires again. The sparks soared far into the air, touching blackness that instantly smothered them.

Obliviously, Jonathan walked among the flames. A few sparks touched his clothing, burning little

305

holes in the material. He brought the back of his right hand up to his forehead, wiping away the glistening sweat.

She heard the thumping. Her own heart beating. A steady sound, until occasionally a beat seemed out of sync. That was when she felt a tug inside her chest.

What the hell is he doing? Elise wondered when she saw that her son was walking in step to her heartbeats.

Chapter Forty-eight

As Jonathan came closer to Jared's colony, he smelled burning flesh. He faltered now and then in his approach, doubting that he wanted to see the terror Yakut had wreaked on this isolated world. He kept pushing on, knowing part of the answer was here among these people, or rather with the priest.

The lights were dimmed. He barely saw figures moving. Stooped and bent, they clung to the shadows. And the smell grew stronger.

He climbed the steps quietly, as if entering a holy cemetery. He didn't want to disturb the dead, which included most of those still breathing. How would they ever return to their former life?

Once he stood on the platform, Jonathan peered

more intently into the shadows, followed the figures as they moved seemingly without purpose.

He softly spoke the priest's name. No response. He raised his voice slightly, and one or two of the figures stopped their movements but didn't turn toward him. They froze, and he could almost feel the way they held their breaths.

"It's me, Jonathan. I'm looking for Jared. Anyone know where I can find him?"

The elderly woman who had been attacked by the child came from behind him. Her flesh was covered with scratches and open wounds. When she slipped her hand inside his, he could feel liquid slide from her flesh to his own. She led him into the dark, where he found himself stepping over inert bodies. Far back, he saw Jared leaning against the tile wall. His eyes were closed in prayer, and the rosary beads he held in his hands were looped tightly around his knuckles.

"Father," Jonathan said.

Jared didn't open his eyes. He didn't move a muscle as the elderly woman led Jonathan closer.

When he was close enough, Jonathan reached out, touched Jared's arm, and called again, "Father."

This time Jared opened his eyes. At first he seemed to see only the elderly woman, but she

308

looked up toward Jonathan's face, forcing the priest to acknowledge the outsider.

"Did you call me 'Father'?"

Jonathan nodded.

The elderly woman released Jonathan's hand and folded herself back into the darkness.

"I'm no one's father. A father would not have allowed this to happen to his children."

"What happened?"

"You saw the child before you . . ." Jared hesitated.

"Ran away," Jonathan said.

Jared smiled. "I wish you had been able to take my people with you. But you did warn me that the child was dangerous. She was such a little girl and so full of power. Several of our strongest men could not hold her down. She appeared to breathe fire. Yeah, like a dragon. Somehow people started to ignite. Hair flared, flesh melted, and bones were singed." Jared unwound the rosary from his knuckles and hung it around his neck.

"Why did he come for us, Jonathan? Was it you who brought him here? Was it Seth? I saw Seth during that frightful battle. He carried the child away in his arms."

"The child that had set the fires?"

"Yes. Seth was naked, his skin all splotched with black and blue marks."

"He had been forced to participate then."

"No. I think the bruises had been given him by my own people when they panicked."

"The bruises wouldn't have formed so quickly."

"The battle raged for hours, Jonathan. Half my people are ash, another third can't walk, and the rest bear some sort of mark.

"Louisa is actually one of the better-off ones." Jared made the sign of the cross. "She is doing her best to help the others, especially those that have lost their children." Jared stared into Jonathan's eyes.

"I'm sorry. I explained—"

"I don't want to hear it again." Jared waved his hand in the air, as if he could clear away the putrid smells that had filled the station. "What do I do, Jonathan? We can't afford medical attention, and most of the people are too afraid to go aboveground to visit an emergency room. What do I do?"

"There's a doctor who has been making house calls on my mother."

"And he will want to come down here? I don't think so."

"More people will die if you don't force them to get help."

"No. I should make the rounds and see who is left."

"You're going to count heads until there's no one left?"

"A few will survive. The others are better off dead." Jared walked away from Jonathan.

"Wait," Jonathan called out, raising a hand to halt the priest. As he did, he saw the dried blood on his hand. Louisa's blood. The brown crust cracked when he stretched out his hand in midair. "Father," he called out, racing after Jared.

He stopped suddenly when he approached a pile of ash and bone. The dead had been collected and placed in a corner of the station near where the token booth would have been. Some bodies still had flesh on them. A leg intact. Or even one side of a body still whole. The smell turned his stomach, but he walked closer to the bodies, curious and intrigued by the disaster. What was the purpose of all this? These bodies couldn't even be used as food to bribe people to become Yakut's soldiers. Wasted lives, serving no purpose, starved of food and education by a society that didn't care, didn't acknowledge its responsibility. Some of the smaller skeletons were paired up with adults. The ones who could be identified. The rest had been heaped together.

"Father," Jonathan shouted, and turned to find Jared.

He found the priest kneeling next to a young man who had no legs. Was it Extreme Unction the priest was giving the young man? Was Jonathan watching another human being die? He hadn't just watched his wife die; he had killed her. Killed her for Yakut. Killed her because he was too scared to face the consequences he acknowledged to himself.

A child sat nearby with her arms crushing her legs to her chest. Her straight, stringy hair was matted and filthy. Her chin rested upon her knees as she waited for her father to die. Jonathan was sure they were related. The features gave that away instantly when the oval blue-green eyes were compared, when the child's short pug nose tweaked with a sob, but most of all when they both managed to cast glances at each other, regretting the future.

Jonathan got down on his knees and tried to pray. No formal words came to him. Instead, he begged God to help this man and child to accept what the next few hours would bring. *Give him strength to face your justice and give her the faith to still believe in you.*

The priest kept muttering his Latin words even after the father ceased to fight for his life. The sentences turned to chanting inside Jonathan's head, and he began to rock back and forth on his knees, lullabied by his childhood memories.

Chapter Forty-nine

"Elise, I'm waiting for you," said Tukay.

"Don't hold your breath," she retorted.

"I don't need to breathe, and soon you won't either."

Elise felt something cold on her forehead. That nurse probably stuck some stinking rag on her forehead thinking that could relieve the terror Elise needed to fight. *This is no fever, lady. This is stronger than any disease medicine is aware of.*

"Elise, why keep me waiting? We both know how tired you are."

"Tired of your bullshit."

"What a cranky addition you'll be, but tough. I like tough, Elise. Tough means you can be cruel when necessary. You can spit in someone's eye without the slightest bit of guilt. Your son would be quite impressed; he doesn't realize how strong you are. To him you're a whining old lady."

"Am not."

"Are you going to stamp your feet and throw a tantrum? It won't do you any good. Those legs of yours can't perform. They're shrouded inside those sheets, resting peacefully now that the doctor gave you medication."

"I wish they'd stop clouding my mind with their drugs. I need a plan."

"You need to give up. Touch my hand, Elise."

"I can't see you."

"Yes, you can. You're purposefully blocking my image. I'm right here, Elise."

"Yuck. You breathed into my ear."

"That's how close I am. Now look at me."

"I already know what you look like."

"And my hand?"

"It's ice. Cold and sticky like ice. You won't let me go if I touch you."

"If you touch me, Elise, you won't want to go. Stay here, Elise. Stay inside your mind with me. Stay forever with me."

Elise felt a chill spread down her left side. Whatever was wrong with her had not been caused by a stroke. This was all Tukay's doing. She could move her arms and legs, she could speak, if only she could rid herself of his spell. There was nothing wrong with her mind. It was her mind he possessed. She had to clear her mind. There were memories that could blot Tukay out. Jonathan as a child.

"Little Jonathan. He was a sweet boy, a bit strange, especially when he'd eat himself. Didn't you know, Elise, he didn't just eat scabs. Your son had a bigger appetite than that. Unusual child. Not as perfect as you would have liked. His mind always wandering far away from his tasks. A shame. He could have been better if you had tried a little harder."

"I did everything I could. You'll not make me feel ashamed of the way I raised that boy."

"Oh, I didn't want to do that. I really want to thank you for raising *my* boy."

"He's not yours."

"He's been mine for many years, Elise. Couldn't you tell? Cindy found out. His feet. Remember her complaining about his feet?"

"She was a tramp to run off with that guy from the motel."

"She didn't run away from your son. He kept her prisoner. Like he's keeping you prisoner, locked in the same room in which she died."

There had to be a way to regain control, Elise kept telling herself. Concentrate on one small part of the body. A tiny move that wins back a minuscule portion of her brain. She bounced her fingers on the sheet to make sure she could still do it. She could. Her toes. She thought she wiggled them. She thought about wiggling them. Someone touched her feet. She had attracted the nurse's attention with her toes.

"What a slow belabored process this will be. Jonathan often ate pieces of flesh from his feet. Have you ever tasted human flesh, Elise? Your son has many times. In one instance he even killed for the taste of human flesh."

Fine, she had her toes going. What else could she wind up? Her right hand made a fist. She opened the fist and closed it again and tried the same thing on the left side.

"I allow you a taste of control, but only that, Elise."

"Bullshit! You wouldn't allow me anything. You've been pushing for me to die. You want me to think I'm weak and can't defeat you, but I'm not stupid. You're in my head because I allowed you in. My own fears broke down the barriers that protected me from you."

"Elise, I am tiring of this. Give me back what is mine."

"None of me is yours, not even the parts that you still rule."

"Think about Jonathan, Elise. Where is he right now? In a dark—"

"Shut up! I don't give a damn where you want me to think he is. I can't save him unless I save myself."

Elise again fisted her right hand, but failed with the left.

She was in a church. An old church. One that had been abandoned a long time ago. The place smelled of bums, tramps, and harlots. *Such a shame,* she thought, walking down the slender aisle. The only aisle, she noted. There seemed to be someone kneeling at the Communion rail, but when she got closer she found only a dirty bunch of clothes. Some pieces were smeared with feces. Others were drenched in streaks of blood. Clumps of jism bound the whole thing together.

She backed away from the mound and looked up at the cross over the altar. A greenish tint blunted the shine of the metal. *Someone should really take care of this place. Needs to be cleaned up,* she thought, opening the Communion rail gate. As she approached the altar, she saw how stained the altar cloth was. She didn't want to know what those stains were from. *Imagine an altar being so desecrated. Who would totally desert a church like this?* she wondered.

A hand rested on her shoulder.

317

"You can maintain the place for me, Elise. This will be your special assignment."

Tukay's voice sounded from nearby, and the hand on her shoulder felt cold.

"This is your church, isn't it?" she shrieked.

"I always get the dregs. The leftovers. Still, I try very hard."

The hand squeezed her shoulder; that was when she noticed that the touch wasn't so cold. "The nurse, the doctor, or Jonathan is touching me. They are bringing me back to them. I'm not inside this church. I'm . . ."

"In the music room where Jonathan killed his wife," Tukay finished. "He has put your bed in the exact spot where she had lain."

"I don't care what he did. I'm going back. I haven't finished with my life. God give me strength . . ."

"To accept the future. Elise, that is what Jonathan is praying for. Strength for you to accept me."

"My future is in that bed in the music room and the hand is too warm to be yours. This hand draws some of the pain from me. And you only know how to give pain.

"This isn't a consecrated church. No, simply a poor imitation of the Lord's church."

"Touch the altar, Elise, and see how real it is.

Touch it. Touch the cloth covering it, touch the metal cross guarding it."

"No. None of that is real. It's a world you've planned to use to discourage people, to force them into despair. And that won't be me. The hand on my shoulder, the voices in the back of my mind. On those I'll concentrate until I've been brought home."

Tukay stepped in front of her and swept his arm across the altar, toppling the candles and the crucifix. The altar cloth he ripped to shreds, allowing the pieces to fall onto the marble steps.

"How real do you think my Father's world is? How real are those wintry days when you bundle up and breathe out smoke? How real the changes of season? From snow comes life. The flowers you pick in the spring, the warmth of the sun on your skin in the summer, and the slow dying of nature in the fall. How real is any of it?

"You want it to be real, Elise, that is what makes it so. I can fulfill dreams you've had that my Father has refused to fulfill. I can give you youth in what you see as an old body. Look at the back of your hands."

Elise refused to follow his command.

"There are no splotches of age or wrinkled flesh. Only smooth, fair skin that is ageless and healthy. Look," he yelled, grabbing her shoulders, and as he did she tightly shut her eyes. "Foolish old woman. So many of you frustrate me in your ignorance."

Elise concentrated on a hand that had moved from her shoulder to her forehead. Someone was brushing back her bangs, rubbing her forehead in soothing, long strokes. No longer did the putrid odors of the church mask the minty smell that seemed to come from the hand. And there was the tickle of voices chilling her spine. Her body sagged but did not fall, for she already was in her bed back in the music room.

Chapter Fifty

"Oh, Doctor, she's blinking her eyes." The nurse dropped her hand from Elise's forehead and stood back to allow the doctor access to the patient.

Elise looked up into friendly brown eyes that stared intently into hers. The gray hair in disarray upon his head gave him a clownish appearance. His eyeglasses had slid down to the tip of his nose, and his lips pursed in concentration. She found that she could raise her right hand to touch the ruddy face. She felt a smile form on her lips, on a mouth that couldn't keep food from sliding out. A mouth that drooped and was near to useless. Not anymore.

She went to raise her other hand, but the doctor warned her against overdoing.

"A little at a time. If I had known a gorgeous babe

like you was going to be rubbing my face, I would have taken a closer shave this morning." He smiled down at her.

False teeth, she thought, catching a glimpse of the plate covering his gums, but what beautiful false teeth.

Elise hadn't noticed the nurse leave the room, but did see her return when the doctor stood to converse with the nurse.

"A woman is here to see the patient. I wasn't sure what to tell her."

"Tell her Elise is not up to having visitors today. A nice potted plant to cheer up this room would be an ideal gift if she wants Elise to know that she's thinking of her."

"She's brought some food along also. Some sort of a stew or something."

"Take it, thank her, and have it for your dinner or toss it, whatever you choose. I want Elise to remain on the prescribed diet."

A burst of heat filled the room.

"What's made it so hot in here?" asked the doctor.

The nurse shrugged. "I left the front door open, but it isn't so warm outside."

"Go see to Elise's visitor, and I'll open a window. Perhaps it's getting too stuffy in here."

Elise wanted to tell the doctor that it wasn't hot

in the room. Tukay wanted them to think it was hot.

"I really must say a quick hello. I promise I won't stay long."

The nurse was fumbling with a large stew pot while trying to prevent a white-haired woman from entering the room.

"Elise," the woman called.

"She can have a few moments," said the doctor.

The nurse hurried off with the pot, and the doctor took a seat at the distant end of the room.

"Remember me? Sylvia?" The white-haired woman crossed the room to stand by the bed. "I baby-sat Jonathan for you when we were young. Remember?"

Elise did recall a skinny girl spoiling her son when he was very young.

"When Jonathan told me how ill you were, I wanted to come here immediately, but they didn't think you should have visitors. I couldn't stand waiting any longer." She rested a hand on Elise's bare arm.

A very hot hand, Elise thought. And the doctor was wiping sweat from his brow. This woman had features similar to the little girl she had been. The eyes so blue, the nose wonderfully classic, the mouth lusciously full. All combined with a shriveled heart. The little girl had had a happy expansive

323

way about her. She'd laughed more naturally than this middle-aged woman did.

"I brought something for you to eat. A token, I know, but I didn't know what else to bring."

A plant, you numbskull, Elise silently answered. The doctor had been right. The room was too dreary, as if she were about to die. As if she couldn't make out the furnishings and the bland colors blanking out the view of the room. Colors. That was exactly what she needed. Bright, neon colors that shouted life. That made her want to stay in this room, in this world.

A slob, thought Elise, as she cast a long look at Sylvia. *Jeans and an old T-shirt, a beige T-shirt. What kind of way is that to dress when visiting someone?* The doctor had taken off his suit jacket; however, he still wore the red and white polka-dot tie. Of course, her son was probably paying the doctor very well; he could have even afforded a tuxedo, but just as this was no funeral, this was no party.

Sylvia noticed that the nurse had come back into the room. "What, no bowl of soup?" Sylvia asked.

The nurse looked at the doctor.

"She'll eat later," the doctor said.

"What is this, a zoo where she eats only at feeding time?" asked Sylvia.

"This is a convalescent's room," he answered.

Elise cheered his reply. She was getting better, not dying. She'd follow the doctor's order, thank you. What the hell did this Sylvia woman know, anyway? She remembered the little girl puking at the sight of blood.

Sylvia took Elise's hand.

"I'll visit whenever I can. Bring more food too."

Elise watched the looks pass between the doctor and the nurse.

With a painful squeeze of the hand, Sylvia said good-bye. How strange her strength, how foul the breath that fell upon Elise as Sylvia kissed her. Elise reached up a hand to push Sylvia away.

"I didn't realize she had regained some of her motor ability." Sylvia looked toward the doctor for an explanation.

"It's been recent. We're hoping for further progress."

Sylvia looked back at Elise. Disappointment clouded Sylvia's expression.

Won't need to be buying me a Mass card yet, girlie.

"I'm sure my soup will sway you in the right direction," said Sylvia.

A brightly colored hydrangea would do more for me.

"Please call before your next visit, Sylvia," the doctor requested.

Mary Ann Mitchell

Sylvia nodded at the doctor and falsely smiled.
I don't like her, thought Elise, *I don't want her to come back. She doesn't care about my getting better. Why?*

Chapter Fifty-one

"What will you do with the bodies?" Jonathan asked.

"We've been watching them rot."

"You're lucky some disease hasn't hit, Jared. And the rats . . ."

"Nothing living comes here anymore." Jared looked up at Jonathan. "Only you."

"We have to dispose of the bodies."

"Are you taking over? Is that what this is about? Are you taking over for him?"

Jonathan turned away from the priest and paced the platform. He couldn't count the number of wounded in need of medical help. Tiles were blackened with ash. Water seeped out from under the bathroom door. When he went over to check, he smelled human waste. He didn't bother to open the door.

The elderly woman approached him cautiously. Her clothes had gaping holes. One of her breasts was exposed, but she didn't seem to be aware. For the first time she spoke to him.

"I am very old. Not able to be of much help, but I will follow you. Father Jared can't cope anymore. He can't defeat Satan."

"And you think I can?"

She nodded her head. "You have managed to make him very angry. He would not be so angry if he thought you could be silenced. Can he even destroy you?"

"I'm not God. If he wants, he can end my life. Probably even steal me into hell. I'll be stoking those fires the Church has preached about."

"Fire is God's gift," she said.

Jonathan pointed toward the pile of dead bodies. "Is that what God's gift can do?"

"Satan uses our own strengths against us. We don't have to let him. That child was a demon that had no skills of its own. It had to use what God created. Evil has no new tricks, no new games to play."

"My mother is bedridden. She has to be fed, washed, wiped, because I dared to play the devil's game. Now what do I do? I fear he will take my mother if . . ."

"He can't take your mother unless she gives up hope."

"She has. I see it in her eyes. When her body experiences tremors, she can't understand what's going on. I try to talk to her, but I never know for sure whether she knows I'm there."

"He could not make you suffer; therefore he tortures your mother."

"This is his way of making me suffer. Believe me."

"No, he's never so indirect. He can't reach you. He can't completely take over your soul.

"Jared's too afraid of Satan. That is why he's down here with us and not battling it out in a real church. He clings to the old language because he needs the magic to make him brave. You don't need magic," she said.

"Hell, I killed my own wife. I ate her flesh. I did exactly what Yakut wanted. My wife died slowly. I went wild with the idea of sharing our flesh. The emptiness of the Communion host banished me from the church."

"See, you do not need magic," she said.

"You are the craziest old lady I've ever met. I gave your grandchild to Sylvia so that she could make a stew for the soup kitchen."

Mary Ann Mitchell

"Why didn't you eat Marissa? You say you enjoy eating human flesh."

"Temptation was there. I touched my lips to her flesh. Licked it with my tongue."

"And succeeded in defeating Satan."

"Yeah, I did." Jonathan smiled.

"Do not become too proud, or Satan will use that against you," the elderly woman warned.

"Will God ever forgive me for killing my wife, for participating in the perversions that I believed in?"

The elderly woman shrugged. "But won't you feel better knowing that you atoned by helping the rest of us?"

"Maybe Jared won't let me wrest power from him." He looked at the milling people around him and found Jared, eyes closed, leaning against the same tile wall where Jonathan had first found him.

"He's tired, Jonathan. He doesn't have the strength or skill to help us," the elderly woman said.

Chapter Fifty-two

The smoke spiraled into the polluted air of the tunnel from the pits Jonathan had the people dig. None had been strong enough to dig for any great length of time; however, each had been willing to take a turn. They had been lucky to find this area of unpaved ground.

"The flames are not hot enough to dissolve the bones. We'll have to cover the bones over with dirt."

"I'm a priest, Jonathan, and I believe we'll all need our bodies on Judgment Day."

"Well, then, you would have to be freshly dead, because those bodies you've buried in the past are not in one piece."

"I want the old religion back. I want the Latin.

331

The strict rules that could be so easier preached than practiced. I want the people coming to me for absolution and believing that I can give it to them. I want organ music resounding through a church with youthful voices singing the praises of God. I even miss those meatless Fridays. I miss Saint Christopher."

"Maybe you can start your own religion, Father."

Jared stiffened. "That's exactly what I don't want. I want to be told what to do. I want to read the Bible and know that it's already been deciphered for me."

"You're a lazy man," said Jonathan.

"Not lazy, only I fear making errors. I fear the temptations of the devil because I was never very good at turning away from them."

"Have you ever felt like killing someone, Father?"

"Please call me Jared. I've told you before I'm father to no one. And, yes, I have committed the sin of hating."

"Have you killed?"

"No, thank God, I have not fallen that low."

"I have." Jonathan saw the shock in Jared's eyes.

"In self-defense, of course."

"No, I plain killed someone because I liked the taste of human flesh and there was no going back."

"You can always ask for forgiveness, Jonathan."

"I can ask, but can I receive it?"

"If you're contrite enough."

"What does that mean? Who measures my contrition? You, in the name of the Lord?"

"I'm merely a tool. I make God's gifts available. His mercy I try to extend to all who come to me."

"By what right?"

"The Church gave me the power."

"The power to establish and maintain all their laws?"

"Man needs guidance, Jonathan."

"Why? Hasn't the Lord given each of us the intelligence to guide ourselves? Isn't it up to each of us to save ourselves? You can't save me. Only I can win the grace to make the right decisions and possibly enter God's kingdom."

"Possibly? You don't sound sure of yourself, Jonathan."

"I'm not sure God wants me in his kingdom."

"He wants all of us to join Him."

"But we must follow the commandments. Heed Papal decrees. Practice our religion diligently every Sunday and Holy Day. Live the way we are told He wants us to live every day.

"Pardon me, Jared. This is how I got into all this trouble. I questioned the power of the Church. If I hadn't bothered to pull apart doctrine, I might still be believing and living the Church's faith. Instead

333

I doubted. I sought for more. Is there nothing beyond the teachings of the Church, Jared?"

"For some of us the teachings make life simpler," said Jared. "We don't have to spend time evaluating our faults against a morality constantly in flux. I don't have to worry about meeting expectations that I haven't even been told about. We can't make our own individual laws and not share what they are with those we live with. There must be a body of laws that we can all agree on."

"What if I doubt the basis for some of those laws?"

"Then it can be debated in a public forum."

"Not within the Church. The Pope is infallible. I can't breathe a word about my doubts without fearing excommunication. And if the Church excommunicates me, does that mean the Church has the right to decide who are God's chosen?"

"Jonathan, we are all His chosen, except some reject Him."

"I've never rejected God, Jared. I did question the Church. There is a difference. They are not necessarily one. And you who defends the Church so adamantly, haven't you doubted the Church? Aren't you preaching your own religion by saying Mass in Latin outside the confines of a church? Isn't that a sin, Jared? And do you consider yourself and your people saved? Or are you dragging your people down to the lower depths of hell?"

Jared's face flushed as he muttered, "And who would cast the first stone?"

Chapter Fifty-three

"I see you are still practicing your laborious exercises, trying to get all your fingers and toes and other appendages to work in some sort of a coordinated fashion."

Tukay stared down at her from the right side of the bed. His long hair fell loosely around his face. The eyes were shadowed, but his mouth and lips were spotlighted by the small lamp on the night table. His lips barely moved as he spoke, but his words came out strong and clear.

Initially Elise had had her eyes closed, concentrating with all her might on her limbs. But at his first word she opened her eyes.

"Haven't gotten very far, Elise. You know this is not just the cliché of mind over body. Some is the illusory confidence that you humans seem to waver in so much. The rest is really physical, Elise. There is physical damage."

"That's what you want me to believe," she said.

He reached out a hand to touch her forehead, and she immediately responded by catching his wrist in her right hand and turning her face from him.

"Nice grip, Elise. Not powerful, but better than your average five-year-old."

She turned back to face him. "Why do you taunt my son?"

"Jonathan. Strange you should think of him now. He is currently berating a priest. Don't think this will win him any bennies from my Father."

"And that's fine by you."

"No, Elise, I love your son. Haven't I told you that already?"

"You want to destroy my son."

"I want to make him stronger. I want him to cast doubts on my Father. I want him to lure the hopeless into giving up."

"He'll not do that." Elise let go of his wrist and held her hand high to see the slow movements of her fingers.

"Elise, come down and visit me. Let me take you to where I command great respect. Where my Father is forgotten and my Brother never existed."

337

"So that I can see more burning bodies?"

"Jonathan is already getting closer to my home. He's digging down as fast as he can. Soon he'll be banished from your world, Elise, and you will be alone."

"God will always be with me," she said.

"Was he with you when you had the stroke?" He smiled, thinking he had won. "He's not a very good friend if he would desert you while your brain was exploding from my touch.

"Are you hungry, Elise? I can give you something to eat. Something not on that stupid diet the doctor has forced upon you."

"That stupid stew Sylvia brought?"

"No, Elise, something far more personal. A taste of my own flesh." Tukay tore off his own bottom lip and brought it to Elise's mouth.

Elise felt her stomach rebel. This morning's bland breakfast with its acid juices that could scar her esophagus, badly laying groundwork for cancerous sores, was coming up.

"Elise, it is fresh," he said clearly. The fact that he had torn a lip off didn't affect his speech. "Fresher than that crap the Church tells you is flesh." A few drops of blood spotted his chin, but on the whole the bleeding had been stanched almost immediately. "There is no other flesh like this. The power that emanates can be felt as a chill down your spine. This will help you to walk, help you to follow your son to my home. Taste it, Elise. Place your tongue upon the unchafed skin and smoothly roll over the manna that can give you new life." He held the flesh to her lips, but did not attempt to force it into her mouth. He guided the flesh along her lips, her cheeks, her eyelids, her forehead, back down her nose, and rested it finally on her mouth. "I baptize you into my army, Elise. March with me. Make love with me. Eat of me."

Elise felt the coldness of the lip, the wetness of the blood that he had trailed across her face. This was the kind of temptation of which her son had spoken; greater than the fleshly temptation of lust. She urged her stomach to disgorge, and when the vomit was released, it came out with such force that she managed to splatter Yakut's face.

Instinctively he pulled back.

"Bitch," he mumbled. "Wanton whore. Mother of the spawn that would lock me away in that blasted hole filled with contempt and pain."

Her own face, spotted with the remains of breakfast, burned from the acid.

His empty left hand came down toward her forehead. Again she reached for his wrist to stop him, but this time her power had been weakened beyond her basic strength. She watched his hand slowly moving down as a claw. As the fat, hairy body of a spider snuffing life from the quivering fly.

Suddenly the door to the music room opened and Tukay became the doctor.

"Doctor, I just received a call from the hospital. One of your patients needs you immediately," said the nurse.

"Later, Elise. I will come back for you later. Think about how I shall return and with no new offers, but with . . ." Tukay recalled that the nurse was still standing in the doorway.

"Oh, I didn't know she had soiled herself," said the nurse, gaping at Elise's face. She scurried into the room, reaching for clean wipes as she passed a waist-high table. "I'll take care of Elise while you get the phone, Doctor."

But he had already left the room. He had vanished into the air surrounding Elise's bed. The nurse was flustered to find that he was gone.

"He's coming back," Elise tried to say. She tried to say the words several times. On the final try the nurse caught the meaning of the jumble Elsie had been pronouncing.

"Yes. Don't worry, he'll be back. I can't believe the kind of recovery you're making. I can tell you for weeks there was doubt about how much of your old self would return. You're really a strong woman," she said, dabbing a wipe around her patient's mouth. That was when she noticed the blood. "I must stop the doctor before he leaves. I'll be right back." The nurse dropped the wipe into the garbage pail that had been brought from the kitchen.

Elise again attempted to speak, but the harder she tried the more garbled her language sounded.

"Slow down, sweetheart. Take your time. I can understand when you enunciate slowly and carefully."

"Don't . . ."

"Don't what? Listen, I have to speak to the doctor before he leaves. Maybe when I get back you'll have relaxed enough to speak."

Disconcerted, Elise watched the nurse pat her right leg and turn to the door.

"Sta . . ." Elise tried again. *He'll be back.* Elise completed the sentence silently.

Chapter Fifty-four

"Where does this go?" Jonathan asked.

The cramped cave appeared to have a slide that descended rapidly. Even with his flashlight, Jonathan could not see the end of the slide.

"That goes down to a lower level," answered Jared.

"How far down does it go?"

"I've never taken it."

"Shall we?" Jonathan asked, turning the light on Jared's face.

"What for?"

"To face the demons."

"I'm not sure we can even walk down that thing, never mind walk back up."

"We may not be meant to come back, Jared. Would it matter?"

"You were talking about your mother just a short time ago. You certainly have something to come back for."

"My mother. Is she safer without me or with me?"

"You are all she has, Jonathan."

"Not true. She has a sister and brother-in-law. They visit five or six times a year. I certainly think they would take my mother, especially since in my latest will, all my wealth has been left to my mother."

"I won't go with you, Jonathan."

"I will," Louisa said.

"You are too old. You'd be more of a hindrance to him than a help," Jared instantly retorted.

"I am so old that I no longer fear death for it is very close to me."

"Yes, as close as Jonathan is to you."

The two men traded irritable looks.

Louisa walked toward the cave.

"There's a cool draft," she said.

"Not as hot as Hades?" Jared said.

She placed a hand on the inside walls.

"It's damp. There are . . ." She hesitated. "Slimy things stuck to the wall."

343

The two men watched as she ripped something off one of the walls. Her hand reached out to show the object to them. Mushrooms. Mushrooms that seemed to bleed a chalky residue.

Jonathan joined her at the entrance.

"You go round up your people and keep them safe until we come back, Jared."

"You're not going to take Louisa with you?"

"Either he takes me, or I will follow," she said.

"And I can stop you, Louisa," said Jared. "You are not strong enough to prevent me from dragging you back to stay with the others."

"I can stop *you*, Jared." Jonathan felt a twinge inside him. Did he want to take this old woman with him? Or did he simply want to demean Jared in front of one of his own? Unsure, Jonathan took Louisa's arm and crossed the threshold with her.

The old woman had been right. There was a draft, and his flashlight lit up the milky mushrooms clinging to the walls.

"Can you manage, Louisa?"

Louisa took the first step down the incline. Her footing was not solid, but she was able to stay upright. He followed each step she took, steadying her when he thought she might fall.

By the time they had reached the end of the incline, both were shuffling along on their rear ends.

"It's flat up ahead," she called back to Jonathan.

The flashlight raked the walls and floors of the new world. Filth spotted the concrete flooring. Tweaking noises warned them that there were rats nearby, perhaps finishing off a meal.

"Walk along here," he said, leading in the direction away from the sounds of the rats.

He felt Louisa's hand reach out and grab the back of his leather jacket.

"Are you cold?" he asked.

"No, the draft is not as strong down here."

As they walked, the scent of incense bled through the stench to reach Jonathan's nose.

"What the hell is that coming from?"

Louisa looked at him quizzically. The old woman had lost the sharpness of most of her senses many years ago.

"Take a deep breath," he suggested.

"I don't think I want to," she said.

"Incense. Smell it?"

She did breathe in deeply, and smiled when she recognized the odor.

Just up ahead, they could make out the figures of men and women, standing with heads bowed and holding hands. As Louisa and Jonathan moved closer, the heads uniformly lifted. He couldn't see any of the faces clearly. The heads were covered by hoods.

"Hello. We're from the level just above you."

Each of the men and women folded back their hoods, and Jonathan felt sick to see the splotches of white hair that barely covered each head. *Are they ill?* he wondered. The ones closer to him turned and allowed him to focus his light on their faces.

Sad, mauled faces. Faces that were neither young nor old. Complexions a pale white that almost seemed to illuminate the tunnel. Eyes either blind or mysteriously unaffected by the glare he shined on their faces. Noses peaked into witchlike points complete with tiny mounds that looked like warts. The mouths drooped on either side, giving them a sad, almost clownish look.

"My name's Jonathan. This is Louisa," he said, taking the old woman's hand in his own to give her and himself confidence. "Have you ever been to the level above you?"

The sad faces looked to each other, but no one spoke.

"Do you understand English?"

A sad face off to the end answered with a voice neither male nor female but terribly haunted.

"We never leave this level."

"At some time you must have been above," Jonathan said.

"Never!" yelled out a voice from within the group.

"Never," repeated the sad face at the end. "We have never been above this level. We are . . ."

The others turned on the sad face at the end to hush the words he was about to utter.

"We came here looking for someone. Do you know a man by the name of Yakut?"

"He is our father," the sad face at the end answered.

Jonathan felt Louisa's hand tighten on his own.

"We want to speak with him. Can you direct us?"

The entire group shook their heads.

A small frail figure came from the center of the group. The hands were delicate and the features softer than most of the others.

"Satan is our father. We have run away from him and remain here to hide."

"You're not hiding. I'm sure he knows where you are," said Jonathan.

"The incense we burn clouds our paths so he will wander but never find us. Sometimes we pray to his Father and Brother. We pray that we may be saved even when we know we are one blood with Satan."

"His Father and Brother are also related to you," Jonathan said.

"No," the frail one answered. "Our father birthed us from human women and distanced us from his own spirit. He comes in dreams to remind us of our weakening powers. The longer we stay away from him, the older and softer, and sadder, we become. Soon we will sit in isolation from each other, unable to call to a sibling or feel the touch of each other's hands. All that is human and weak we possess."

"Why do you stay here? Why not go up a few levels and try to build a home for yourselves?"

"What awaits us up above? And how are we to mingle?" The frail form removed the robe. Breasts shriveled into flattened circles covered a small area of her chest. Her ribs poked at the flesh trying to escape. From the waist down her body was covered with white hair.

Jonathan couldn't lie to them.

"You must have hated your father to leave in such a hopeless state."

"He hates us because we are not beautiful." All the figures bowed their heads as if shamed by the woman's words.

"Do you have a name that I may call you?" Jonathan asked.

"He numbered us as scientists do with experiments. I am fifteen."

"What happened to your mothers?"

"They could not birth us and survive. Only six's mother did, and she no longer moves about. She sits in one place all day long, and blood constantly

348

flows from the open wound between her legs."

"How did you escape?"

"We were led by a young man. Naked, he arrived and walked freely through our father's caves. He did not seem frightened of things he saw. He seemed already maddened by his own world."

"Naked, you say. What was his name?"

"Seth. He spoke often with his invisible lover. We would find him at night masturbating to the whispers of his own words. The name he spoke was always the same. Florry."

"I know him. I need to help him. To free him from the prison in which your father has placed him. I fear he is there because of me."

"But he is not a prisoner. He walks where he wants and speaks to all he pleases. We tricked him into showing us the way out by offering him a vision of Florry. We tapped his mind and were able to manifest his woman as a reality when she existed only inside his head. We stole the vision from him, but promised to give it back if he would lead us to the next level. We left him with nothing. We could hear his wailing as we disappeared through the tunnel."

"Poor Seth. He must be insane." Jonathan spoke to himself, but all the others heard the words.

"Insanity will protect him. Our father reveres insanity. He most probably finds Seth to be a diversion when he wonders about his own powers."

"And does he doubt himself at times?" Jonathan asked.

"He is a failed god, sir," the figure at the very end said quickly.

"Do you remember where the entrance to your father's world is?"

"Yes. We have marked the place with symbols we have heard he hates," the female figure said. "Even though he passes through whenever he wants, we still discourage his coming."

"Take us to the entrance."

"We never go near the entrance. We do not want to be tempted to return."

"Why would that be a temptation?"

"Our powers would be reinvigorated. We could visit the graves of our mothers and learn to pray at their headstones. But he would walk among us, touching us, branding us with his sins."

"Then tell me how to get there. Describe the path, at least."

"You would go to bring back your friend Seth?"

"He may not want to come back with me. I must learn more about your father. How to stop him from robbing lives. How to contain his evil to a very minor space."

"Like his Father and Brother, he is everywhere and nowhere. He shows himself only when he means to. You cannot sneak up on him. You offer no surprises to him."

"Your father has taunted me for a long time. I must know why."

The female figure looked at her siblings on either side of her. Only now could Jonathan recognize the color of their eyes. Blood red like their father's.

"This woman is not your mother."

"No," said Jonathan. "Why do you mention my mother?"

"Is she still alive and sane?"

"She is ill right now. She had a stroke and was left paralyzed. But up until a short time ago she was quite healthy."

"And your father?"

"He is dead. Been dead since I was a teen."

"No, he is not dead."

"Are you going to tell me he's living down in the tunnel with your father? It wouldn't surprise me. Certainly wouldn't surprise my mother."

"Your father has always been and will always be."

"My father died from too much lard and too much drink."

Fifteen picked up her robe and wrapped it around her shoulders.

"I am embarrassed and humbled," she said.

Louisa struggled to release her hand from Jonathan's.

"You are the devil's son," Louisa whispered. Her breaths changed to panting as she tried harder to pull away. Jonathan found that he couldn't let go of Louisa's hand. She grounded him. He depended on the touch of her skin.

"I am not his son, foolish old woman. How could you believe that?" He became frenzied attempting to keep Louisa quiet. He held her to his body, searching for her warmth, for her humanity. He felt her body go limp, and eased her gently to the ground.

Chapter Fifty-five

"In Nomine Patris, et Filii, et Spiritus Sancti. Amen."

Jonathan heard Jared close his prayer as he walked into the cove in which Jared had chosen to hide. Louisa was light, her weight so little that he barely remembered that he carried her body.

"My God! What happened, Jonathan? Is she all right?" Jared ran to relieve Jonathan of his light burden. People crowded around the priest, reaching out to touch Louisa, but hesitating when they were within a quarter inch of her cold skin. "What happened to her?"

Jonathan let his body drop to the ground.

"Answer me! What the hell happened?"

"She died."

353

"How? Did Satan touch her?"

"Not Satan himself."

Jared laid Louisa's body in the arms of a young woman and rushed at Jonathan, grabbing the leather jacket, attempting to pull Jonathan to his feet.

"Tell me exactly what happened!" Jared's voice echoed in the alcove. His sweat streaked his forehead and his scent filled the close quarters.

"Get away from me." Jonathan attempted to push the priest away, but was surprised by the priest's strength.

"No. You took one of my people down into that hole against my wishes. I want to know what happened."

"We met his children."

"Whose children?"

"Yakut's." Jonathan felt cold. He attempted to pull the leather jacket around him, but too much of the material was in Jared's grasp. "I held her close. To my heart. She crumpled in my arms. I don't . . . think . . . I . . ."

"You killed her?" Jared's voice was low. His disbelief reflecting Jonathan's own.

"They made her afraid of me. There's no reason to fear me. None. I promise. An old woman's heart gives out. That's normal, Jared. Nothing I did."

"What did these children say?"

Jonathan mechanically related the story.

"Are you his son?" Jared asked.

Jonathan looked up at Jared. He could not see the man's face clearly because of the blur of tears. His son? The people down in that hole were probably people who had given up, retreated from society, and now they believed they were Satan's children only because of the lives they had led.

"Jonathan, we have to think about this. You wanted to know why he hounded you. You wanted to know why he would hurt your mother."

"He hurt her to hurt me."

"I know. You have to talk to your mother. Maybe she can give you some hint as to what he wants from you."

"She can't talk. She's paralyzed. She wouldn't have lived had she birthed his baby. Only one lived, and she . . ."

"I know what they told you, but he seems fixated on you, Jonathan. Please, maybe you'll find some way to communicate with your mother. Go to her. She must miss you by now."

"I am there or I am not. What is it to her?"

"Jared," the young woman holding Louisa called.

Jared released Jonathan's leather jacket and went to help with Louisa's body.

"The Last Sacrament. You haven't given her the

Last Sacrament yet." The young woman's eyes pleaded with Jared.

"I'll get my vestments." Jared threw a single glare at Jonathan. "Go to your mother."

Jonathan stood. Satan's children had helped him to crawl back up the slide with Louisa. They had warned him against coming back. At some point, they warned, he would not be able to return to the surface. His father would have that strong a hold on him.

His father. The concept was ludicrous. His body was normal except for the self-inflicted scars. His appetite for human flesh was shared by other humans. No. He could not be related in such a way to Satan. Perhaps they meant figuratively. Then he couldn't deny being his son. But certainly not born of the Devil's seed. His mother would never have consented. Yakut didn't wait for consent, Jonathan reminded himself. He could have assumed the shape of his father's body and his mother would have accepted him as her husband. These so-called children of Satan simply wanted to be rid of him, and this was their way of scaring the hell out of him.

356

Chapter Fifty-six

The stillness of the music room frightened Elise. She knew Tukay would be back. Next time he would take her life. Hell! She would fight for life and win. She was that strong. She was that pissed off.

Elise continued to try to move more and more of her body, and she found with her confidence she was able to succeed. Tukay might be losing his grip on her mind. In his frustration . . . Her paralysis didn't matter any more to him, because she would soon be dead. But he'd wanted her dead from the start, and she had won.

Her hands were moving easily now, and her legs were able to bend at the knee without assistance.

She threw the sheet to the floor and attempted

to use her arms to bring herself to a seated position. Still too weak. She had no time to waste. Her arms had to be strong. No pain, only a dull ache, as if her extremities had fallen asleep and were just starting to wake.

Halfway to a seated position, Elise began rocking her body. Momentum could complete this drudgery. Momentum, a simple scientific . . .

"Mom."

Elise almost fell back into a prone position, but managed to keep the rigidity in her arms.

"My God! What are you doing? I mean . . . When did this happen?" He walked swiftly to his mother's bedside.

Usually he couldn't fool her. The others would see the mask, but she normally saw Tukay for what he was, but was this her son?

He reached out a hand to touch her shoulder, and she grunted and pulled away.

"I know you want to do this yourself, Mom. I'm sorry." He let his arms fall back down to his sides.

"Go," she attempted to yell, but the word came out as a high-pitched whisper.

"Mom, I have to talk to you. It's urgent. About Tukay."

"Back," she said, and looked around the room. The chair where the nurse normally sat was empty. "Sit," she softly commanded.

He backed up several feet and dropped into the chair.

"Mom, I spoke to some . . ." She watched him hesitate. Obviously he was choosing his words carefully. "Some beings calling themselves the children of Tukay. Do you know anything about them? Has he ever mentioned them to you?"

She shook her head.

"I apologize even before I ask the question. Did you have sex with anyone besides Dad nine months before I was born?"

"Ten."

"Ten months before, you did?"

"No, idiot. I told you many times that you were a ten-month baby. And no, I didn't sleep with anyone else. I wouldn't have done that. I had pride in myself." The words were coming out smoothly, but the volume was still way too low.

Jonathan sat stunned, staring at his mother.

Elise made a grand effort to push herself to a seated position, and succeeded. She saw her son almost stand to assist, but she was sure her glare prevented him from coming over to her.

"How do I know you are my son?"

Jonathan moved forword in his seat to hear her words.

"Mom?"

"How do I know you're not shape-shifting and really are Tukay?"

Jonathan groaned and leaned back in the chair, easing his head against the back curve of the chair.

"Well? You expect me to trust you?"

"If you can't recognize your own son, then I may as well give up."

"Where have you been?"

"The tunnels."

"Tunnels?"

"The tunnels of the subway system."

"Riding?"

"No, Mom, I was walking through the tunnels. Some of the tunnels lay below where the subway runs."

"Why the hell would you do that?"

"Please work with me, Mom. I need so much information and you are my main source."

She squinted at her son, peering through the mask. Only there was no other face, only her son.

"Mom, is there any chance I'm someone else's child?"

"Adopted?"

"Yeah, even that."

"Even. You think I sleee . . ." Damn, the stutter. She wouldn't give in, not when she was regaining everything. "Sleep" came out as a scream. She smiled. Happy to hear her own voice at an above-normal pitch.

The door to the music room opened, and Jonathan chased away the nurse.

"Mom, do you ever remember seeing Tukay before?"

"Bastard."

"Yes, but have you ever run into him in the past?"

"You think I would have been tricked by him a second time?"

"I want to know what he wants with me."

"With you? It's me he's been attacking," she said.

"Only to reach me."

Elise paused to think about this.

"Awake or asleep, he visits me. He threatens my life."

"I don't think he will kill you. He wouldn't have you to use against me, and you're the last person who would mean enough to me to force me to . . ." Jonathan shrugged.

"I don't like him. He seems evil."

"He's Satan, Mom."

"He is not human." She stopped. Satan. Yes, that was the answer. He had supernatural powers. Satan. As her recuperating mind plowed through the conversation they had just had, she realized her son thought he was the son of Satan. "I sent you to Catholic school. I gave you money each Sunday for the collection. You were always eager to go to church. I never forced you. You received the sacraments. Do you think God would have allowed you to receive the sacraments if you were Satan's son?"

"Possibly."

"Nonsense. Satan is God's enemy."

"And son."

"Angel. He created Lucifer as an angel."

"Listen, Mom, he told me a story."

"And that's all it was." Without thinking, she brought her legs over the edge of the bed.

"Mom, take it easy."

Her feet touched the floor and she stood.

"I'm not going to let you be fooled by him anymore. He sits and taunts you and you're unaware. We can drive him away." Elise looked down at her feet and took a solid step. "I just did."

"Bring your mother down for a visit, Jonathan. Bring her down to see your siblings." Yakut stood across the room from them.

"Old woman, you can walk because I am tired of you," he went on. "I said that I would come back for your life. Remember?" He took several steps toward her.

Her son placed himself between them.

"Such a brave son you have raised for me, Elise. If your mother had consorted with another man, do you think she would admit it to you?

"Such a liar, old woman."

Her gut pained her. Her mouth was dry.

"She eagerly embraced me. Many times. Her flesh sweated. Her skin tingled with the touch of my . . . What would you expect, Elise? A hoof?" Suddenly his hand was the hoof of a goat.

Her legs felt weaker. He was playing the game again with her. He wanted her to lose faith in herself. She wouldn't. She watched his hoof turn back into a hand.

Yakut chuckled.

"No, Elise, you are playing a game. I am not."

"Get out of here. Whatever you want from me, keep separate from my mother," Jonathan said.

"I've already had your mother. The warm moisture between her legs insured your birth."

"No, Jonathan. None of this is true." Her hand reached out and touched the back of Jonathan's shirt.

"She wasn't difficult to corrupt. You remember how lazy she had been? Always sending you off to church and returning herself to bed to fornicate. Ah, and remember when she didn't even get you off to church and you came up with a fascinating alternative to Communion. All on your own, dear son. No help from me. Instinct led you to an answer. I merely watched.

"But didn't I choose the perfect mother for you?

One who would put you in positions that forced you to use that instinct."

"I don't believe you," Jonathan said, taking a step toward Yakut.

"Believe the old woman behind you. Speak up, old woman, before you expire."

"I don't know what the hell he's talking about, Jonathan. Your father was Steve. No one else."

"The hoof you didn't remember, old woman. What about . . ." A patch suddenly appeared over Yakut's right eye.

"No, no. That was a fantasy. A story in a novel. Not real. He was a fantasy from my imagination. I clung to him in my sleep."

Yakut took off the patch, and Elise watched a bloody hole fill up with an intact eyeball. The patch Yakut threw at her feet.

"Not a novel, Elise. I was your lover and will always be your lover. Even with your wrinkled skin and drooping breasts, I will continue to be your lover. I always will be there when you call."

Jonathan flung himself upon Yakut, ripping at the shreds of Yakut's clothes, attempting to land punches on solid flesh. Yakut lifted Jonathan's body and held it in the air.

"Our son, Elise."

"Put him down. Please, put him down. You can have me. Don't hurt him."

Chapter Fifty-seven

Jonathan woke atop his mother's bed. The linen beneath him was wet from his own sweat. His arms and legs ached as if he had done a long day's work of heavy lifting. Slowly he raised his body to a seated position. The room was stuffy, full of a damp, close smell that washed his flesh. Steam had clouded the windows, and he reached out a hand to clear it away, except the window was too far away for him to reach.

His hand. He stared at the hand held out in front of him. The shape, the texture was his own, but it was covered with blood. A sticky dark blood corrupted his fingernails and knuckles, dripping down onto the back of his hand. When he raised his other hand, he saw the same mix of flesh and dried blood.

The sheets, spotted with dark stains, were wrinkled and torn. Jagged cuts in the sheet revealed the mattress cover below, the quilting also stained the deathly color.

He opened his mouth to call out for his mother, but his skin was tight around his lips. His jaw ached, his tongue felt coated.

"Mom?" He didn't yell out the name. He carefully pronounced the syllable, sure that she would not answer. "Mom?" he repeated, already saying a prayer for her.

He didn't want to move, didn't want to see anything or feel anything else. Then he noticed the smell of the room. How could it have taken so long to smell it? Perhaps because the smell was so familiar. So familiar to this room. Shit, urine, and bloody flesh.

He looked down at his shirt and saw that most of the buttons had been ripped off. His chest hair was sticky with blood.

"Mamma, please," his voice cracked. A sob caught in his throat. "Mamma." He wanted her to rush to the bed, hold him, console him, take away the frightening dream.

He could barely move; his stomach was full as if he had eaten an immense banquet.

"Mamma." His eyes watered, tears didn't fall, and his eyes hurt from the buildup of tears.

He leaned over the side of the bed, and was almost relieved to see the nurse's bloody body lying still on the floor. Intact. Her body was bloody from wounds, but intact. No one had even nibbled on her fingers. But he felt so full.

"Mom," he yelled, sure now that he did not wear his mother's blood.

Until he reached the foot of the bed.

He recognized the ring on her finger. He had given it to her one Christmas. The pieces of material around the body were the same color as her nightgown. Her right foot still carried the bunion that she'd been so afraid to have removed. Her legs networked with the purple varicose veins that had pained her so much in the last year or so. Her stomach with the bulge that she blamed on her being pregnant with him for so long. Ten months. She never let him forget. Ten months she'd carried him inside her belly. Ten months he'd depended completely on her body for life. Her breasts flopped outward away from her heart, away from the hole in the middle of her chest. Ragged hole, not smoothly cut, but ravaged by a madman.

It was all there before him on the muddy-colored throw rug. All there except her face. That was gone. Strips of flesh and cartilage missing. Gone. Not lying next to the dead body. His stomach felt so full.

Jonathan fell to his knees, but couldn't remember

how to pray. Couldn't remember a single prayer, but one.

"Our Father," he began. "Who art in Hades . . ."

"Our Father," he began all over again. "Who art in . . ." In the subway tunnels, he remembered.

Chapter Fifty-eight

He walked the tracks, an exploding vision of his mother's blood. The smell of him attracted more rats than he usually encountered. Rats scurrying behind pillars. Rats peeking out, waiting for him to drop.

He passed the spot where Jared had taken his people. No one there now. Had Jared fled knowing that Jonathan would come back? He paused to look inside the alcove. They had taken everything with them, even poor Louisa. He was sure that Jared had taken the time to give her Extreme Unction. He wished he could be assured of the last sacrament when he died. What would it matter if someone said a prayer over him? God would never accept him in His midst.

He was surprised that tiredness did not overcome him. He could keep walking these tunnels another twenty-four hours. He turned back onto his path and continued.

There were nine rings in Dante's hell; how many would he find here? Rumor had it that there were seven levels. Of course, no one had seen them all, but everyone assured him of the seventh level, Yakut's level.

He found the path to a lower level. Intently he searched the darkness around him. His brothers and sisters, would they be waiting to bid him goodbye? They'd know he wasn't coming back to them when they saw him. His eyes had become accustomed to the darkness; he hadn't seen daylight in days. He didn't miss it anymore. There was nothing for him aboveground, nothing able to pull him back. He had covered his mother's body with his own silk robe, folding the material around her body, draping it so that not a speck of her could be seen. He didn't want to see his mother anymore. The nurse he never touched, and he doubted that he had killed her. Too clean, flesh still intact. If he had killed her, he would have mauled her body, filled his gut until he no longer could move. He would have fallen asleep on the floor between the bodies, unable to force more flesh down his throat and unable to part from the meat he had for so long desired. No, the nurse had been Yakut's kill.

Movement up ahead. A wraith flowing in a cloak. Moving cautiously. Had he been spotted. *Brother, sister, come bid farewell, for I will sacrifice myself for you and for mankind.*

Many wraiths began to gather round him, holding their cloaks closed, their father's eyes staring out at him from beneath their hoods. They didn't block his way, or speak a word. One, small in height, reached out a hand to touch his arm. The others pulled the small one back.

He wanted to see his brothers and sisters one more time in the naked glory Yakut had given them.

"Disrobe for me, please," he whispered, turning to face the wraiths he had passed. "Disrobe so that I can remember you when I face our father."

One by one the robes fell to the floor. The sparsely covered heads and hirsute bodies were exposed, ugliness triumphant in these bodies. His father's mistakes or his father's lust before him? Perhaps both, he thought. Or simply God's vengeance.

A brother lifted a cloak from the floor, his own, and offered it to Jonathan to cover the shame and guilt that stained his body, more ugliness than the brothers and sisters ever needed to hide.

"I killed my mother. I ate of her flesh." Jonathan

raised his hand high so that everyone could see. "I carry her inside me now as she carried me."

"We usually kill our mothers at birth. You have delayed what was inevitable," said the brother still offering the cloak.

"I will not hide my sin," Jonathan said. He brought his hands down in front of him and looked at the stains. "She had bled for me many times, but this was the last time."

"You have far to go. We will not keep you." He heard the voice come from the group before him, but could not know which one had spoken.

He turned his back on the cloak and on his family. Instinct would lead him. He didn't need brothers and sisters to direct him.

He stumbled on to paths that took him down deeper into his pain. And yes, he felt his father's hell burning very near. He knew he neared the entrance when naked Seth approached him. Seth's flesh was soiled with dirt, blood, and feces. The smell of Seth made Jonathan's breath catch for a second.

Playfully Seth skipped in front of Jonathan as a child would on a long-delayed walk. Seth would turn periodically to make sure that Jonathan followed.

And I was going to bring you aboveground. Jon-

athan smirked with the irony. Instead, Seth was
taking him down.

He didn't notice the entrance to Hades until he
was upon the opening, so dark was the hovel Yakut
called home. Jonathan thanked Seth for bringing
him this far, and asked whether he would be joining
him for the rest of the journey.

The young man skittered around Jonathan, his
eyes crazed, wearing a ludicrous smile.

"I understand you come and go at will in my father's home. I could use the company for my last
journey."

"Florry isn't there," said Seth with a petulant
child's voice. "I bring her with me." He pointed to
his forehead. "But she never wants to stay."

"I don't blame her. Why do you keep coming
back?"

"I have nowhere else to go. You promised—"

"You don't need me to take you aboveground,
Seth. You know the way; all you need is courage."

"And a heart and a brain," Seth said. "Florry read
me that story a long time ago when she could read
to me. Now she stands near me, sullen all the time.
She laments that her little statues are all gone." He
came closer to Jonathan and lowered his voice. "He
destroyed every one of those statues. He left nothing for me to take to her. Once I cried. Now I never
do. Florry thinks that is a sin. Crying will make me

human, she says. Can you cry, Jonathan?"

"Not anymore. Now I come to do my father's bidding."

"Much is sad," retorted Seth. Without warning, Seth threw his arms around Jonathan. "I wish that I could cry for you."

"It would be a waste of your tears, dear friend."

Jonathan's mother's caked blood fell to the ground in flakes. When Seth pulled away, his skin was speckled with Elise's blood. Tiny pinpricks clung to his hairs and to the sweaty flesh.

Now we both carry my mother's blood, Jonathan thought.

"I liked the singing Jared's people did," said Seth.

"Why don't you go search for Jared? He would be able to . . ." *Able to what?* Jonathan asked himself. Offer protection when there is none?

"He understood Florry, but never me."

"He offered to take you in."

"A long time ago, when I was not supernatural. Now he wouldn't want me near him."

"You're not supernatural, Seth. Demented maybe." Jonathan smiled, ruing it from the moment he spread his lips.

Seth shook his head, his face turned very serious, his eyes peering into Jonathan's mind, trying to see the meaning of the words.

"I didn't mean to offend, honest."

With all his pride shattered, Seth still managed to stiffen his stance and raise his chin into the air.

"You'll always be a child, Seth; unable to be guilty for anything you do. Even for deaths you may cause. I envy you, Seth."

"Florry said envy was a sin."

"I am awash in sins. Is there one I have not committed?"

Seth shrugged, giving serious thought to the question.

"Where does Florry like to be taken?" Jonathan asked.

Enthusiasm burst from Seth's eyes. "There is a place several levels up where no one visits. Only Florry and I know the place. It is quiet and cool and he can't see us."

"You mean Yakut?"

Seth nodded. "We cram our bodies into a niche and hold each other. She tells me she can feel my heart beat. I tell her that's because it must work twice as hard for her and me. You see, she doesn't have a heartbeat anymore."

"She doesn't need one as long as she has you."

"I tell her that. She smiles and holds her palm to my chest and I can feel my heart beat faster, vibrating the air around us. We like being alone together. And she's healed. Her skin is unblemished and the swelling has gone down in her tummy. Way down. I joke that she is almost a toothpick."

"And does she laugh, Seth?"

"She smiles and pulls me closer and I am in heaven with her instead of here in hell." The sadness in Seth's eyes spoke of the brief flashes of sanity that tortured him.

"Go to that place now, Seth, and kiss her on the cheek for me. I can find my way on my own."

Chapter Fifty-nine

The air heated up swiftly once Jonathan crossed the
threshold into Hades. The smell of seared meat inflicted the air with a tang that sparked his hunger.
The walls pulsed out their presence, a steady
pounding against the air. Wind whistled in sweltering heat; the spongy floor was unable to firm up
completely due to the high temperatures. He
slogged through a slop that contained the rancid-
ness of all the wrongs done upon the earth. His feet
would stick once in a while in the sludge that splattered the bottoms of his jeans. And the smell was
always there, a constant companion reminding him
of the taste of flesh.

As he peered deeper into the darkness, he could
make out a face every now and then. The ages var-

ied, but the expressions were the same. Happiness faded from the lives of those who followed Yakut. Mold seemed to grow on the chins and brows of the people, strands of long leathery filament waving in the pressure of the hot air. He attempted to walk toward one face; the eyes blinked and the face disappeared.

Are these people the dead or merely those who have been enticed? he wondered.

Sobs spread from the distance, linking the scared souls together, dry sobs that couldn't spare the tears in this hothouse.

A figure to his right rocked back and forth, caught up in his own meditation on life as he must live it now. The male body was thin, bruised with welts, and covered with maggots from the corpse he hugged so close to him. The figure almost hid in the darkness, except for the brightness of his teeth, which were revealed under drawn-back lips. The whites of his eyes were dulled by the anguish that paralyzed his body.

"You finally made it."

Jonathan turned and faced Sylvia. "What the hell! I thought Yakut never brought you down here."

"He has leaned on me for a few favors and I have managed to win my reward."

"Staying down here for eternity with him?"

"All of this could be so easy, Jonathan. Accept this world and free yourself to move into your father's love."

"Yakut loves no one. He destroys, he rips apart the beautiful, and flushes the truth down the sewer."

Jonathan heard the man move, heard bones rattle to the floor. He feared taking his eyes off Sylvia. She would possibly lay hands on him, mar him with her own sins, cry out in the feel of his flesh, and spoil his body with her diseased fingertips that bore the germs of death.

"Where is he, Sylvia?"

"You've barely entered his home, and already you make demands." Sylvia seemed disappointed in his manners, disappointed that he had not yet fully accepted this life. "He doesn't wait for you, but expects you to come."

"And what will he do when I face him?"

"Give you anything you want." She smiled as she spoke the words.

"I want my mother and Cindy back. I don't want the hunger that has driven me to this point. I want him to take it away. If he is so powerful, then he should be able to accommodate me."

"He can if you truly know what you want or what you should want."

"Nothing I've said means anything to you?"

"Cindy and Elise were leeches sucking you dry. You had no time to think past the encumbrances of those relationships. Now you are free, Jonathan. No one wishes to stop you from your work." She moved closer to him.

Her white hair was worn loose, the color emphasizing each stray strand. She brought her own smell with her when she approached, different from the hellhole odor that had struck him as soon as he had entered. There was an unusual sweetness, too sweet, spoiling the freshness that seemed clustered to her clothes and body. She smelled of honeysuckle and sweetened vanilla, both too strong to be contained within the tunnels.

She held her right hand out to him palm up.

"See my palm, Jonathan."

He saw torn flesh in the center of her palm. Open flesh, recently wounded.

"This is how I proved myself to him."

"By slashing your hand open?"

"By offering my flesh to a caged rat." Sylvia's eyes sparkled. "The rat was hungry, and I gave of my flesh. Now he knows that I will do anything for him."

"This was some sort of trial he put you through?"

"Not a trial, Jonathan. I showed my belief in him by feeding his tiniest of followers."

"People come down here and instantly go mad,

380

don't they, Sylvia? On my way here I met Seth. And I think you two have tied in the craziness challenge."

"Seth is useless." Sylvia pulled back her hand and buried it deep in the pocket of her jeans. "His brain cells were deficient at birth, and are just getting fewer and fewer with time."

"Yakut is using him, though."

"He is still good for errands, but only for that purpose. He can't fill the voids waiting for us, Jonathan. We have the capacity to firm up Yakut's hold on the earth."

"You, Sylvia? Since when have you become so important?"

"I always have been."

"Did Yakut tell you that, or is it some delusion that you're fixated on?"

"He needs you, Jonathan, and I have helped to pull you in."

"How? By letting me help out at the food kitchen? By chopping up a baby I innocently brought to you? By seeking to taint my mother with his flesh? And what happens when I refuse to serve him? What will he do with you?"

"He doesn't want you to serve. He wants you to rule. Rule the earth for him in your human form. Cast doubt upon the familiar and bring in chaos, Jonathan. That's what he wants."

"In that case, I am insulted. He sends you to beckon his prince, his Antichrist, to him? Why doesn't he come himself? If he thinks I am capable of accomplishing so much for him, then he should be here to greet me, not an inferior servant such as yourself."

Sylvia's eyes flamed with rage.

"I don't need you, Sylvia, and neither does Yakut. We're far more powerful than you can imagine. You want to tutor me." He laughed loudly. The echo of his laughter set off waves of agonizing pain through the tunnels. Screeches from children could be heard peaking over the disharmonious cries.

"I am here to make your passage easier, Jonathan." Sylvia's lips were thin, tight.

"You're here to make yourself indispensable, but you failed to do that, Sylvia. Failed because you're much too human, too enmeshed in the wants of man. Yakut could care less about the people you say you are helping. It makes it easier for those people to be used and discarded. What do you think would happen if I attempted to take your life? You think he would rush to your aid, or take glory in the hunger that feeds my violence?"

Sylvia took a step back away from Jonathan. He could see her legs almost buckle.

"You have no champion, Sylvia. No one cares about what happens to you. As we know, the people aboveground would be better off without you, without your feeding them their own kin. If I destroy you, I do a favor to all those homeless who come to you in innocence." He took a step toward her, and he watched as she steeled herself to not move away from him. "I frighten you, Sylvia. Why? Because you know I share the evils that so attracted you to Yakut? Because I too am able to hate and I despise you?"

He took several more steps toward her. They were practically touching when he spat in her face. She closed her eyes and stood taller, refusing to back away from him.

"Do you think that I am frail enough even now that I would not rip you apart?" he asked.

She opened her eyes and stared into his with defiance.

"Humanity no longer clings to my bones, Sylvia. You make a mortal mistake by thinking that." He reached out and grabbed her throat with his right hand, pressing lightly against her skin. "Still you foolishly refuse to believe that I could destroy you. Or do you believe Yakut will suddenly come and rescue you?" He looked around them and saw nothing but the darkness that filled the air.

"No one comes to be your savior, Sylvia. What do you think of that?"

"There are many folded within the darkness," she said.

"I'm glad, because your flesh is not worthy of me. The body smell tells me that you went rancid long ago. What I feel in my hand is greasy with your fear. And your flesh has aged beyond ripeness."

Jonathan could feel breath all around him, the panting of the starved, the desperate.

"Who wants this flesh I hold in my hand?" he asked.

Scrawny bodies slipped out of the dark, ribs almost breaking through flesh, fingers so thin that nails barely had any flesh to cling to. Mouths were gaping open, showing teeth cracked and splintered by use.

"Many have come to be served, Sylvia. You did it so well aboveground; try to do as well here."

"I haven't anything to feed them," Sylvia said, her control almost breaking in the heat of the surroundings.

"You have the ultimate gift for them. A gift that you've coddled for years, saving it for these people."

"They will not touch me, Jonathan. They daren't."

"They will when they smell your blood." Jonathan raised his left hand and slashed down across her face, leaving skin gaping open on one cheek.

"Already they are restless. Their feet seek to come closer. Their hands reach out in childlike desire. Look at them, Sylvia. Tell me you don't see starvation in their eyes." Jonathan used his right thumb to yank her chin first to the left, then to the right. "Look at the spit wandering down all those jaws. Listen to the puppylike whines they've started to make. Whimpers really. And you still are not afraid?"

Sylvia brought her hand up to touch her ripped cheek. Her eyes squinted in pain when her touch confirmed the damage he said he had done.

"Please, Jonathan, you don't know him as well as I do. You need my guidance around him."

"He's my father, isn't he? How much closer could we be? We'll embrace as father and son, isn't that what's supposed to happen? You're useless now. I am here where he wanted me and have come on my own."

"No, the things I did paved the way for you. Without me, you still wouldn't know what the hell he wanted. And I know more, Jonathan, so much more that can ingratiate you to him."

"That flap of loose skin on your cheek is disgusting. Tear it off."

"I warn you that you won't survive without my help."

"Sylvia, neither of us will survive."

"You must."

Jonathan sensed the crowd closing in on Sylvia and himself. The smell of their breath sickened him, but no more than the woman standing in front of him. When he raised his hand to touch her cheek, she protected her skin with both her hands.

"Just a taste is all they need, Sylvia, and they will dutifully complete the servings."

Quickly he threw her to the ground and fell on top of her. Using her hands, she tried to fight him off, but she was not strong enough. He ripped at her clothes and gouged chunks of flesh from her body, tossing it to those who waited. He lifted himself off her and stood. She attempted to follow, but masses of bodies swarmed over her flesh.

Jonathan backed away from her screaming. It did not take long for silence to come back.

Chapter Sixty

The quiet was brief, for suddenly applause was sounding from behind him. He turned and saw a handsome man of spectacular beauty. The features were precise, the hair long, full, with rich highlights. The naked body was well proportioned, with rich, pale, hairless skin. Beauty existed in every movement the man made.

It was the eyes that revealed the identity. This was Yakut with the burning red eyes that glittered happily at him.

"You've done well, son."

Jonathan stood and gaped.

"My beauty comes from my Father, Jonathan. The same as your skill to make those around you suffer comes from me."

"You forced me to kill my mother." Jonathan felt his hands close into tight fists. For the first time since entering Hades he noticed his own sweat. Drops slipping down from his forehead; ribbons covering his body.

"I never forced you to do anything. I simply watched you develop into a true son. And your mother begged to be taken."

"Taken instead of me. I remember her words."

"You don't remember her crying out in pain, begging for her freedom from the torture? 'Spare me, dear child, this horror.' Those words do not cling to your memory?"

"No, Yakut. I woke on her bed innocent."

Yakut laughed. He approached the feasting behind Jonathan and drove the squirming bodies away. Left were a few bones and unrecognizable organs.

"We should be alone for this meeting, son."

"Jonathan is my name, and my father was—"

"Shut up. You tire me. That man you lived with wiped your ass, kept a roof over your head, and kept you healthy. But he did it all for *me*. He never shared a single cell in common with you. The instant he saw you, he suspected that something was off. He would watch you play and feel a separateness from you. Your skin never softened to his touch when he laid hands on you. Warmth was never sparked when he was alone with you. He cast you aside when he felt threatened by you, keeping his distance especially as you grew older."

Jonathan's eyes watered.

"Oh, never loved by Daddy, sweetheart," Yakut went on. "So wrong. I waited impatiently for you to achieve the promise I knew you had. Many times I was tempted to come to you. I didn't. I waited for you to call me. Inside that church on that rainy night, I came to fulfill your wishes."

"Not my wishes, your desires." Jonathan searched the dark around him. "This is not Hades. This is just another tunnel with tracks running through. Trains may never have passed through, but this was all built by men, human men. You veil this place to look like your own hovel. It is not yours. These tunnels belong to man, and in turn to the Father that created them. You're weak, so feeble that you don't even have a home. If I'm your son, I am ashamed. You have nothing to pass down to me except the blackness of your future."

"You are here to fulfill the prophecy."

"Then the prophecy was a lie."

Jonathan remembered something Seth had told him when he first entered the tunnels.

"Don't ever step on that third rail. What a gooey mess if you do. I've seen people do it. On purpose or not, I don't know. But their extremities explode.

The head pops like a balloon. The hands and feet disappear into a bloody mess."

Jonathan had to see through the fog Yakut had built within these tunnels. Just as with the unused tracks above, he was sure electricity flowed down here.

"Don't, Jonathan," Yakut warned. "Too many eons have been spent preparing for you."

"Yes, all those mistakes I met. Did you try to hide them down here with you? I'm surprised you didn't simply destroy them. Ah, but your ego wouldn't have allowed that. They were all part of you. An aspect of you."

"They left because they were embarrassed to be seen by me. They wanted my love. However, you saw them, Jonathan, they were freaks. No beauty to their bodies or their souls. Worthless souls that not even my Father wants. So they will live on in memory of . . ." Yakut paused. "My failures. That is how God punishes me."

"Beauty? You treasure beauty? Of course you do. Your Father praises it. He also embraces the ugly, Yakut. That you can't do, because you create only ugliness."

"You are beautiful, Jonathan."

"No. A man who causes pain to those who need to be helped? A man that can kill what he loves most? A man that takes vengeance when he could

390

have given pity? You have no idea of what beauty is. I have seen beauty and marred it. Scarred my own flesh that was so precious." Jonathan began to pace. He needed to find the escape. He hoped that God would grant him oblivion, for he knew the Lord could never invite into heaven the perpetrator of cruelties that Jonathan had perfomed.

"There will never be an end, Jonathan. Eternity belongs to every man, even when he is partly a god."

"I'm no god. A half-breed. Yes. I mingle humanity with the envy you have. Instead of uniting with your Father and Brother, you chose to prove that you can be more. When will you understand that you cannot?"

Jonathan tripped. He caught himself before he could fall, but he knew the tracks were beneath his feet. He judged the distance between the tracks and located where the third rail would be.

"I will not stop you if you attempt this," Yakut said. "For in the attempt you prove you are useless to me."

Jonathan kicked off his shoes and positioned himself just a step away from the third rail.

"Good-bye," Jonathan said, and took that last step.

And I heard a voice from heaven saying unto me,
Write, Blessed are the dead which die in the Lord
from henceforth: Yea, saith the Spirit,
that they may rest from their labours;
and their works do follow them.

THE BOOK OF REVELATION

Sèphera Girón

House of Pain

The house looks so normal. Just a charming home in a small town — perfect for a young couple starting out together. But this house was built on the site of an unspeakable series of murders, butchery so savage that the brick walls of the basement seemed to flow with blood. Tony was just a boy then but he stood and watched as the notorious house was demolished. Now he's a man, and he's brought his beautiful young wife with him to live in the new house built on the site, without telling her of its hideous secret. Still the nightmares come to her, visions of horror, suffering and perversion, drawing her down to the basement, to a dank tunnel that lies beyond a wall. What calls to her from inside the tunnel? What waits in the darkness to be unleashed?

___4907-4 $6.99 US/$8.99 CAN

Dorchester Publishing Co., Inc.
P.O. Box 6640
Wayne, PA 19087-8640

Quenched

MARY ANN MITCHELL

An evil stalks the clubs and seedy hotels of San Francisco's shadowy underworld. It preys on the unfortunate, the outcasts, the misfits. It is an evil born of the eternal bloodlust of one of the undead, the infamous nobleman known to the ages as . . . the Marquis de Sade. He and his unholy offspring feed upon those who won't be missed, giving full vent to their dark desires and a thirst for blood that can never be sated. Yet while the Marquis amuses himself with the lives of his victims, with their pain and their torture, other vampires—of Sade's own creation—are struggling to adapt to their new lives of eternal night. And as the Marquis will soon learn, hatred and vengeance can be eternal as well—and can lead to terrors even the undead can barely imagine.

___4717-9 $6.99 US/$8.99 CAN

TAINTED BLOOD

MARY ANN MITCHELL

The infamous Marquis de Sade has lived through the centuries. This master vampire cares little for his human playthings, seeking them out only for his amusement and nourishment. Once his dark passion and his bloodlust are sated, he moves on, leaving another drained and discarded toy in his wake.

Now Sade is determined to find the woman who made his life hell—and destroy her. His journey leads him to a seemingly normal suburban American house. But the people who live there are undead. And when the notorious Marquis meets the all-American family of vampires, the resulting culture clash will prove fatal. But for whom?

DRAWN TO THE GRAVE — MARY ANN MITCHELL

"A tight, taut dark fantasy with surprising plot twists and a lot of spooky atmosphere."
—Ed Gorman

Beverly thinks that she has found something special with Carl, until she realizes that he has stolen from her. But he doesn't just steal her money and her property—he steals her very life. Suddenly she is helpless and alone, able only to watch in growing despair as her flesh begins to decay and each day transforms her more and more into a corpse—a corpse without the release of death.

But Beverly is not truly alone, for Carl is always nearby, watching her and waiting. He knows that soon he will need another unknowing victim, another beautiful woman he can seduce...and destroy. And when lovely young Megan walks into his web, he knows he has found his next lover. For what can possibly go wrong with his plan, a plan he has practiced to perfection so many times before?

____4290-8 $4.99 US/$5.99 CAN

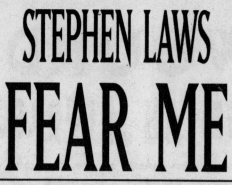

STEPHEN LAWS

FEAR ME

Gideon loves women...to death. He seduces them, uses them horribly, then discards them, drained of their very lives. Until the day three women disobey him and dare to fight back, to seek revenge, leaving him in a pool of blood. Releasing them at last from his depravity.

The women don't know that Gideon can't be killed that easily. They don't know what he really is. He has returned to seek vengeance of his own, and their mere deaths will no longer be enough to satisfy him. He will make them pay dearly for crossing him. But first he will destroy everyone they love.

- -

FIEND

JEMIAH JEFFERSON ✠

In nineteenth-century Italy, young Orfeo Ricari teeters on the brink of adulthood. His new tutor instructs him in literature and poetry during the day and guides him in the world of sensual pleasure at night. But a journey to Paris will teach young Orfeo much more. For in Paris he will become a vampire.

Told in his own words, this is the story of the life, death, rebirth and education of a vampire. No one else can properly describe the endless hunger or the amazing power of the undead. No one else can recount the slow realization of what it means to grasp immortality, to live on innocent blood, to be a fiend.
